THE LAST HOT TIME

THE LAST HOT TIME

JOHN M. FORD

TOR® A Tom Doherty Associates Book New York

THE LAST HOT TIME

Book design by Heidi M. K. Eriksen

Edited by Teresa Nielsen Hayden

A Tor Book
Published by Tom Doherty Associates, LLC
175 Fifth Avenue
New York, NY 10010

www.tor.com

Tor® is a registered trademark of Tom Doherty Associates, LLC.

Library of Congress Cataloging-in-Publication Data

Ford, John M.
    The last hot time / John M. Ford.
        p. cm.
    "A Tom Doherty Associates book."
    ISBN 0-312-85545-1 (hc)
    ISBN 0-312-87578-9 (pbk)
    1. Emergency medical technicians—Fiction. 2. Criminals—Fiction.
  3. Elves—Fiction. 4. Chicago (Ill.)—Fiction. I. Title.

PS3556.O712 L37 1993
813'.54—dc21   00-056763

First Hardcover Edition: December 2000
First Trade Paperback Edition: November 2001

Printed in the United States of America

0 9 8 7 6 5 4 3 2 1

L THE AST HOT TIME

SEPTEMBER

The Triumph TR3 was running sweet tonight; Danny Holman had been fiddling with it for a week straight, but he'd tinkered with it near nonstop for the eight months he'd owned it without any really definite results. But now he was doing—well, nearly sixty—through the September night, all alone on I-80, a wire-wheeled golden bat out of hell.

Danny saw a lighted truck stop about eighty miles into Illinois. He was pretty sure he could get to Chicago on the gas he had, but the truck stop was the first place he'd seen open since dark. No sense getting caught short. Not after what it had taken to get this far. He pulled the TR3 onto a ramp with heavy weeds to either side.

The station looked like it had been huge, once. There were at least a dozen pump islands out of service, lots of cracked concrete and dead light poles, and some hollow buildings. A big brick shell still had a dark MOTEL sign. There were ten tables in the restaurant, and room for forty more. A big red-lettered sign by the counter said IF YOU ARE UNDER 21 DO NOT ASK FOR BEER. WE PUNISH CRIMINALS. *Who's we?* he thought, but no one gave him a problem with his cheeseburger and berryade. There was another sign that read WE HAVE COFFEE, with HAVE on a separate card. Below that it said PRICE NEGOTIABLE.

A skeletal old man filled the Triumph's tank, then wiped the windshield and headlights. "Goin' home?" he said, with a look at the luggage in the little car's passenger seat.

"No," Danny said, without thinking about it.

"Well," the man said, "then it ain't too late to go home."

"I s'pose so." Danny didn't want to start a string of lies with the guy, and he supposed that anything he said would have about the same effect.

"If you need directions . . ." The old man nodded toward a cardboard box, between a rack of oil cans and the end pump. A card said THE ONLY MAP YOU NEED. The box was full of Gideon Bibles, black and green, probably from the motel. Danny'd seen the same box in Iowa, half a dozen different times and places. He paid the attendant and drove on.

The road was empty. Every half hour or so he slowed down for a reflector barricade marking off a patch of crumbled pavement or collapsed embankment or a mass of burnt-out vehicles too big to remove. There was a little fingernail of moon, making foggy gray shadows on the concrete, but mostly the night was black on black, with a few lone stars on the horizon, barns or one-crossroad towns. A couple of the towns had signs, the old white-on-green reflective ones. He didn't turn off. Towns like that had shot at him in the county ambulance with the lights going. The odds wouldn't be any better now.

Maybe, Danny thought, Illinois was different.

Nope. It would be different where he was going.

He flipped on the radio and started scanning with the knob. There was noise with long dead spots between, no change there. He got a ripple of piano music and an unintelligible voice, but it slipped away.

Then rhythms came up clear, and a voice Danny knew: one of the WGN night people. Danny smiled. This was the sound that had kept him sane, in his room, with the earphones stuffed in tight and muffled with gauze so that no one else would hear. He could ride the beam all the way now.

A record came on. The car hummed and Danny did too.

> None of you knows what to do
> You better move it 'cause I'm coming through
> Everybody's sayin' that the kid's insane

I'm doin' ninety miles an hour
In the breakdown lane

As the road rose up to meet the car, Danny saw an edge of orange light on the distant horizon. It reminded him of a night fire call, last summer, when a barn and silos had gone up a county over. It had taken a couple of hours to cover twenty miles, to find a road somebody hadn't blasted or blocked for some weird local reason. When they got there, the VFD had given up trying to put the fire out and was just holding it back from the farmhouse.

One of the firemen led Danny and his partner to a covered pickup. In the back were a woman wobbling between numb silence and screaming fits, two little kids who just wanted to watch the fire, and a teenage boy with second-degree burns on his hands and arms who didn't want to be treated and *really* didn't want pain meds. After a while Danny understood the boy needed something to fight, and the pain was all he had. If he lost that, he might just break down.

Some of the VFD guys had burns and smoke, so the paramedics went to work on them. Danny's partner asked the fireman he was bandaging where the farmer was.

The man twisted his face around, and then said, "When we said there was nothin' we could do for his barn, he just up and walked into it. Captain tried to knock him down with the stream, but he just kept goin'. I mean, we tried, but—"

Up ahead of us walls and wire
We're gonna take 'em like a house afire
Everybody's sayin' that the kid's insane
I'm doin' ninety miles an hour
In the breakdown lane
Wolves are gettin' hungry, let 'em off the chain
Doin' ninety miles an hour
In the breakdown lane

Danny fiddled with the radio again, trying to get some news about the glow ahead. The orange light was too big to be a burning house, or even a whole town. What the heck *could* it be?

Headlights flashed in the rear-view. There was a big car back there, gaining on him. Danny thought about giving the guy a run for his nickel, but he was already getting enough crosswind to make the Triumph wobble, and besides, the car behind had asked permission. He dropped a gear and slipped into the right lane.

The car pulled up. Danny took a look. He saw headlights like chrome buckets, a hood like a coffin, bow-wave fenders over white-sided tires, and running boards six feet long: a car straight out of a James Cagney movie.

The near front window was down, and a face showed in it, lit by green dashboard glow. Danny saw weirdly sharp, foxlike features, long white hair.

An elf. A real, honest to . . . whatever elf.

The elf raised two long thin fingers and the car rolled on. Danny tapped his hands on the wheel, feeling a charge right down in his gut. Elves. Fast cars with power to burn. Next stop Chicago.

Just ahead the road made a tight right, notched through a low hill; the big car's headlights spilled across the blasted rock face. Danny dropped back a little farther; this wasn't necessarily a divided highway anymore, and—

Halfway through the curve, the Triumph's lights picked up the other car, dead ahead in Danny's lane: it was another high-wheeled box like the first car had been, it was blood red, and its lights were out.

Just as the two big cars in front of Danny were side by side, white fire spat from the side of the red one. Danny heard the guns above the wind, like saw blades going through pine. The red car spun its wheels and shot away through the darkness toward the city glow beyond. The dark car bucked and wavered, but somehow kept to the road until it was clear of the rock face; then it bumped over the left-hand shoulder and came to a stop on the roadside, tilted nose-up, headlights aimed at the treetops.

Danny braked hard, pulled off the road to the right, and stopped. He opened the door, looked around: no more traffic. His working stuff was in a red roll bag behind the seats; he slung it and sprinted across the highway.

Crazy patterns of holes were punched across the side of the car and starred the dark windows. Danny heard a groan from some-where in the rear. He grabbed the door handle, got it open. A soft light came on inside.

The rear space was as big as a normal car's whole interior. There was a sofa-sized rear seat, and against the front wall, just below a glass divider, were folded jump seats and a wooden cabinet holding cut-glass bottles. One flask was smashed, and Danny smelled whis-key.

A woman was sprawled on the backseat. She wore a sapphire-blue gown and a short white jacket. There was blood all over them, and on her short, white-blond hair. Her head rested in the lap of a small man in a dark suit with wide peaked lapels, a silver shirt, and a shiny black tie. A broad-brimmed hat hid his face. Danny zipped the kit open.

"Cloud," the man said.

Danny felt a movement past his left ear. He jerked, got some-thing in his hand, turned. There was a white-fleshed, thin man—the elf he had seen in the dashboard light—just beside him, in a blue leather cycle jacket and a long dark scarf. The elf was holding a short-barreled pump shotgun. Its muzzle was what had flicked past Danny's ear.

Danny had automatically grabbed a pair of angled shears, to cut access to the wounds. Its metal was warming in his hand. It looked pretty lame compared to the elf's gun. As if that weren't bad enough, the bent metal made Danny think of Robin, and he'd come up here to not do that anymore.

The suited man looked up. He was black, with a sharp chin and nose, large dark eyes. He said, "You have excellent reflexes, young man. Do you know how to use that equipment?"

"That's why I brought it," Danny said, calmly enough. He'd heard *Ain't you awful young for a paramedic?* often enough that it didn't sting any longer, not much.

"You'll see to the lady." He spoke without an accent, but with an odd rhythm. He put the woman's head down, very gently, and moved to the jump seat opposite. The elf hadn't moved.

Danny shoved his brain back into Trauma Mode. Airway first. The woman sucked in a breath, and the dark well of blood in her flank sucked and bubbled. Through the lung. Bad. "Excuse me," he said, stuck a penlight between his teeth and bent down to check beneath her. No exit wound. One hole to seal: less bad for the moment. An ER would have to worry about where the bullet was.

A couple of long rips with the shears got the white jacket out of the way. Danny ripped open a pressure bandage, peeled the blue satin away from the hole. There was nothing between the thin slick fabric and her skin. The pad went on and he leaned on the sucker. He tore off some tape one-handed and sealed it down. She heaved another breath, coughed, but the bad noises stopped.

Danny took inventory. The scalp wound looked minor, a bullet crease or a flying sliver; it was clotting okay, not a priority. There was a nasty clip out of her upper left arm. He could see bone.

The door by the patient's head opened. A big man in a black bush jacket leaned in. There was a Colt .45 in his hand; it looked small there. "Looks clear, sir." His voice had some Irish in it. "Ruthins. Mighty hunters. Fah." He turned his head and spat. "Norma Jean?"

The small man said, "The young man seems to be doing well by her."

"The young man could use a hand," Danny said, feeling the sweat on his hands and face. "Can one of you guys hold her shoulder? Really firm, and don't let go if she screams."

The big man leaned into the car. "Reducin' the fracture?"

"That's the idea."

The man nodded and put his hands on the woman's upper arm. Danny pulled, clenching his teeth against the sound of grating bone, but the woman didn't yell, just grunted. He got the dressing and splint in place. "That's it. Thanks."

"Think nothin' of it."

"Her name's Norma Jean?"

"Around here," the small man said, "names are something one keeps to oneself. We *call* people things." He indicated the big man and the elf in turn. "This is Lincoln McCain. And Cloudhunter Who Keeps His Sisters' Counsel, though Cloudhunter will do. I am called Mr. Patrise." He spelled it.

"Danny Holman."

"You're a . . . medical student?"

"I'm a paramedic."

"That means you have a license."

"Yeah. Can I show it to you some other time, please? She needs a hospital."

"Yes. And yes."

The big man, McCain, said, "Cook County's closest."

"Not secure," Cloudhunter the elf said. His voice sounded like the wind in high grass.

"I'm afraid that's right," Patrise said. "It's always at awkward times that one is reminded of one's weaknesses."

McCain said, "Michael Reese, then."

"Fine." Patrise said to Danny, "I assume you're used to working in a vehicle? The car rides smoothly, and it'll get better as we get closer to the city."

"City?" Danny said. "No, wait, my car's out there, and my stuff."

Mr. Patrise said, "Nothing you absolutely need in the next few hours." He did not seem to be asking.

"I can't leave my car here!"

"Yes, you can. I personally guarantee its safety, and that of all your belongings. They will be brought to you by morning. Anything you need before then will be provided, and by that I mean anything. You will find me a properly grateful man." Patrise looked past Cloudhunter, out the car door. "Besides . . . you haven't been to the Levee before."

"You're from the Levee?" Danny said, too quick. It was a stupid question, with an elf in the car. "Uh—no, never."

McCain said, "Your car may not work once it hits the redline, then."

"What about yours?"

"Ah, we're dual-fuel," McCain said. "Don't worry. She looks like a nice machine. She'll be cared for."

Mr. Patrise said, "Cloud, I'll ride in front. You stay here." Cloudhunter nodded, pulled down the jump seat, and shut the door.

McCain moved aside to let Patrise get out, then leaned in again. He pointed to some buttons on the backseat bar. "This one keeps the light on. Lighter here if you smoke. Help yourself to what's left of the stock; there's cold beer below." He picked up the broken decanter, flung it away into the dark. He shut the door.

The car started. It bumped a few times, then found the road; the ride was very, very smooth. Danny wiped some of the blood from Norma Jean's scalp wound; it really wasn't too bad. He put a small dressing on, deciding to leave cutting her hair to the hospital team. In the dim light he could hardly tell Betadine from blood.

He looked up. Cloudhunter Who Keeps His Sisters' Counsel was sitting absolutely still, the shotgun across his knees. Only his silvery eyes moved, shifting like mercury. Danny couldn't see a thing through the tinted windows, not even into the front seat; he had heard that elves had night vision, or some kind of special vision.

"Mr. Cloudhunter—"

"No titles," the elf said. "Cloudhunter is fine. Cloud if we get to be friends."

"Cloudhunter, could you put that thing away?"

"The Ruthins might try again." The elf's voice was softer now, more like human. "Not much use put away."

"Yeah, I guess."

The eyes shifted again. "The Urthas like to plot," he said, still more softly. "Urthagwaed's clever and likes to be seen so. Long Lankin, or Iceberg Jack, Glassisle, Rhiannon—any could find a nice human lad, good with the kingsfoil . . . have him finish whatever needed finishing."

Danny didn't say anything. Assuming he understood what the elf was saying, there was no point in arguing with it.

Norma Jean groaned, stirred. She gurgled out a half scream. "Easy, now, easy, Norma Jean," Danny said, and put a hand on her shoulder, pressed just slightly. She sighed as the pain defocused. The blue dress had covered her breasts maybe halfway, before Danny had started cutting.

"Is she in pain?" It was Patrise's voice through an intercom grille.

"I don't think she's really conscious. But—is there a blanket back here?"

"Drawer under the seat."

As Danny got Norma Jean covered, Patrise said, "Can you give her something?"

"You mean for pain? I've got aspirin and benzocaine cream. No good here."

There was a pause. The woman's head trembled.

Mr. Patrise said, "I'd like to see your license now." A little drawer slid out of the dividing panel. "I'm not questioning your ability."

Danny got out his wallet. "You want my driver's license, too?"

"That would be all right."

He put the cards through. "Ah," Patrise said. "Do you see this birthdate, Lincoln?"

"Okay!" Danny said. "Okay, so I'm still nineteen, all right? The stuff's all real and the car's really mine. It's only a few weeks to my birthday—"

"It certainly is," Patrise said. "October thirty-first. All Hallow's Eve."

Cloudhunter's head turned.

Mr. Patrise said, "Hallowseve. Holman, Hallownight. That's a fine alias. Doc Hallownight, I think." He laughed. It was a pleasant sound. "There are already several Docs on the Levee, there always are. Oddly enough, few of them ever have MDs." He laughed again, and Danny found himself wanting to laugh too.

After about fifteen minutes, Danny could see the glow of the burning sky through the dark windows. They were apparently traveling at high speed, seventy at least, but the car seemed barely to be moving. Danny looked at his watch. The liquid-crystal display read FEAR. Danny blinked, angled his wrist to catch the light. 2:28 AM. No wonder he was seeing things. He'd been driving for nearly nine hours straight before all this.

He said, "How long till we get to the hospital?"

McCain's voice said, "Ten minutes."

"Can I have my IDs back now?"

"Mr. Patrise is rather tired."

Danny's watch said 2:30, and then RAGE, and then 2:31.

At 2:40 they drove into a brightly lighted garage. An ambulance was parked nearby. Cloudhunter opened the door. A moment later, Norma Jean was on a gurney and Danny was giving the ED team the lowdown: "We have a woman, early twenties, two gunshot wounds to the left flank and upper left arm, punctured left lung . . ."

Somebody, probably a resident, nodded to Danny by way of acknowledgment and the team closed him out. Nothing new about that. He looked around for Mr. Patrise and the other men, but they had disappeared. He wandered out into the waiting room.

It had the usual litter of old magazines, empty cardboard cups, and smokers' debris, and an unmanned counter of ancient varnished wood. The room smelled both musty and of disinfectant. As he started to feed change to the drinks dispenser, a woman's voice said, "Don't do that. Even if you *are* near a hospital."

A muscular, dark-haired woman in surgical scrubs, stethoscope draped around her neck, was standing in a doorway. "You're Doc Hallownight?"

"Daniel—uh, yeah."

"Lucy Estevez. I'm the lucky bozo in charge of the Knife and Gun Club tonight. It was pretty quiet until you got here." She held out a hand and Danny shook it. "Come on back and have some actual coffee. It's probably just as toxic as the machine stuff, but at least it's free."

They went back to a nurses' station, facing a row of a dozen curtained cubicles, about half of them with signs of occupancy. Dr. Estevez poured coffee from a heavily stained pot into two mugs bearing the names of drug companies; one was advertising an antihypertensive, the other a stool softener.

It was real coffee, as strong as he'd ever tasted it. It made Danny's chest burn and his head stand up and cheer. "Thanks."

"McCain said you were a paramedic."

"Yeah."

"Hey, relax." She told him a story about a motorcycle decapitation, down to the last splintered vertebra and drop of O-negative. He told her one about a disk-harrow accident. He'd had the conversation before, at Adair County. He relaxed. He knew this place.

Dr. Estevez got a bottle of peroxide and a towel to take the blood off Danny's denim jacket. She fingered his blue chambray shirt. "I think this one's had it. Mind accepting a loaner?"

"Sure." He was given a blue scrub shirt, found a bathroom to change in. In the mirror, there was more blood on him than he'd realized. He rinsed his chest and slipped the shirt over his head. It was stamped STOLEN FROM MICHAEL REESE HOSPITAL.

When he came out, Dr. Estevez was emerging from a cubicle. "The young lady ought to make it," she said. "You do good work."

Danny nodded.

"I mean that. You did it all dark?"

"There was light in the back seat."

"I mean, you didn't use any magic."

"Huh?"

"Never mind. You're from the country?"

"Duz it show s'much?" he drawled.

"When you came in, you said, 'We've got a woman.' One of the local people would have said, 'white female.' "

Danny thought hard about that. Things were going to be different here. People were going to be different, in more ways than one.

Dr. Estevez said, "I don't suppose you're looking for a job. We can always use another van jockey."

"Well, actually, I just got here, and . . . I guess a job sounds pretty good."

"The pay's fair, but I guarantee the hours stink worse than anything you're used to. And you know the New Paradigm?"

"No."

"There are never enough of us, so if you bring somebody in and don't have another call right away, you can get drafted as an ED assistant. OR too, sometimes. And you do know which end of the baby to grab?"

"Did it for real once."

"Good enough. Anyway, it's all the fun of being a first-year trauma resident, without ever getting to be a doctor."

"We did all that at home. We didn't have a name for it."

McCain appeared from somewhere in the back of the ward. "Mr. Patrise wants to see you, Doc."

"Offer's open," Dr. Estevez said, and went into one of the cubicles.

McCain led Danny to another cubicle. Cloudhunter was waiting outside, holding a hand inside his coat. Danny had no doubt there was a weapon tucked away there. The elf opened the curtain and Danny went in.

Patrise was sitting up on a bed, his shirt off. His chest and arms were very thin, and his dark brown skin had the blue-gray cast of heart disease. EKG wires ran to a monitor; Danny saw a slightly abnormal rhythm, probably valvular trouble.

On Patrise's right chest was a black bruise the size of Danny's palm.

"You didn't tell me you'd been hurt."

"A ricochet. My coat stopped it." Patrise tilted his head back. His face was delicate, even-featured, thin-lipped. His hair was black and combed straight back from his forehead, caught in a silver clip at the back of his neck. "Some first night in the big city, eh, Hallow? What's the time?"

Danny looked cautiously at his watch. It showed just numbers. "Three-ten."

"Little late to show you the bright lights, then. But you're still going strong. That's good. Night people are at an advantage on the Levee. Lincoln."

McCain looked in. He had a broad, rocklike face, all planes and crevices. His eyes were sharp blue. When he looked at Danny they seemed friendly enough; Danny didn't want to see unfriendly on McCain.

Patrise said, "We'll go by the club; Doc can shake some hands."

McCain nodded and left. Patrise said, "They always treat your clothes like something dangerous. Find my shirt."

It was on a hanger nearby. The label said TURNBULL & ASSER. As he helped Patrise put it on, he realized that it was silk. He had never in his life seen a man's silk shirt.

Patrise fingered the rip in the shirt above the bruise on his chest, touched one of the EKG wires glued to his skin. "Shut that gadget off. I don't want them thinking I've died. Too many people have ideas already."

Danny switched off the monitor. Patrise peeled the electrodes off, buttoned his shirt.

"Mr. Patrise, the doctor on duty offered me a job here."

"I'm not surprised. Lucy can see competence a mile off. I'm

sorry to disappoint her. Don't worry, Lincoln will make the excuses." He paused. "Perhaps it wasn't clear: you have a job. With me. Personally. There's no room for moonlighting." He pulled on an elastic-sided shoe. "You'll have plenty of your own time, but you work *for me*. Understand that and you'll have no cause to complain."

"Mr. Patrise, this is—I mean, I just drove into the city. You don't know me, it was just an accident—"

"There aren't any accidents." Patrise examined his slim hands, rubbed away a bit of electrode paste. "You have options, of course. You could work here. It's a nice place, if you don't mind the pay and the hours, the homicidals and the positive Wassermanns, all that. And, too, Norma Jean's family is Gold Coast, and they'll probably want to express their gratitude in a concrete way. But you'd regret it." He looked up, smiling. "That isn't a threat: I won't *make* you regret it. You just will." He stood up, wavered a little; Danny caught his arm.

Patrise looked up at him, eye to eye. "As for not knowing you . . . ask me again in a month if I know you. Cloud."

Cloudhunter pulled the curtains open, held Patrise's coat. At the nurse's station, McCain was signing some papers. Dr. Estevez waved as they passed. "Have fun, Doc," she said. "If you ever get tired of the good life, give me a call."

They got into the car, Patrise and Cloudhunter in back, McCain driving. Through the clear glass in front, Danny could finally see the city. A long building with lit strips of stairwell would be the hospital; beyond it was the hollow concrete shell of a structure just as large. McCain turned into a broad street lined with burnt wood, broken bricks, empty windows, lit only by the car's headlights and the orange sky hovering low above everything.

"People live out there?"

"Not so you'd call it that," McCain said. "This is the Boneyard. The Penumbra if you're in a fancy mood. Went in the big shakedown. You saw the first big wreck back there? They blew that as a firebreak, to save the hospital. Now it's too far out of the World and the Shade both for either to care."

There was more red in the airglow now. "It burns like this all night? Every night?"

"Nothing's really burning. The light's something from the

change. Witch stuff, not my department. We'll lose it once we're really inside. We're almost to the river now. Watch."

The car climbed a bridge approach. Danny could see red light turning water to blood. Suddenly the sky was black, with the fingernail moon descending. Stars came out as Danny's vision adjusted. He looked back. The river still had a pink tinge.

The little moon, without competition, washed down dark walls to wet pavements. Here and there a streetlamp glowed, and a bit of brilliantly colored neon flared. Motorcycles were parked in clusters, and a few of the boxy old-style cars.

Danny saw a multiple, hunched movement, as of something huge and dark and formless slithering down an alley—or else just a group of people, keeping their backs to the wind.

"Was that—"

"Probably. Where're you from, Doc?"

"Nowhere."

"Been there many a time. Little dull, but no cooking like it. Where?"

"Okay, Iowa. Adair, Iowa. Know anything you didn't know before?"

"Adair, Iowa. The James brothers pulled their first big robbery around there, didn't they?"

"Yeah. Yeah, they tried—but they robbed the wrong train."

"Ah, well, everybody has to start somewhere, eh?" McCain laughed, and Danny felt himself relax.

Then McCain said in a dead cold tone, "Where you start is knowing that all the attitude in your little farmboy body don't come up to the top of my shoes. Got that?"

It hit Danny like a fist. "I guess I'm learning."

"If you can learn, then it'll all be right. 'S'how it goes." McCain's voice was back to normal.

"Earlier—when Cloudhunter had the shotgun on me—he would have blown my head off just like that, right? No warning? Is that how it goes?"

"When you mean to kill somebody, only a damn fool gives him a chance to disagree. And only a damn fool pulls a gun without meaning to kill somebody." McCain turned, smiled—not all that reassuring a sight—said, "Ease up, Doc. You did a good job tonight.

You work for Mr. Patrise now. There's no better friend you could have on the Levee."

"Are we friends?"

"I do sincerely hope so."

McCain stopped the car in front of a lighted building with a violet awning that stretched from the curb down stairs to a double glass door. Massed electric bulbs spelled out LA MIRADA.

The door was opened by a man in a white top hat and tails. "Good evening, Mr. Patrise. Mr. McCain, Cloudhunter. And good evening to you, sir. Your coats?"

Patrise said, "Pavel, this is Doc Hallownight. A full member of the club with all privileges."

"Delighted to meet you, Mr. Hallownight. What will you be drinking?"

"A beer. Please."

"Your brand, sir?"

"Uh—anything. Have you got draft beer?"

"Of course, sir."

The entryway was lit by brass towers that threw light against the white sculptured ceiling. Brass vases of fresh flowers stood in niches along the wood-paneled walls. The corridor led to a double door of glass, frosted in geometric patterns, framed in chrome.

That door was opened by a blonde girl in a white blouse and an extremely short black skirt. "Oh! Mr. Patrise!"

The name stopped everything in the room. The few people there all turned.

The room was large and circular, with a domed ceiling that was black with twinkling stars. The outer part of the circle was three steps higher than the center. On one side of the upper ring was a black glass bar, backed by chrome and mirrors and endless ranks of bottles; a woman in a white shirt and red bow tie was mixing drinks. A man and woman leaned against the obsidian bartop, interrupted in conversation. On the other side were dining tables, all empty but one where two men in dinner jackets and two women in astounding gowns were seated.

The lower circle was a glossy black dance floor, empty. At the rear of the room was a bandstand with a white grand piano; a woman leaned against the piano, toward a man seated at the keyboard.

None of them looked like elves, but there was enough glitter and cool light that Danny was hardly sure.

Patrise went to the occupied table. One of the women said, "Patrise, how good to see you! You won't believe the stories that have been going around tonight." She sounded very drunk.

"Then you must tell me sometime, Tonia," Patrise said genially. "Hello, Erika. Bob, Warren. Have you had a good evening?"

They agreed that it had been splendid, that Fay had been in top form.

"Then you must consider it on the house. Always a good time here."

They were dazzled at Patrise's graciousness, and oh my was that the time, they'd all turn into pumpkins, good night, good night.

The woman from the piano was running across the dance floor. She wore a low-cut, ruffled black blouse and a gold metallic skirt; she held the skirt up to run, her golden high-heeled sandals clacking on the black surface, which reflected her image full-length, two people tap-dancing sole to sole.

"Patrise, oh God, Patrise," she said, flung her arms out and hugged him. "Oh, God, you're here."

"Of course, Carmen, dear." He put his hands on her wrists and unwound her. "Meet someone new. Hallow, this is Carmen Mirage. Carmen, meet Doc Hallownight. We had a little to-do with the Ruthins tonight, and Doc saved Norma Jean's life."

"Ohh . . . where is Norma?"

"I'm afraid she'll be going home now."

"Oh, that's so sad . . . but you saved her? That must have been very brave."

Danny said, "Well—" and then Carmen's arms were around him. She was very warm, and wore a potent cinnamon perfume, and she hugged *tight*.

"Pleased to meet you," Danny said past the lump in his throat.

"You mean that isn't a tongue depressor in your pocket, Doc?" Carmen said. "Or maybe it is." She laughed and finally let him breathe. He couldn't think. He looked down at his scrub shirt and jeans, here among all the satin and silk, and felt like he was knee-deep in pigshit and had a live chicken tucked under each arm.

The bartender had arrived with a tray of glasses. Patrise and

Cloudhunter had brightly colored drinks in tall frosted glasses, McCain a mug of coffee with whipped cream. Danny got hold of his beer, took a gulp. It went down just fine.

"Doc, this is Ginevra Benci." He gestured at the woman with the drinks.

She was a little shorter than Danny, with intensely black hair, dark blue eyes. She couldn't have been much older than he was. Her black skirt came to just below her knees, her legs and ankles showing pale and delicate.

"Hi, Doc."

He looked up at her face. She was smiling. "Hello."

Mr. Patrise said, "And Alvah Fountain at the mighty Bösendorfer." The young black man at the piano waved. His hair was done up in a mass of long, slender braids.

The two people who had been at the bar were approaching. The man was an American Indian in a wide-shouldered suit and a flowered tie. The woman was petite and Japanese, with dark hair coiled up and held with jeweled pins; she wore a tailored suit and a black turtlenecked shirt, calf-high boots of light brown suede. "Evening, Patrise," the man said. "Is this an open party?"

"Of course. Doc Hallownight, Lucius Birdsong of the *Chicago Centurion—*"

"Syndicated worldwide through GNS," Birdsong said.

"—pen sharper than a Trueblood arrow. Tongue, too. And Kitsune Asa, the Tokyo Fox."

"Welcome to the Levee, friend," Birdsong said, and shook Danny's hand. "What's the matter? Aren't you going to tell me you read and admire my column every day?"

"No."

"Fair enough."

The Tokyo Fox said, "You're a doctor?"

"I'm a paramedic. What do you do?"

"Right at the moment, I drink standing up. Pleased to meet you, Doc."

Patrise said, "Where's Fay?"

Ginevra said, "She went home right after her set."

Patrise said, "Yes?"

No one spoke. Then Miss Asa drained her glass, put it on Ginevra's tray, and said, "About two AM a couple of my-mama-eats-ambrosia Ruthins came in, with a side dish of Vamps."

Carmen said, "You said the rule was—"

"I know," Patrise said calmly. "Ginevra, get the lady another drink. Ruthins, attended. No Highborns?"

"Nope." The Fox shrugged. "They were hinting that you wouldn't be coming home tonight. Didn't seem to get the rise they wanted, so they left after Fay sang. People started drifting out after that. Last half hour it's been just us and that mooch patrol you saw."

"Who took Phasia home?"

Lucius Birdsong said, "Stagger Lee."

Mr. Patrise spread his hands. "Another hot time in the old town. I think it's time we went home too, ladies and gentlemen: I believe I'll have to be seen by a few people today, upright and walking in my own semi-solid flesh."

Birdsong said, "Is that typewriter of mine still under the bar someplace?"

"I couldn't find an open hock shop," Patrise said, and the two of them chuckled at whatever the joke was. "Ginevra!"

"Yes, sir, almost ready," she said, whipping a cocktail shaker.

"Pavel will shut down in front; you serve Kitsune and Mr. Birdsong as long as they want, then lock up. You've been on golden hours since two. And take tomorrow night off."

"Yes, sir. Thank you."

"Cloud, see Miss Mirage home. Lincoln, Hallow, let's go."

They got into the car, Patrise alone in the back. With the Mirada sign switched off, all the world seemed dark, the big car's headlights just pushing the blackness aside for a moment.

Danny said, "The Ruthins are a big elf gang, right?"

"One of them," McCain said. "Red's their color. You see a red leather jacket, you take care."

"The car that shot at you was red."

"You're observant. Yes, that would have been the Ruthins. Unless it was someone else who wanted them blamed."

"Is there some kind of gang war going on?"

"Conflict, I'd say. And there's always conflict. War, now, well. They'll cut each other up as easily as a round-ear. You heard there were gang elves in the club tonight: they can come right in as long as they follow the rules. Not like the pure-Ellyll clubs."

"What's an—ethyl?"

"*Ellyll.* Not that I can say it right, either. That's an elf name for elves."

"And Miss Asa said something about Vamps. That can't be what it sounds like . . . can it?"

McCain's voice was suddenly tense and quiet. "Vamps are human or halfie kids who want so bad to hang around no-shit-real live elves that the elves let them. The price is that you get a taste of elf blood."

"You mean, like, literally."

"I mean real literally. There's something in their blood that hits mortals like heroin. Slurp, you're hooked, and you'll do anything for another little sip. So the elves think up in-ter-est-ing things for you to do. Be real careful around the Vamps: an elf'll kill you for the sake of a joke, but a sucker'll kill you and never know why."

The car turned sharp right, went down a ramp. A steel door rolled up before them, and they drove into a concrete bunker of a garage. There were half a dozen cars parked, none as big as Mr. Patrise's, but all in the same old-time style. The garage was only about half full. As they got out, Danny saw a row of motorcycles, some with sidecars: big Harleys, BMWs, classic Indians.

A man in coveralls was cleaning the parts of a Thompson submachine gun. Laid out on a table near him were two pistols, several knives, and a black metal crossbow.

Mr. Patrise said, "Good morning, Jesse."

"Morning, sir. Glad to have you home."

"Have Stagger Lee and Miss Phasia come home?"

Jesse looked at a wall clock with a round white face and a swinging brass pendulum. The glass case read REGULATOR. " 'Bout two hours ago."

They walked on to an elevator lined with panels of etched bronze. It began rising. "Hallow will be in the north wing with us," Patrise said. "Good morning to you, gentlemen."

The door opened. McCain stepped out, waved for Danny to follow. They left Patrise behind.

They were in a broad, carpeted corridor, with Art Moderne geometric wood on the walls and overhead lamps of marbleized glass. It looked about half a mile long.

"In here." They went into a room lit by a hard white downlight. It shone mostly on a telephone switchboard, dozens of sockets and a row of plugs. A refrigerator-sized safe was in the corner. A woman was sitting at the switchboard, wearing a headset. "Hi, Linc."

"Hi-de-hi, Lisa."

She moved her right hand out of shadow, put down the revolver that had been hidden there and picked up a coffee mug. "I take it things are all right now."

"Norma Jean got hurt. But she'll be okay, thanks to this guy. He's gonna be moving in with us. Twenty-four."

McCain made the introductions. Lisa picked up a phone and spoke softly while McCain went to the safe and twirled the knob. Danny saw Lisa reach under the switchboard, and the safe door opened. McCain closed it again, came away holding a key on a white tag.

"Give me your left hand."

Danny did. McCain squeezed the end of Danny's ring finger, and he felt a stick. A drop of his blood plopped onto the key tag, which seemed to suck it up like a sponge. The tag glowed for a moment. It was blue now. McCain pressed the key into Danny's palm.

"Lisa, call Michael Reese at six, find out how Norma's doing. Then call her folks."

She made a note. "Anything else?"

"No changes otherwise. G'night, Lisa."

"Good night, Linc. And you, Doc."

As they walked down the hall, McCain pointed at the key Danny was turning over in his hand. "Nobody but you can use that now. You need somebody let in, let the staff know. Just pick up the phone in your room, you'll get Lisa or whoever's on the board."

"Is 'hi-de-hi' code for 'everything's okay'?"

"Good thought. Sometimes it is. Know anything about the witch works?"

"Magic?" McCain nodded. "No."

"You'll find out soon enough if you've got the Touch. If you do, you'll be able to find the key with it. Enough stuff, and you can zap it to you. Here's your room."

Danny waited, then looked down stupidly at the key in his hand. He opened the door.

The room was about the size of the one he'd grown up in, paneled in rich dark wood. Desk, table, big closet door. The sofa would fold out to a bed, or maybe there was a wall bed, a Murphy.

"Front parlor," McCain said. He rapped a knuckle on a wall panel and it swung open. "Coat closet. Next one's the gun cabinet, there's a trick lock on that. We've got an infirmary downstairs, but you might want to keep a crash kit ready in here."

He opened the "closet door," went through into a room three times the size of the entry, fully furnished, with a bar and kitchenette at one end. Danny still didn't see a bed—wait, there was another doorway. This place looked bigger than the house he'd grown up in.

McCain opened the little refrigerator. "Isn't stocked; tell the kitchen what you'd like. Bar's probably dry too. You a beer man?"

"Yeah." He didn't have a clue if that were true: he'd had beers with the fire and rescue guys—everybody knew his age, but nobody said anything. And he'd split a pint of Wild Turkey bourbon with Robin once, before the accident. They had to sleep it off in the field behind Rob's place. He couldn't remember now what dumb excuse they'd come up with after that, but Rob's dad was—well, you could believe he'd been eighteen once.

McCain stood up, opened a drawer, took out a tin box. "Matches." He pointed to a tall-chimneyed kerosene lamp in a reflector on the wall. "You know how to light those?"

"Yes." That was true; he had grown up in Tornado Alley.

"The power's usually pretty good, but this is the Shades. We like to save our generator juice for real emergencies. If you turn out to have the witch gimmick, keep that in mind." He put the matches away. "Bedroom's that way; Lisa called and it should be ready." He went to the entry door, leaned against it, said gently, "Yeah, I know you've got about six million questions. Anything that won't wait till tomorrow?"

"When's breakfast?"

McCain laughed. "Hey, this is your house now. Breakfast's

when you wake up and get hungry. The dining room's a floor down, or you can call to have it up here." He looked aside. "That's how it is here: you do as you please—unless it's Mr. Patrise asking."

"You're telling me I just lucked into all this."

"Mr. Patrise says that people make their own luck, and I think I agree with him." McCain knocked wood. "Not to worry, is it? If you're dreamin', you'll wake up somewhere else, won't you? G'night, Doc."

"Good night, McCain."

After McCain had gone, Danny wandered into the bedroom, into carpet up to his ankles. There was custom cabinetry all around the walls, another desk, and an oversized four-poster bed in carved walnut. His great-grandmother had a bed like that. Her heirs had done everything short of spill blood over who would get it. The covers were turned back, and a white plush robe and a pair of gray pajamas were laid out on the spread.

He picked up the pajamas. Silk. He decided he didn't want to put them on without a shower first.

The bathroom was all glass and chrome and silver-veined black marble. The tub was marble, with taps like spaceship controls; the shower was completely separate, a cylinder of glass block with multiple heads to spray from all directions. Somehow the stone floor was warm.

Washed and in the slippery gray silk, he slipped between the sheets. There was a console at the bedside that controlled every light in the apartment. A dial selected music channels: jazz, jazz, classical, swing, opera, jazz—wasn't this the city? Where was the rock? He got some electric folk and listened for a while. One song was about somebody named Matty Groves and somebody else's wife, another about a bandit on a mountain who got seriously screwed over by a girl.

He snapped off the lights and lay there, stone awake.

Lights on, robe on. A midnight snack—okay, a five AM snack—couldn't hurt. At the last moment he remembered to get the key out of his jeans and stuff it into a robe pocket.

The heavy oak door made no sound at all. Danny looked up and down the hall. The elevator was to the right. So was Lisa's switchboard room. There must be stairs someplace, especially if the power went off and on. He turned left.

The last door had a glass panel. He could see stairs beyond. He paused to look out the window at the end of the hall. It had bars outside, and steel shutters. He couldn't see very much—what looked like a hedge, maybe a moonlit garden. He went down the stairs.

The hall here had less wood, more crystal and steel. There was an office, that must be a library . . . dining room, yes.

There was a flutter of light just at the edge of his vision, and he turned, half-thinking of Cloudhunter's shotgun at his head.

He saw a woman. She was wearing a black and gold kimono tied with a fringed silk sash. She looked up at Danny, and his heart crashed straight into his brain.

She was the most beautiful woman he had ever seen, so much so that he had trouble actually *seeing* her—the eyes drew him to the lips, and then the chin, the ear, the throat, without a stop to register any of them fully. He tried to speak, but his tongue wouldn't engage and a blimp was docked in his throat.

She smiled. He ached, he hurt, he thought he would drop to his knees. She walked away from him, down the hall. He didn't quite see her go; she was just *gone*, and a man's voice said, "Is there something I can get for you, Mr. Hallownight?"

The man was a butler in a perfect gray uniform. Danny felt the sweat on his own palms, his gasping, his locked-and-loaded erection. "Was that—ff—Fay?"

If the butler saw anything untoward about Danny, he gave no sign of it. "I didn't see, sir. Miss Phasia is retired for the night, but it could have been. Can I get you something?"

"A sandwich . . . roast beef? And a glass of milk."

"Certainly, sir. And might I suggest something to help you sleep?"

"Yes."

"I'll have it sent up at once, sir. You know you can telephone us at any time."

Danny climbed the stairs slowly. When he got into the hall, a girl in a gray uniform was coming out of the room. She paused to hold the door open. "Good night, sir."

"G'night."

There was a tray on the bedside table with a rare roast beef on dark rye, pickles and chips, and a glass of milk with a brown sprinkle on top. Danny sniffed it: nutmeg, and doubtless something under it. Something to sleep on.

Well, he had something, and he couldn't sleep on it unless he stayed flat on his back all night. He looked dizzily at the bed: no, not in those crisp clean sheets. He walked into the bathroom, stripping as he went. The floor was warm to the skin.

He cleaned up, took another couple of minutes' worth of shower, and crawled into bed. He took two bites of the sandwich, which was of course delicious, drank the milk-and-whatever in three gulps, and sank into sleep like quicksand, fully expecting to wake up, naked and damp, somewhere else.

But he didn't: same bed, same bedroom. A sliver of light ran around the drapes. He got hold of his watch, which read PAIN; he threw it across the room. The bedside clock's hands pointed to ten past five. PM, presumably.

He sat up, shook his head, dragged the robe on and walked around the apartment, just checking.

The two bags he'd had in the Triumph were in the entrance room, and the closet door stood open with a couple of paper laundry covers inside. A note was pinned to one of the bags:

> *Your cases were opened briefly, to check your sizes. Mr. Patrise instructed that you were not to be awakened, but if you rise in time, he will be pleased to see you at La Mirada for dinner at eight o'clock. If these clothes do not suit, please call me at your earliest convenience.*
>
> *Boris Liczyk*

Danny ripped the paper open. Inside was a wide-lapel suit, with pleated trousers in a deep gray-green, a tan silk shirt, and dark golden tie. At the bottom of the closet was a package of underwear and socks, a pair of wingtip shoes, and a black leather doctor's bag. Behind the suit he found a pale-tan trenchcoat, with the full complement of buckles and buttons, and up top a matching snap-brim hat.

On the desk was a pocket watch on a chain, and a leather sack of coins. Danny had read that paper money wasn't worth much in the Shadow; it was barter, or metal.

It was crazy. It was all plain crazy. He moved to check out his own bags, then decided why bother? What did he have worth *this* crowd's stealing?

The bathroom cabinet had shaving stuff, aspirin and cold pills, a box of rubbers, and some of those sponges girls used. He showered again, shaved carefully, dressed in the new outfit. It all fit nicely, and felt good, crisp and sharp and *good*. The shirt collar was a little tight, and Danny had never been able to manage a tie knot, but he didn't care. There was a full-length mirror in the bedroom: he looked at himself for a long while, jacket off and on, coat and hat off and on. He experimented with the hat angle. Even his hopeless red hair seemed to look right. The freckles—well.

He hung the coat and jacket up and went downstairs. In the dining room, he found a short, thin man with gray hair, in a perfectly creased navy-blue suit and a red scarf at this throat—ascot, that was it. The man turned.

"Good day to you, Mr. Hallownight. I am Boris Liczyk." It came out *Lizzik*. "Did you sleep well?"

"Yes, thanks." Danny began to wonder if there was a way to turn off the solicitude.

The man looked Danny up and down. "It's not bad, not bad— is that how you usually stand, sir?"

"I guess so. Would you call me, uh, Doc?"

"Certainly, Doc. I'm Boris. Now, if you'll just hold still—" Liczyk adjusted Danny's suspenders, pulling the waistband way up. He pinched a seam of the shirt sleeve, and Danny felt a chill down his arm. It passed in a moment. "*Don't* move, now." Liczyk did the same to the other sleeve. Then he put his hands on the collar, and at once the collar wasn't tight any more. Another touch smoothed the tie knot. "Yes, that's better. Do have me show you how to knot a tie. Do the shoes fit?"

"Fine."

"Mm-hmm. You didn't bring the jacket down."

"No, but it fit just fine."

Liczyk gave a blink of a smile. "Do you expect to be wearing a shoulder holster?"

"I—uh—well, no."

"Good. They're intractable. I'm sorry, I'm probably keeping you from breakfast."

"No, it's okay. I guess I'm having dinner in a couple of hours."

"True. Some juice? Some coffee?"

"Yeah, coffee. And maybe a glass of orange juice."

"Why don't you take them in the north garden? And I'll let Mr. McCain know you're awake."

It was pleasant in the garden; the sun was about to disappear below a building, but the still air was warm. The plants were still surprisingly green, with dashes of color from late-season flowers. There was no view. Brick walls twenty feet high, topped with iron points, enclosed it completely.

McCain entered. "Not bad," he said. "Boris always likes having a new body to work on. You know you're in for a full custom fitting."

"Did he use magic on this?" Danny described the work on the shirt seams.

"That's his Touch. All he works with is fabric. Seams, cigarette burns in the carpet . . . He's a wizard with drapes, he is." McCain grinned. "What, did you think it was all throwin' lightning bolts? Come with me. Bring your coffee."

They went down to the garage. The TR3 was there, hood propped open. Jesse the mechanic was leaning over the engine.

"You tune this thing yourself, ki—Doc?" Jesse said.

"When I can get the parts."

"Yeah, that's always the trouble." He pointed at the engine block, at places where the metal looked unnaturally shiny, or glowed a deep cobalt blue. "Wasn't any way to go dual-fuel—space, mass, architecture—and you needed new lifters anyway, so I put in sensitives, and bound a desire to the fuel pump. That should get you through any short-term tech failure." Jesse closed the lid. "She's a pretty car, Doc. I wouldn't do her wrong. Turn her over yourself."

Danny slid in. He noticed that a couple of familiar dings were out of the panel, and the rips in the soft top had all been mended.

He started the car. It caught on the first try, and sounded slick as iced snot.

"Take her 'round the block," McCain said. He held out two slabs of plastic: a driver's license and paramedic's card, new ones with his new name. Danny tucked them away, saluted, and put the Triumph into gear.

He got up the ramp, turned onto the street, upshifted. She liked it.

The low sun bronzed the corridors of glass and brick and the stumps of broken skyscrapers. The near buildings were mostly clean and cared for, with here and there a notch of fallen stone. Beyond, there were walls holed with empty windows, holding up nothing, and bare metal frames, twisted like dust devils petrified. Above the near rooflines, Danny could see the tops of skyscrapers: they were dull, and dark, and looked ravaged. Not one seemed to be intact.

A cluster of five motorcycles went by the other way. The riders had this-and-that leathers, not a helmet among them, streaming long hair and tassels and bits of chain. One was a bare-legged bare-foot girl. They revved, popped wheelies, split to flow around the Triumph, hooting and hollering. Something bounced off the soft top and crashed against the pavement. Danny drove on, checked the mirror: they gave no sign of doubling back.

He saw the lake then, across a band of highway and a line of wrecked buildings. It roiled, green and whitecapped, more like pictures of the ocean than any lake Danny knew. It faded out into darkness to the east.

He stopped on a bridge, got out of the car for a look around. The river was low, with sludgy banks littered with broken concrete and old metal. There had been a whole series of bridges toward the west; about half of them looked intact, the others just pilings, or collapsed and partially cleared. One looked as if something had bitten out and swallowed its span. Somewhere upstream—no, downstream; the water was, illogically, flowing *out* of the lake—a cargo ship was beached and rusting along the waterside, tilted twenty degrees over.

To the southeast there was a green park, little smokes curling up from among the trees. At least it seemed like something people were doing. He couldn't tell how far the park went; beyond a certain point, maybe a mile and a half away, the world got vague, like a running watercolor. A long way off to the southeast the sky was just a long smudge of smoky color. Danny had been to the Paint Pots at Yellowstone Park once, all steam and sulfur and colors; it was like that, but stretching for miles.

A breeze whistled through the bridge ironwork. It was the only sound there was. There was nobody *here*. The emptiness, the loneliness was awful.

A dull metallic sound came from beneath the road. Contraction? Loose bolts? Trolls?

He got back into the car. Up ahead was more iron, framing the street. He took a right, and the sun went out: the street was framed and roofed by metal lacework, big riveted girders. The elevated railroad, Danny realized. There didn't seem to be any trains running, though he saw a couple of station signs, and a stairway with people sitting on the steps.

Danny drove as straight as he could back to the house, down into the garage. McCain and Jesse were playing cards.

"The stuff you put in," Danny said, "does it work, outside? I mean, where there isn't magic?"

"Sure," Jesse said. "Not so well, but better'n spit 'n' baling wire." He put a card down.

McCain picked it up. "You know what—"

"Yeah, I know what baling wire is!" Danny shouted.

Both men were looking at him. Neither had any kind of meaningful expression.

Danny said, "I'm sorry."

"For what?" McCain said. "Now, Jesse, he's gonna be sorry. *Gin*." He tossed his cards down. "What do you say we go down to the club now? You'll have a better look before the crowd gets there, and we can get a head start on the evening's serious purposes."

"Without Mr. Patrise?"

"Oh, he'll be there. Get your coat . . . and grab your hat. . . ." He sang the last four words in a terrible baritone. "And don't forget your black bag, Doc."

The took the Triumph, McCain folding with care and some difficulty into the passenger seat.

"Left up here," he said. "So, magic or not, you like how she drives?"

"Oh, yeah. I, uh, she doesn't seem to have as much power, though."

"That's 'cause you're partly on spells. They don't have the kind of power you get from high-test gas." He chuckled. "Sounds funny, don't it? You think about magic, thunderbolts, splittin' the Red Sea. And some of it's like that. I hear in Elfland—but we'll never see that. In the Shades it's rickety, and when you tie it to machines it's rickety-tickety. Tin."

"Mr. Patrise's car seemed to have plenty of go."

"Mr. Patrise's car is particular. The others are mostly wood and fiberglass. The kids who can afford 'em ride bikes. But you can't see Mr. Patrise on a bike, now can you?"

They parked in an alleyway and walked the last block to the club, coats flapping in the cool air. Somebody in a cap and a frowzy jacket hustled by, carrying something in brown paper tucked tight under his arm. Danny wondered if he were a Vamp. He supposed he'd have to learn to tell that.

A few steps before they reached the awning, the electric sign came on. Abruptly there was movement at every edge of Danny's vision: people rounding corners, moving deeper into shadows or changing the ones they already had. A few people came out of darkness, too: all of them dressed up, dressed to kill.

"Mr. McCain!" one of them said, a man in a broad-brimmed hat and a cowboy duster, walking with a woman in a fringed jacket and tight skirt of white leather.

"Sheepscry. And Miss West. Good evening." McCain tipped his hat. The man lifted his. He was an elf, ivory-skinned, silver hair—not gray but metallic silver—slicked back, small round glasses with black lenses.

Miss West, who was human, said, "I would imagine this is Doc Hallownight." Her hair was black and white in jagged stripes, and there were a dozen silver studs in her left ear.

"Yes, miss," Danny said, and lifted his hat crookedly. "May I ask how you knew?"

Sheepscry said, "The inimitable Birdsong wrote about you."

Pavel opened the door. "Good evening, everybody! It's cold outside, not in!"

The ceiling stars shone specks of light around the room. Alvah Fountain, in a brocade jacket, was playing "Hey Bartender" at the piano.

"Draw one, draw two . . ." Danny muttered.

"Don't mind if I do, Doc," said Lucius Birdsong, sitting at the end of the bar.

McCain said, "Later, Doc," and moved off.

Danny said, "I heard you wrote about me?"

"Shaker," Birdsong said.

"What's your pleasure, Mr. Birdsong?" the bartender said. He had pointed elf ears, and pale, not pure-white, skin, black hair with patches of steel-blue at the temples. Danny had heard that elves and humans could interbreed.

Birdsong said, "Another one for me, and—is the doctor on duty?"

"Beer, please."

"And a *Chi-Cent*, Shaker. Unless you've used them all as bar towels."

"Wouldn't think of it, Mr. Birdsong." Shaker reached under the bar and produced a paper.

The paper had the feel of industrial toweling. Danny's thumb smudged the ink, which had a distinct chemical smell. The CHICAGO CENTURION—*For This Price, You Don't Expect a Tribune* banner, with pictures of eagles and trumpets, was a coarse linoleum or wood cut.

"As your fellow doctor Sam Johnson put it," Birdsong said, grinning, "it's not that the puppy tap-dances like Honi Coles, but that it has any rhythm in the first place. That's how *I* heard it, anyway."

THE CONTRARIAN FLOW

by Lucius Birdsong

I'm sure every devotee of this pillow-stuffing re-members what Mark Twain said about newspaper obit-

uaries and exaggeration, so I shall merely note for the
record that when that well-known gentleman Patrise entered the La Mirada nitery in the small hours of this
morning, he was accompanied neither by the sound of
clanking chains nor by cherubim strumming six-string
Rickenbacker harps.

Witnesses report that an innocent bystander (or
rather bysitter—whatever has happened to the standards
of marksmanship in Our Fair Levee?) was seriously injured in the incident that inspired all those campfire stories, but was ministered to by an able young man known
as Doc Hallownight, of whom Our Fair may expect to
hear more anon.

Personal to the Lousy Shots: Mind how you treat
Doc. He did you a big favor.

"Sing ho, for the Fourth Estate," Birdsong said, and tapped his
glass against Danny's.

The beer he'd been given was a medium brown color, with
thick foam. Danny tasted it carefully; it was slightly heavy, a little
sweet. He thought he could actually get to like beer like this.

Birdsong finished his drink. "Good night to you, friend."

"Where are you headed?"

"They're showing *His Girl Friday* at the Biograph. Miss it and
they revoke your press card." He paused, looked Danny in the eye.
"Circulate, Doc, circulate! Everybody here wants to meet you, and
those that don't aren't worth meeting anyway." He tapped the
newspaper. "Thank me later."

Danny looked around for McCain, Cloudhunter, someone he'd
met last night. The piano was playing something jazzy but slow.
He turned to Shaker, saw that the bartender was wearing a lapel
button that read HALF THE BLOOD, ALL THE CIVIL RIGHTS.

"Does Mr. Fountain take requests?"

"Sure does, sir."

"No sirs. I'm . . . Doc."

"You got it, Doc. Just tell Alvah what you want."

Danny went down the steps to the glossy, empty dance floor.
"Evening, man," Fountain said without missing a note.

"Could you play something . . . that, you know, rocks out a little?"

"Nothin' easier, man. You got yourself a girl to dance with?"

"No."

"Well, maybe by the second chorus."

"Yeah, maybe. Thanks."

"Cool runnings, Doc."

Danny walked back to the bar, hands in his pockets. Halfway there, he could see Shaker setting up another beer for him. As the glass touched the bar, hammer chords came down like thunder, and everything stopped. Fountain had kicked into "Great Balls of Fire" like the world was gonna end in three minutes five.

Couples were pulling each other away from their tables. A woman with a tenor sax came out of nowhere and swung in. High heels banged and elflocks shook. Even the waiters were twirling.

"Good Golly Miss Molly" followed hot, and "Roll Over, Beethoven." Some of the dancers were spending more time airborne than on the floor. Danny just stood there watching, the beer going warm in his hand.

"—gotta hear it again today," Shaker said in his ear. "Oh, come on, Doc! It ain't a movie."

There was a black-haired girl in a deep blue dress, one of those flapper dresses that ended in long points, showing and hiding leg at once. "Do you dance?" Danny said, half hoping she'd knock him on his butt for asking.

"I'll try," she said, and he saw that it was Ginevra Benci, the bartender from last night. She held out her bare white arm and he took it.

There was one extraordinary pair of dancers on the floor, a man with dark, dark skin in a pure-white suit, large but totally graceful, and an elf woman in a black sequined flapper dress like Ginevra's, who moved as if she was boneless. Danny tried to follow their style, ridiculous as he felt. After a moment, he realized that the man was looking at him; Danny felt his collar tighten, but the big man winked and nodded, and the couple started doing steps Danny could follow with relative ease.

By the second chorus, Danny and Ginevra were actually moving as a unit, off each other's toes. Danny hadn't done this since—

well, he'd done this, but he had never enjoyed it before.

The piano crashed, the sax cried, and the music stopped. Everybody applauded, even the waiters. Ginevra tugged Danny's arm; he turned and saw Patrise in the doorway, clapping furiously.

"Delighted you could both make it," he said. "And that you kept each other busy. Come up here, let's get to dinner."

Danny looked at Ginevra; she looked slightly away from him. Had Patrise told her to be his date for tonight? There were four couples plus one at the table: the two of them; McCain and an older woman, certainly over thirty, in black and pearls, introduced as Chloe Vadis; Cloudhunter and Carmen Mirage; and the two expert dancers, whose names were—that is, who were called Matt Black and Gloss White. Patrise sat alone at the head of the table.

Other people took the cue, drifting up to the tables and the bar. Fountain had gone back to a slow swing tune. Two couples were still dancing, half melted into each other.

Danny ordered a rare steak. McCain had his well done, with a lobster tail on the side. Ginevra had chicken salad, Gloss a dinner-sized Caesar, Matt a rack of barbecued ribs. Chloe Vadis was brought some kind of multicolored pasta dish. Carmen just had a little fruit cup, and Cloudhunter didn't eat at all. Patrise had a half duck glazed orange he carved like a surgeon.

There were occasional bursts of conversation as they ate; people came by to say hello, to admire Matt and Gloss's dancing, to mutter into Chloe's ear. Patrise had a compliment for every compliment, a quick answer for every question. He gave things a center. Danny still felt one part in three dreaming. He looked at Ginevra. Ginny. He wondered how she felt.

Carmen stood up. So did Cloudhunter. "Well," she said, "here goes nothing."

Patrise said, "Knock 'em dead, *primoroso*."

Cloudhunter took Carmen's hand and kissed it. She shut her eyes for a moment, then went around the curve toward the stage, disappeared through a curtain. Cloudhunter bowed and followed.

As the plates were cleared away, the room lights went down. Candles flared to life on the tables—like magic, Danny thought, and then let go the "like." The music stopped, and the last dancers left the floor.

A soft-edged spotlight showed Cloudhunter on the bandstand. He was wearing a blue velvet tailcoat and white tie, boots with silver trimmings. "Ladies and gentlemen," he said, sounding like the rise of a summer storm, "Miss Carmen Mirage."

He stepped back. She came out, bowed at the light applause, and began singing, a slow, torchy tune.

> *Tell me what my true love loves*
> *'Cause I want to fit him*
> *Like my hands in gloves*
> *Will he get in motion*
> *For a carol of devotion*
> *Or a cooing like a soft gray dove's*
> *You know I can't take the waiting*
> *Or the silence or the doubt*
> *So will you tell me what my love's about*

Carmen had a nice voice. She seemed to be pushing hard, as if she really wanted the crowd to break down and cry for her.

> *Tell me what my true love needs*
> *Should I dress in satins*
> *Or in old gray weeds*
> *Would it suit his style*
> *To be Emperor of my Nile*
> *On a barge among the whispering reeds*
> *Even Moses wouldn't travel*
> *Without spying out the land*
> *So will you tell me where my love's heart stands*

Everybody applauded. Someone whistled. Carmen took a bow, went off, came back for another bow. Another spot came on, moved around the room, stopping on Matt and Gloss. More applause.

"Would you mind?" Patrise said.

"Should have had one less rib," Danny heard Matt say, but they stood up to applause. Matt took off his jacket (there wasn't a speck of barbecue sauce on it) and they went out on the floor. Gloss White whispered to Alvah. He nodded, cracked his knuckles with a flourish, and barrel-rolled into "Saturday Night's Alright for Fighting."

Matt and Gloss danced: they moved like fury, they lit things up. When he spun her round, cometary light followed them. By the chorus, the crowd was up, shouting "Saturday! Saturday, Saturday!" and hell, it was Thursday. Finally they pressed back-to-back for a tap routine that seemed to take place in air. And there was a cheer. The dancers took their bow, scrambled out through the door Pavel was holding open.

"Coffee, I think," Patrise said. When it was poured, he held up his delicate china cup and said, "Once upon a time, when you had to go to the Shadow country for a drink of anything worth going out somewhere to drink, they served it in teacups. Now the World drips whiskey, and we slip the coffee over the line."

Danny said, "Was there a Levee—" He stopped, afraid he'd said something out of turn.

But Patrise smiled. "The first Chicago Levee existed at the end of the nineteenth century. But the Shadow regions have always been, and always will be. It's . . . other places that come and go."

Carmen reappeared. "How did I do?"

"You did," Patrise said, "And you do, and you are." She leaned down to kiss him.

Matt and Gloss came back, in fresh outfits, still all white, all black: Matt in a loose cotton suit over a crewnecked shirt, Gloss in a shiny ebony skintight, with thin satin straps that crossed and wound to her throat, and an oval of elf-white midriff showing behind a gauze panel.

"I must speak to Boris," Patrise said, as if to himself. Then the spotlight was on the stage again, on Cloudhunter.

"Ladies and gentlemen," he said, and now his voice was a faint breeze on a still pond, "friends of all lands and all origins, La Mirada is pleased to present . . . Phasia, the Voice."

Cloudhunter stepped back, out of sight. There was absolute silence. Danny felt his heart hammering in anticipation of god knew what. The curtains opened. A woman in a plain white bareshouldered gown stood in a column of light. She was pale, but not an elf; dark brown hair fell in curls around her bare throat, and her eyes were piercingly blue in the downlight.

It was the woman he had seen last night . . . Danny thought. The face was the same, he was sure, but she did not have the extreme, unreal, frightening beauty he had seen then. Maybe he had been dreaming.

She raised her arms, curling long thin fingers with bright red nails, and began to sing.

No, this had to be the dream.

There was a singer Danny's mother had liked, a woman with a multiple-octave range who could use it all as an instrument, making silly pop lyrics sound profound, meaningless be-bop-a-lula syllables meaningful.

There weren't even distinct syllables now, just a continuous flow of sound. Danny could faintly recognize the tunes: they were, had been, "Orange Blossom Special" and "Walk On By" and "Can't Help Lovin'," but that didn't matter either; with the voice, the Voice—it was silly to call it *pure music*, like saying rain was pure water and the sun was pure light, so a rainbow was—there it just *was*, and Danny thought how much better it would be to be blind than deaf. It was hard to move one's look away from Fay, but Danny saw Alvah Fountain sitting straight up on the piano bench, his hands folded, his fingers knotted tight enough to snap right off. He wasn't playing a note, so where was the music coming from?

She wound down to the last note of a song that was "My Funny Valentine" when it had words, and they all woke up, back where they had been, wondering what they had done in their sleep. Phasia took a sweeping bow, and the curtains closed on her. Danny wondered why there was so little applause—why the walls weren't cracking with it—and when he tried to clap, found that his hand wouldn't move, and hurt. In a moment he realized it was because Ginny was squeezing it in both of hers. She was crying.

He fumbled the silk handkerchief out of his pocket and gave it to her. As she wiped her face, he noticed the dampness on his own cheeks. He saw Mr. Patrise watching them.

Patrise said, "Why don't you take the lady home, Hallow? This has hardly been a quiet night off for either of you."

Ginny nodded and looked into her empty coffee cup. Danny wobbled his chair back, went to stand by Ginny's. She took his hand and stood up.

Patrise said, "Ginevra, you're not on duty tomorrow, are you?"

"No, sir. I would have been working tonight, but . . ."

"That's fine, then. Hallow, we will be working, but not until quite late."

"Yes, sir."

"Then good night."

Pavel brought their coats, lifted his topper as he opened the door.

"It's cold," Danny said. The sky was mostly low pink clouds, with a few holes. Mist drifted across the street.

"It's almost Halloween," she said. "Is that why you're called Hallownight? 'Cause you got here on Halloween?"

"It's my birthday. Halloween is, I mean."

"Oh. I had a friend whose birthday was the Fourth of July. They always had her party a couple of days early, nobody wanted to have two parties at once."

"Yeah, that's a good idea. Down this way." They turned into the alley. Danny heard a scuffling, then feet running away. He looked up and down the street, into the darkness past the car, but didn't see anyone. He thought about taking Ginny's hand, but just put her between himself and the nice solid wall. He pointed to the Triumph. "Here it is."

"Oh, it's cute! I haven't seen one like this."

"It's mine. I brought it with me from home."

"A guy with his own car," she said, faraway. "My grandma used to talk about when all the guys had their own cars, you know, before Elfland and stuff." She walked around the TR3, looked at the rear plate. "Iowa, huh."

He opened the door. "Where you from?"

"Ohio. Since my mom and dad broke up. But I was born in Italy. My dad was Navy, with the Med Fleet."

"That sounds neat. I mean, well—was it?"

"Sometimes. Dad took me around Europe, when he could. We went to Paris four or five times. The Shadow there's called the Rêve Gauche. Do you get that?"

"Sorry."

"It's . . . I'll tell you another time. I think my favorite city is Florence, though. Florence is beautiful. The art, and the buildings . . .

Elfland didn't come back there. They say they don't need it."

He helped her get into the car, then got in himself. "So then your name's really—"

"Oh, no. My name—my dad's name—was Artensteen. Ginevra da Benci is a woman in a painting by Leonardo da Vinci. I don't look anything like her, though. Mr. Patrise called me that." She gave him a small, nervous grin. "He said, 'You can't be the Gioconda. You smile too much.'"

"The Jo—I'm sorry, I'm stupid."

"The heck you are. You know the *Mona Lisa*?"

"Sure."

"Same painting. She's also called *La Gioconda*."

He started the car. "So, where do you live?"

"Aren't you going to take me home?"

"Well, yeah, as soon as I find out where it is. *Oh.*" He banged his knuckles on the steering wheel.

"I mean, I think you're a nice guy. And Mr. Patrise has always been really good to me."

"Oh." He heard something clatter down the alley, turned to see what it was. Nothing. His heart was so loud he had to check that the car was still running. "Which way do I go from here? To get to your place?"

She pulled the shoulder belt across her breasts, cinched it. Danny looked away. She said, "Back out of the alley, then right."

After a few blocks, she said, "It wouldn't be the first time for me. I'm not scared." She tugged at her coat. "Do you want to?"

"Yeah. Yeah, I do. But not because somebody *told* you to."

"Turn right here."

"You're not—you won't lose your job, or anything, if—"

"I'm not one of Chloe's girls. Left, you can't get through down there. Did Mr. Patrise ask you to—well, heck, do anything with me, except drive me home?"

"No."

"Stop the car."

He did, expecting her to get out. Instead she turned to look directly at him. "This is *important. Listen.* I came out here a year ago last summer. I didn't have a car, I hitched. I thought I was gonna have to go work on the street, or—I don't want to tell you what I thought about doing. You ever been crazy, I mean, just *crazy* over the way things were, so *anything* else looked good?" Her voice was rising. Danny knew why.

"McCain picked me up. I knew who Mr. Patrise was; everybody on the Levee does. So I thought, yeah, sure, one night on clean sheets. But Mr. Patrise gave me a job. And Shaker taught me how to tend bar. So if he *told* me to lie down for you, I'd *do* it, okay, Doc?" She breathed in hard, clenched her hands. "He's taken me to dinner a couple of times, and I mean *dinner*. Everybody who works for him gets things like that. But this is the first time—do you want to know what he said?"

"I guess I do."

"He said, 'Hallow's new, and he's alone, and that's not right. No more right than that you should be alone. See what happens.' "

"You said you'd—"

"That was a long time ago," she said. "I guess we'd better move on, huh?"

Danny started the car again. Ginevra said, "Up here, on the right."

He pulled to the curb in front of a brownstone apartment block, torch-shaped lamps flanking the door. She sat there, buckled in tight. "So I guess nothing happens tonight, huh?"

"Not tonight."

"I could make you some tea, or something."

If he went up there, he surely would not come down until morning. He didn't dare even touch his seat belt, and he surely could not touch hers.

She unfastened herself, turned as much as the little car would allow, her face just inches from his. "You're really sweet. And you want to be nice, and I like that. I appreciate that. But you're on the Levee now, in the Shadow. You have to know nobody cares one way or another. Nobody but us." She kissed him. "Hey, redhead, you're hot."

He didn't move.

"You wanna safeword out, Doc?"

"What do you mean?"

"Have you got a word that means 'really stop it, right now'?"

"I never heard of that."

"Oh," she said, and Danny understood that he was missing something important. "And I haven't seen any reason to use mine. Well. Let me tell you how to get back to Mr. Patrise's house. You really don't want to get lost around here." She spelled out the directions; he tried to remember them. Then she got out of the car.

His body made him call out, "I'll see you again?"

"Oh, jeez, Doc. Sure."

He waited until she had gone up the steps and entered the building before starting the car. You could have, he kept thinking all the way back, you *could* have. Nobody. Would. Have. Cared.

"She wasn't *afraid*," he said out loud, as he passed a cluster of people warming themselves around an oil-drum fire. It brought him to the edge of laughing, and the tension got him home.

He woke up a little after eight the next morning. When he went down to the dining room, Phasia was there, sitting at the table in a long flowered gown. There was also a man Danny hadn't seen before, wearing shirtsleeves and suspenders; he had short brown hair, large dark eyes behind round-rimmed glasses. He ate scrambled eggs and home fries with his left hand and wrote on a pad of graph paper with his right.

"Hello," Danny said.

Fay looked up from her egg cup and toast. She was still very beautiful, especially when she smiled and her crystalline blue eyes twinkled, but the fabulous glow was not there. Danny wondered if he had really seen it at all.

The man scratched his head with the eraser end of his pencil and looked up. "You must be Doc. I'm Stagger Lee. Sit down and join us."

Danny did. One of the staff was there instantly to take his breakfast order.

Stagger Lee said, "You're up kind of early. I thought you were out at the club last night."

"I came back early."

"Oh. I'm just finishing up for the night." Danny noticed that Stagger Lee's shirt was badly wrinkled, and one of his suspenders was flapping loose.

Fay folded her napkin and stood up. Stagger Lee was on his feet at once; Danny did likewise.

"Staganess day toll," she said, or something sounding like that. "Doc well be dockelnight, sorge do well." She made a small, nervous gesture with her hand and left the room.

Stagger Lee said gently, "I guess you haven't heard Fay speak."

"I heard her sing last night."

"No. Not the same."

"Phasia," Danny said, understanding. *"Aphasia."*

Stagger Lee said, "Yup," dragging the syllable way out. "I guess we could sit back down now."

Danny's pancakes and bacon appeared. Stagger Lee said, "Excuse my company while you eat; I need to get this done before I drop over. You know we're going to be out late tonight. You might want to get a couple of hours' sleep this afternoon."

"Does Mr. Patrise party every night?"

"Not every night. And I wouldn't call this evening a party, at least not the way you mean." He worked a while longer, then said, "Are you a poker player, Doc?"

"I know how."

"There's a game Monday night. You'll be welcome." He glanced up. "Unless Patrise wants you then?"

"He hasn't said."

"Right." He sat back, drinking coffee and examining his notes. As Danny finished his breakfast, Stagger Lee said, "I've got the infirmary keys. You ought to get your bag like you want it before tonight."

Stagger Lee led the way out of the dining room, absentmindedly hitching his loose suspender. "Know anything about magic?"

"They tell me it works here."

"True. Not always well, but it works."

The infirmary was in the south wing. It had white enameled cabinets, a desk and examining table out front; in back was a room with two hospital beds, and another room fitted for light surgery. None of the facilities seemed to have seen much use.

Stagger Lee said, "Some of the staff have first-aid training, so if you ever need a hand down here, give the switchboard a yell.

And there's me." He disconnected a small ring of keys from a larger one, jingled them in his fingers. "Glad to pass the buck, to be honest."

"Are you a doctor?"

"Not an MD." He unlocked one of the cabinets. It was full of supplies: vials, boxes, syringes, tape. "I'm just the general tech guy around here. Have you ever heard of Stagg Field?"

"Where the nuclear reactor was."

"Bingo. It's not there any more, but I went to what's left of the University of Chicago. Just in case," he said with a grin, "you thought I'd shot somebody on account of a hat."

He took some boxes down from a cabinet. "This is goldenrod unguent, for all-purpose healing; it works best on elves, but you can use it on humans. Piñon gum's for abscesses and infections. Boneset leaf, you may have seen that before in the World. . . ."

He held up a fabric-covered object a little thinner than his thumb. "This is a tarantelle cap, for serious systemic poisoning. You use it like an ammonia inhaler: crack it under the nostrils, have the victim breathe. And then get clear: they'll start dancing like crazy to drive out the poison."

"You're kidding."

"Empiricists don't kid, Doc. I've seen it work. I mean it about the getting clear, too. If the patient's busted up physically, you've got a judgment call, because the tarantelle doesn't care about a few broken bones. But remember that we've got poisons here like nothing you ever saw in the World."

"Magic," Danny said.

"These aren't spells. Most of them are old folk remedies on our side of the fire; some even work—piñon kills *Staph aureus*. They just work better here, like penicillin works better in the World. That's the other thing: magic's unreliable here in the middle, but so is penicillin. The only things you can really always rely on are mechanical closure, sutures and tape, and usually the simpler antiseptics, alcohol and iodine. You're going to see some really bad scarring around here. Don't let it get to you."

Danny thought of Norma Jean. He thought of Rob, too, of course.

Stagger Lee held up a glass vial of what looked like colored glitter. "This is fairy dust: broad-spectrum illusion powder. The Shadow uses a *lot* of this stuff. Did you see people at the club who looked like they were glowing? Dust."

Okay, Danny thought, that was it. That explained Phasia's appearance, her light.

"It's also a euphoric, psychologically addictive."

"Psychologically?"

"You can't *prove* dust has any somatic effects. But it sure does hook people."

"What am I supposed to do with it?"

"Comfort the dying." Danny couldn't tell if Stagger Lee was joking or not. "Meanwhile, back at reality ..." Stagger Lee unlocked another cabinet, pointed to boxes of hypodermic cartridges. "Meperidine, haloperidol, straight morphine—synthetics don't work as well on elves."

"I can't carry that stuff."

"Why not? You've got a license."

"Sure, but I'm supposed to have authorizations."

"*Doc.*" Stagger Lee sounded amused. "You can carry any of this stuff you want, and prescribe it any way you want, to anybody you want, at least on this side of the Fire. You have all the authorization there is." Danny got the message. "Okay. Atropine, lidocaine, most of the rest of it you know better than I do. There's a reference library over there. Down here's bicarb in a heart needle pack, though the only coronaries I've ever seen Shadowside were so coke-boosted they needed the bomb squad more than CPR. It's your call, but most of your cases are going to be trauma, and combat trauma at that."

"How about IV fluids? And blood?"

Stagger opened another cabinet, revealing racks of solution bags and accessories. "The plastic bags are hard to come by, even for us. We've got a glass still and autoclavable bottles, though they're a pain to haul around. Remember what I said about trauma?"

Danny nodded.

"So you understand the problem?"

"Yes."

"Wish I had a good answer for you."

"Thanks."

"Don't mention it."

"How about blood?"

"Mm. Anybody told you about elf blood?"

"It doesn't mix."

"Sure doesn't. Somebody down in the New Carré gave a human patient who would have died anyway a unit of *gwaed gwir*. . . . Well, like I said, he would have died anyway. Don't even think about transfusing between Truebloods; the class and race situation's too complicated. They don't mingle."

"Truebloods . . ."

"Elves."

"McCain called them Ellyll."

"Yup. Short course in nonhuman nomenclature: All elves are Truebloods, or *gwaed gwir*. Ellyllon—that's the plural—are a kind of minor nobility. Almost all the elves you see on this side of the gates are Ellyll; the lower orders can't come across and the higher ones rarely bother. You might think of the Ellyll as like the nothing-special European nobles who went off to the New World a few centuries back, looking for adventure and easy loot.

"Once in a while a High-born elf—an Urthas—comes over to our tacky little reality. It's not polite to mix them up with the Ellyll, but you're not likely to. High-borns are conspicuous. And if you do goof, they're probably not listening. Get it?"

"Got it."

"Good. The only other sort of Trueblood you might see are the Mani; they're a service class, who fetch and carry for the Urthas."

"What do I say to them?"

"They're easy to get along with. Very mission-centered, and either you're the object of the mission or you're not there. Even if you are—do you talk to postage stamps?"

"How many of the . . . Truebloods speak English?"

"All the Urthas and Ellyllon can, when they feel like it. Their own languages—I know of forty—aren't available for mortals to study. But there's Ellytha, which is like a trade language; humans can learn it, and it's okay if you don't speak it very well, because heck, humans aren't supposed to speak the beautiful elven tongue very well. They don't even mind if we call it 'Elvish'. There are dictionaries and recordings in the library downstairs, if you're interested."

Danny nodded.

"Okay, let's finish up here. I have got to get some sleep." Stagger Lee pointed to a clipboard inside the IV cupboard. "All us mortals in the house are typed; list's here. If you need a withdrawal from the bank, Mr. Patrise can arrange that."

"Is there anything Mr. Patrise can't get?"

"He's got me. And you." Stagger Lee yawned. He tossed Danny the key ring. "The house is about as safe as anywhere on the Levee, so you don't absolutely have to lock up every time you go out the door. Your call."

"These aren't—anybody can use them?"

"No, we don't tag those keys. If you got hurt, you wouldn't want us to have to fool around getting the door open, right?"

"Right."

"Just take care of 'em. See you tonight."

"Yeah."

Danny stood in the infirmary for a little while, looking around at all the stuff with no rational idea of what to do next. Finally he put it all back on the shelves, locked the cabinets, and went over to the library shelf. He got out the *Merck Manual*, the *PDR*, and all the books on emergency medicine, called the kitchen for a pot of tea in his rooms. They politely asked if he wouldn't rather have coffee. He agreed, and went upstairs to study.

By noon he had worked out a list. He took the black bag downstairs, then had a thought partway through loading it, and went to the dining room. McCain was there, eating a sandwich and reading the *Centurion*. He hummed and nodded. "They said you were up early. You know about—"

"Tonight, yeah. I'll be awake. What are we gonna do tonight, anyway?"

"Raise some hell. It'll be interesting." He gestured at a pitcher of iced tea, and Danny poured himself a glass.

Danny said, "Miss Phasia talked to me this morning. How long has she been like that?"

"A couple of years." McCain looked up suddenly. "She talked to *you*? Was anybody else here?"

"Stagger Lee. But she spoke to me: she said my name, or tried to."

"She hadn't ever seen you before. Not close."

"Well—" Danny told McCain about the previous night, the encounter in the hall. "I couldn't understand it, until Stagger Lee told me about the fairy dust."

"You thought that was *dust?*" McCain looked terribly intense. "Let's go down to the infirmary."

McCain shut the infirmary door behind him, and leaned against the frame, head tilted as if he were listening for a sound in the hall. "Piece of friendly advice. Seeing Fay that night—forget it happened." Danny started to interrupt, but McCain stopped him with a raised finger. "I know it was just an accident, and all she did was smile. Leave it at that." He didn't sound angry; he sounded concerned.

"Okay."

"Okay." McCain relaxed.

"Can you tell me what happened to her voice?"

"She used to be a singer," McCain said, almost offhandedly. "Pretty good one, as I hear. Then one night after a show, she said something to piss off an Ellyll. Big boss in the Glasa gang."

"What did she say?"

"I wasn't there, but I imagine it was something like No. Elves get upset easy anyway. So he cursed her. They do that. Crumpled her speech up, like you heard."

"And . . . her singing voice? The one I heard last night?"

McCain tapped one hand on another. "I stay clear of the witch ways, mostly. But I know it doesn't work right, here. Elves forget that, a lot. And some say it's to do with innocence—she hadn't done anything to bear cursing—but I don't know, it's not my idea of justice.

"Understand, she's like that with all words: she can't speak, or understand right, nor write nor read. When you're around her awhile, the understanding starts to come. And there's the Voice." He stood away from the door.

Danny said, "The elf who did it . . ."

"He didn't know how to undo it. Away from home they don't know how their own magic works. He's dead now."

"Aren't elves, you know, immortal?"

"They don't die of old age. But nobody ever dies of that in the Shade." He looked at the door to the surgery room. "If they can crawl back to Elfland, all the holes close up. This side, they die just like anybody."

"Okay," Danny said, because he didn't want to hear any more of this, "thanks for telling me, Lincoln."

"Wait. Fay trusts you: she doesn't talk to people she doesn't trust. You know what a glamour is?"

"Not something to do with movie stars?"

"No. It's a magic, that changes people's senses. The Voice is a glamour." McCain paused a long beat, as if considering something long and hard, then said, "It can show itself in other ways. You follow?"

"Yeah. Thanks."

"Don't mention it." McCain looked up, with just a little smile. "Really." He opened the door. "This place got everything you need?"

"Sure."

He nodded, paused again. "Oh, yeah. Can you shoot?"

"A rifle. Twenty-two."

McCain shook his head. "There's a range down in the garage, if you want to learn. 'Sides, didn't you always want to shoot a Tommy gun?"

"Well . . ."

"Thought so. Jesse'll teach you."

"Should I?"

"Can't hurt. Not tonight, though. See you, Doc."

It was a few minutes before midnight. "September gave up early," Stagger Lee said, and breathed out fog.

Stagger had driven Danny around town for twenty minutes or so, in one of the wobbly lightweight cars. They parked in an alley. Stagger Lee carried a black nylon shoulder bag. Danny had his red paramedic's bag; the leather doctor's kit was fine for carrying a few essentials, but too small for a serious trauma kit. And besides, he knew his own bag. He and Stagger wore dark topcoats and hats. So did the two people on the street corner ahead. Danny saw the glow of a cigarette, no faces.

"Evening, brethren," Stagger Lee said, cheerfully though not very loud. "Have you seen the true light?"

"Shinin' like a beacon," a woman's voice said.

They were in a warehouse district. Windows were barred at ground level, or bricked up. Webs of razor ribbon caught the moonlight, and the hard shine of bare electric bulbs.

The four of them walked a block, and met two more people: McCain and Patrise. Patrise carried a silver-headed cane. There were nods, a hi or two. They kept walking. Then Patrise gestured with a gloved hand, and they stopped.

Patrise tapped the cane on the sidewalk. A fluid shape slid out of the darkness: a small figure in a wide-brimmed hat and a long cloak. The hat tilted up; Danny saw a flash of lace, and a face. It was Kitsune, the Tokyo Fox.

"Around the corner, two doors along," she said. "This is as close as I get."

"Naturally," Patrise said. He took a step, and the Fox's cloak swept; Danny was aware that something had changed hands. Then the Fox hurried on into the night, almost floating, with no sound at all.

The group moved on, around the corner, to the indicated door. It was a hinged steel door, with a massive padlock. There was no light or sign of life from the building. The woman who had joined Danny and Stagger Lee kept on walking. Patrise gestured at the padlock, and Stagger Lee reached into his bag.

Stagger wrapped a length of soft metal ribbon around the door hasp. He looked at Patrise, holding his hand arched. Patrise nodded. Stagger Lee moved his hand, and a match flared; the thermite caught, there was a ring of white fire and a spray of sparks, and the hasp and padlock dropped into Stagger Lee's gloved palm with a plop.

McCain grabbed the edge of the door and flung it wide open. Light spilled out. Patrise walked through, just as if it were La Mirada. The others followed.

The warehouse space was more than two stories high, lit by bulbs in green tin fixtures; cardboard and junk sheetmetal had been duct-taped over all the windows. Toward the rear was a dimmer space, a metal framework, and stacks of crates. Up front was an assembly line, snaking back and forth around the floor.

At one end, a young man took empty bottles out of crates. Another pushed them along rollers; they stopped below a glass tank of red liquid, with a long rubber hose leading from it. Another person dribbled a half inch of the red stuff into a bottle, then sent it along to another station, where the bottles were topped off with clear fluid from a tube attached to an iron tap. At the next stop, the bottle was capped, shaken to mix the contents, and placed in a wooden case. Another worker leaned on a hand truck, staring into space, presumably waiting for the case to be filled.

None of the workers seemed to have noticed the intrusion. They just kept on shoving, filling, stacking. Their clothes were battered, ragged, filthy; they wore ruined tennis shoes or none at all. Danny could see that the capper's hands were scarred and bleeding. Some of them looked like part-elves, some human, but their skin was so dirty, their eyes so red and vacant, that it was hard to be sure who was how much of what.

He looked again at the tank of red fluid. He knew well enough what it was. The workers were Vamps; the red stuff was elf blood, cut with water to make it go farther. This was where the addicts got their supply.

A woman in a red leather jacket appeared on top of a stack of crates. She had a clipboard in one hand and a long-barreled revolver in the other. Her hair shone blue-white; her skin was the color of bone, her eyes silver. She wore black jeans with a hip holster, and army boots.

"What the fuck is this supposed to be?" she shouted, in a chiming voice that might otherwise have been beautiful. "If you're coppers, you can just—"

"Not at all, madam," Mr. Patrise said, tipping his hat and bowing from the waist. "Not a copper button among us. We're merely a community interest group. North Side Citizens' Sanitary Committee, at your service."

He gestured with his cane, and Stagger Lee went to the kid who was filling the bottles. Stagger took the hose from the boy's hand, not roughly; he just stood there, looking slowly around.

Stagger Lee gave the hose back. The Vamp took it in both hands and stuck it in his mouth. The red stuff dribbled down his front.

Patrise said, "Grossly unsanitary, madam, I'm sure you'll agree. I'm afraid we'll have to file a formal complaint."

"Complaint?" the Ellyll woman said, still stuck between anger and puzzlement. Then she drew herself up straight, and her hair seemed to crackle and spark. She threw down the clipboard and brought up the pistol. "Why don't you complain about *this,* asshole?"

To one side, windows near the roof crashed in. Glass and cardboard fell away, and the tall woman Danny had seen earlier stepped onto the high platform, holding a tommy gun. She was flanked by two bulky men wielding axes.

The woman fired, a long spit of yellow flame and a noise like a chainsaw. There were little explosions from the crates below the elf's boots; splinters of glass flew, and the red stuff bled from the crates. The elf shrieked something, not in English, ran to the back of the warehouse and dove out of sight.

"Lincoln," Patrise said, and McCain's Colts were instantly in his fists. He fired once, and the tank of blood exploded. All around the room, the workers' heads came up, scenting the air. They converged on the puddling fluid.

"Hallow," Patrise said, "you and Lincoln clear the area. Ladies and gentlemen, let's file our complaint."

Danny and McCain rounded up the kids from the bottling line. They didn't respond to speech, but followed numbly when herded along. McCain led the way to the street: a canvas-covered truck had pulled up before the door. Cloudhunter got out of the passenger seat, swinging his shotgun. The Vamps let themselves be loaded aboard, and the driver took off.

Danny said to McCain, "What was that? Withdrawal?"

"Outsider's Disease. Sometimes they turn nasty—Loop Garous. But they don't use the violent cases for work like this."

Back inside, the gunner and axmen had come down to ground level, and the other man had produced a crowbar and sledgehammer from under his coat. Stagger Lee was examining the machinery.

"Here," he said, and the hammer struck once hard; a whole section of the assembly line collapsed.

Cloudhunter handed his gun to Patrise, who said, "Thank you, Cloud," and began firing into the crates, smashing more glass, sending up sprays of fluid. He handed the gun back, and Cloudhunter reloaded it, as the axmen continued the job. Stagger Lee had strapped on a dust mask and taken some canisters from his bag. He began spreading powder over a pile of cardboard crates and wooden pallets.

There was a crash from the rear of the warehouse, then a movement: a figure in red and black, running straight at them, at Patrise. Cloudhunter took a step, leveled his shotgun: it clicked. He let it go and raised his empty hands. There was a blinding sweep of light, a clunk as the shotgun hit the concrete floor, and a yelp like a hurt animal. The running figure fell down.

Cloudhunter suddenly had his long jeweled knife out, and in front of him lay another of the Vamps, wrapped in the elf-woman's jacket, his head nearly severed.

"Loop Garou," McCain muttered to Danny. "Everybody's got a job to do."

The Ellyll woman, in a white shirt, appeared from around a corner and fired. Cloudhunter jerked, doubled over. McCain's pistol was out then: he fired twice, the woman screamed, and then the Colt jammed. McCain started walking forward, clearing the jam, ditching the magazine and slamming in another. But the woman had disappeared again.

"Cloud," Mr. Patrise said, and woke Danny up. He dashed to Cloudhunter's side, unslinging his bag. The elf was in a half-crouch, right arm pressed to his chest, left hand still holding the knife at guard. "Can you sit?" Danny said. "Here, lean against this."

Cloudhunter had taken the hit in the upper left chest, just below the collarbone. He was still bleeding freely. One of Danny's books said that the elf vascular system was close to human. Aorta? Not a direct hit, or Cloudhunter wouldn't have been standing, and there was no arterial spurt.

Danny got Cloud's jacket open, cut away his shirt. Cloudhunter's neck scarf was wrapped around his upper chest. It was a hard silk, blue with points of light in it. Danny couldn't find a tear, and no blood seemed to have soaked into it; it was driven in—

A memory floated up, something about silk in wounds. The Mongols, that was it. They had worn tightly woven silk shirts. Arrows didn't tear the silk; they would still make wounds, but a tug on the fabric would bring the arrow out clean.

It would be worth a try—later, when they weren't under fire. "I'm going to dress this just as it is for now," he told Cloudhunter. "If I try to get the bullet out now, you might start bleeding. That wouldn't be good, here." At the edge of his vision, Danny saw some of the Outsider's workers shuffling about. *Yeah*, he thought, *it sure wouldn't.* He pulled out the bandaging supplies, and a pair of angled scissors to cut away the excess silk.

"Don't try to cut that," he heard Patrise say. Danny looked up, then felt the metal spring apart in his hand. The hinge rivet was sheared, and the lower blade clattered to the concrete floor.

"I guess not," Danny said.

Mr. Patrise said, "Don't worry about that now. You're doing very well. Please proceed."

Danny said to Cloudhunter, "I'm going to pin up your arm. You need to move as little as possible until I can see to it at the house. Okay?"

"Yes," Cloudhunter said. His voice was thin and tight.

Danny reached to the bag, loaded a morphine cartridge into the hypo carrier. "And something for the pain."

Cloudhunter said, "No."

Danny hesitated. He could see the stress on the elf's face, in his eyes. "Yes," he said. "Just for the pain. I won't knock you out."

"It's all right, Cloud," Patrise said, bending down. "We're almost finished here."

Cloudhunter nodded. Danny gave the shot. "Thank you," the elf said softly.

Patrise said, "Rudy, Katherine, bag detail and follow with Stagger Lee. Where's Sam?"

"Went with Linc," one of the others said, and indicated the back of the warehouse.

Mr. Patrise tapped his stick. "Hallow, can you follow them carefully?"

"I've been in fires."

"But not firefights, I think," Mr. Patrise said. "However, you are no longer needed here, and you may be there. Go on."

Danny gathered up his kit and moved toward the back of the warehouse. There were crates of empty bottles, coils of tubing, crates of God knew what. Through a doorway he saw a doctor's examining table with an IV arm board. That would be where the supply came from. There had been at least a couple of quarts in the glass tank. Losing two quarts of blood was fatal, if you were human. Maybe they pooled it. Or—

He felt a cold breeze. To his right a few steps was an open door. He looked through. There was an empty lot beyond, and in the distance a low stone wall, some trees beyond. He clenched his fingers on his bag and walked through the doorway.

"Dance with me, mister?" a woman's voice said, right in Danny's ear.

His spine froze and he tensed for a bullet or a blow, but there was just an instant of silence, and then the voice again: "I've gotta go home soon, but I'd really like one more dance. You look like a nice fella. Please?"

Danny turned. A girl was standing just a few steps from him, wearing a long beaded dress that sparkled in the moonlight. She held out her hands. "Come on, mister. Just one more. Before they miss me at home."

Danny heard a grunt from behind. He turned. The wounded elf-woman lurched out of the doorway, toward him. Danny ducked to one side; his foot hit something and he lost his balance, tumbling over as the woman just brushed by him.

"Yes, you'll do," the girl's voice said. "Let's dance."

Danny struggled to get up; his foot was caught in a root or cable of some kind. A hand touched his shoulder, and he twitched. "Take it easy, Doc," McCain said, and helped Danny stand. He pointed a finger. "You find her like that, or did you take her down?"

The elf was lying face-up a few yards away. Her hands were clawed at her throat; she was absolutely still. The girl in the beaded dress was nowhere in sight.

"I didn't . . ." He tried to explain about the girl in white.

McCain looked into the distance, and said, "Oh."

"I know I saw her."

McCain went to the fallen elf, drew one of his guns, aimed very deliberately between the woman's eyes, and fired. He put the gun away. "I believe you," he said, with no irony at all, and crossed himself.

"I don't get it."

"Her name's Resurrection Mary," McCain said, and tilted his head toward the stone wall. "That's Resurrection Cemetery over there. Usually she's on Archer Street, but I guess it was a slow night."

"Okay, but I still don't know where she went."

"She got what she wanted and went back where she came from, Doc. What's the matter, don't you whistle in graveyards in Iowa?"

Danny stared.

"You go on back," McCain said. "Night's not over yet."

When Danny reached the bottling floor, everyone was gone except for Mr. Patrise and Stagger Lee. Stagger was wiring up what were pretty obviously explosives. "That's it, sir. Good night."

"Good night, Stagger," Patrise said. "Come with me, Hallow."

Danny and Mr. Patrise got into the big car. The woman Patrise had called Katherine and Cloudhunter sat in front; Katie drove them away. About half a block down, there was a muffled sound of thunder, and a shimmer of orange light behind them.

At the house, Danny took Cloudhunter to the infirmary. Mr. Patrise followed them. The Ellyll removed his shirt, showing a slender, very angular chest. By human standards, there wasn't much musculature, but Cloudhunter was certainly not weak; Danny touched his shoulder and felt wiry hardness beneath the skin.

He had Cloudhunter lie flat, got a pressure bandage ready in case of serious bleeding, and unwound the blue silk scarf. With a firm, even pull, it came out of the wound, displaying the flattened slug like a piece of jewelry in a shop window. The bleeding was minor.

Danny opened a tube of goldenrod salve, looked at it skeptically. Stagger Lee had made some pretty wild claims for the stuff;

Danny supposed it was at least an antiseptic. He rubbed some on the broken skin.

The oozing blood just stopped. The bruising began to fade, and Danny could *see* the edges of the hole crawl toward closure. He blinked, thinking he must be too tired to see straight, but there it was. With a nervous glance at Mr. Patrise, who was watching silently, halfway smiling, Danny applied a gauze dressing and reslung the Ellyll's arm.

"Do you think you can rest okay, Cloudhunter? I think that's what you need more than anything."

"Call me Cloud," the Ellyll said, and nodded. "I will have some . . . camomile tea."

Danny laughed. "My grandmother used to make camomile tea."

"Was she wise?"

"Yeah," Danny lied.

Mr. Patrise said, "The tea will be in your room, Cloud." He yawned. "It's been a busy week. I think we'll all just relax for the next couple of days. Good night." He went out.

Danny said, "You'll be all right in your room, Cloud? If this starts to bleed at all, or hurt, call me."

"I will, Doc. You have my thanks."

"Oh. It's my job now. Here, don't forget your scarf." He folded the blue silk, then felt the hard spot within it. "You want the bullet?"

Cloudhunter stared at him in a way that was deeply unsettling.

"I, uh—I knew some people who'd keep things like that. Luck, I guess."

Silently, Cloudhunter accepted the piece of metal, closed his fingers over it.

Danny tried to think of something else to say. "That's really beautiful silk."

Cloud said something that sounded like "Nancy." Danny supposed it was a word in the elf language.

The phone buzzed. "Infirmary."

Stagger Lee's voice said, "Doc, are you still working in there?"

"No, just finished."

"Would you stay there, please? There's another job."

"Sure." Cloud nodded and left the room. "Who's—" But Stagger had hung up. Danny hadn't seen anyone else hurt. He paced a bit, then looked around at the cabinets and refilled his bag, adjusting the load—fewer pills, more wound closures, an extra inflatable splint.

A few minutes later there was a knock at the door. Stagger Lee came in, followed by two of the gray-coated house staff. They were carrying a zippered black bag. From its size and weight and the way it folded, Danny had no doubt of what was in it. Without a word it was carried into the surgery room, dropped on the table. The bearers left. Stagger Lee had hung up his coat; he went in, unzipped the bag.

It was the dead elf woman.

Danny said, "What's this for?" He remembered something McCain had said: *If they can't crawl back to Elfland, they die.* "She won't—I mean, she isn't going to—come back."

Stagger Lee looked faintly amused. "She's quite permanently dead. We need the bullets out." He uncovered a tray of surgical tools. "It'll wait till tomorrow, if you're really worn out, but the job won't get any prettier."

"The bullets."

"Yes. It doesn't have to be done neatly. Just get them out intact." He exhaled. "I am in serious need of a scotch. Can I get you something?"

"Just some coffee. Please."

"Be right back." He stopped at the door. "Wait. You were taught all about body-fluid safety, right?"

"Yeah, sure." Danny looked at the body. "Don't touch the blood, right?"

"It won't soak through unbroken skin. But yeah, don't."

Danny pulled down his suspenders and took off his shirt. There was a waterproof apron hanging against the wall. He reached for a pair of surgical gloves, then found a heavy rubber pair.

The body was wearing a white cotton shirt with ruffles down the front, and thin leather bands with silver buckles wrapped around her forearms. Danny cut away the shirt front with scissors. He cut off the straps, too, so he didn't have to look at them.

There was a hole near the heart, another on the left flank, by the floating ribs, a third in the abdomen—when had that happened? He was impressed that the Ellyll had gone so far with those wounds. The wonderful silver hair was matted and vile. McCain's shot to the forehead seemed like overkill, unless it was something to do with the pale girl. . . . There were a couple of long bluish marks around the throat that didn't make any medical sense, but he put the question aside.

He had seen plenty worse, riding the van, in the County ER, learning the trade. Shotguns. Traffic accidents; a little bullet had nothing on a pickup truck for kinetic energy. And farm machinery was hell on muscle and bone.

Death made a difference, too. A dead body didn't move or pulse or clutch or moan. When the life had faded out under you, after you'd pounded and stuck, breathed and fought for it, you felt something. You couldn't let it last, because there'd be another run any minute, but it was bad while it held on. A body you just found, though—when the bullets or the truck bumper or the tons of corn falling down the silo had finished the job before you got there— there was nothing but the taxi ride to the morgue. Meat delivery, some of the guys called it.

Retractor, probe. He thought he heard a click, but there wasn't enough light. He tossed the probe down and opened drawers until he found a headband light. Yeah, there the little bastard was. Dissecting knife. Forceps. He examined the slug: it hadn't deformed much, looked like an ordinary hardball. At home, people had mostly used hollowpoints on each other. He tossed it into a steel basin, where it gave a rolling clang.

The other chest shot had gotten behind a rib. Danny got a spreader on the bone, cracked it out. Hemostat, to pull back the mangled heart wall; it was tough and kept slipping. Light on metal. *Clang.*

"Coffee's on," Stagger Lee said, and put a big china mug on the counter.

"Thanks. Halfway there." The coffee was muddy-looking, and had a sharp, sweet smell. It burned the back of his throat, not with heat.

"What's in this?"

"Irish. Just drink it slow. The comfort of mankind."

There was brown sugar in it, and thick cream. It did taste good. Danny took a long sip of it, then noticed his glove left a bloody print and wrapped the mug in a towel.

The bullet in the lower thorax was deep. He undid the woman's belt, started to unfasten the fly buttons, then just got the shears and cut his way in. It wasn't anything like undressing her. Meat forgave everything. He made a Y-shaped cut, pulled back the points and got retractors and elastic on them. The liver was a strange coppery color, and he didn't see a spleen.

Stagger Lee said, "You know what you're doing. I just dug like Fred C. Dobbs."

"You do this often?"

"When it needed doing."

Danny thought about objecting to the answer, but didn't. "What's it for?"

"Mr. Patrise didn't talk to you about this?"

"No."

"The body goes back to the Ellyllon. Sometimes they take it over Division to Elfland, sometimes not. It's their fancy Borgia politics, nothing to do with us." He looked down at the deep incision. "We take all of our stuff back."

The third bullet went into the pan.

Stagger said, "Do you need help?"

"No."

"I'll be in the other room. I quit being curious about brains a while ago."

"Go to bed if you want."

"No, I'll wait."

The knife went around the forehead, the scalp peeled back. The electric skull saw buzzed right through the bone. The brain didn't look any different from a human's, not that Danny's job had involved much neurosurgery. He was getting tired. He used the long-bladed knife and cut out a wedge, as from a watermelon, pried out the bullet and shoved the section back. He put the bowl of skull back in place and tugged the scalp down. "That's it," he said. "What now?"

"That's all," Stagger Lee said. "I'll call to have the body collected, get the maids to clean up in here."

"I can do it."

"We've got maids. You're a specialist. Get your—" He looked at the mug with its pink stains, wiped it, carefully poured the contents into a paper cup. "Here. Call it a night. Remember, poker game's Monday. Let me know."

Danny didn't object. He carried the coffee up to his room, took a short hot shower and fell into bed.

Something didn't add up right about the bullet business. It might be true about sending the body back to Elfland, it might even have been true about removing the World stuff; but it didn't *feel* true—at least, not like all of the truth.

He didn't think anymore, he didn't want to. He slept.

OCTOBER

The weekened passed quietly. Cloudhunter's arm was visibly stiff, but he was healing—impossibly well by World standards, though there would probably be a scar. Danny studied his books, especially the few thin papers on Ellyll medicine. He had also found a primer on the Ellytha language, and was working on basic expressions.

In high school, Danny had taken a couple of courses in French, taught by the girls' basketball coach during free-activity time. The teacher said that Danny had a real talent for languages. But there were only four other students in the class, all girls, and after two years it was dropped. The following year, girls' team sports were cut too—"not for ladies" was what the principal said, though there were some other, odd whispers—and the coach left town.

Danny saw Fay at Sunday lunch, and she spoke a few words to him. He thought there surely must be someone, if not around the house then somewhere on the Levee, who knew sign language. He had been told that it was not quite word for word; would that get by the spell? Then again, would there be any way of teaching her?

He went down to the garage, thinking about taking the Triumph for a drive. As he entered, there was a muffled ripping sound that bounced around the concrete. He couldn't be sure, but it sounded like automatic gunfire. He looked around quickly, trying to locate the source among the echoes. Then he remembered that there was a gun range down here. Not quite dropping his guard, he went around a corner.

There was a tall woman there—really tall, somewhere over six feet—in a red flannel shirt, black vest and jeans, blazing away with a Tommy gun. Danny recognized her from the raid on the bottling plant. She turned her head. "Hi," she said.

"Hello. I'm . . . Doc."

"Just a sec." She pulled off her soundproof earmuffs. "Hi," she said again. "You said you were Doc, right?"

"Yeah."

"We didn't have a chance to get introduced the other night. I'm Katie Silverbirch. Long Tall Katie if I'm not there to hear it." She pulled the magazine out of the Thompson. "Come to play?"

Danny gestured at the weapon. "I never shot one of those before. I was going to ask Jesse about it."

"Jesse's busy, I think. But he taught me, and I can teach you. If that'll do."

"That'd be great. Thank you."

"Get yourself some goggles and a set of muffs. Right over there."

When Danny was equipped, Katie showed him how to load and work the gun. "You've basically got two useful stances. If you really want to hit targets, you hold it like a rifle, bring it up to your eye, like this. If you can brace against a corner, that's even better; gives you some cover, too." She lowered the weapon to just above her waist, leaned forward on the balls of her feet. "Hipshooting isn't very accurate, but if you've got to charge through a door, it makes the bad guys duck. And a Thompson throws so much lead you'll probably hit *something*. This is the way." She leaned into the gun and fired a burst, tearing the midsection out of the paper silhouette at the end of the range. She handed Danny the gun. "Try it."

He did. The Thompson bucked like a firehose under full stream, but he clenched hard and got some of the bullets into the target.

" 'S'okay," Katie said. "What do you think made all those other holes in the wall—moths?"

"How long did it take you to learn?"

"Awhile. But I was handling a chainsaw when I was four. It's all in the control."

"Four?"

"My folks are loggers, up in Michigan. The Peninsula."

"That's the skinny north part, right?"

She laughed. "Right. How about you?"

"Farmers. Iowa."

"Came 'bout as far. Call strong down there?"

"What do you mean?"

"The call to come here. You know, to where the magic's strong. My Mama calls it medicine. She's Ojibwa. Try changing out the magazine." As Danny did, Katie said, "I didn't know what it was at first. I just had some dreams, and a funny feeling when I saw clouds in the south. But Mama knew. She said to Dad, 'Girl's had a vision. She's gone go.'

"My dad, he's a big old Finn, but he's got medicine of his own. . . . Anyway, Mama packed me up, and said goodbye. Dad drove me to Green Bay, to the train station, and he said goodbye. Don't think he could have done it with Mama there. The way he did it, he could go back home and tell Mama I'd gotten on the train all right, everything was fine. So what did your folks say, when it happened?"

"They didn't want me to go." Danny put the gun down, thinking hard. He thought he'd gone away on his own account. What did it change if something had made him do it? "We argued a lot about it."

"Oh." Katie chewed on her lip, and then said, "I got scared, on the way. I got off the train when it stopped in Milwaukee, and I thought about just not going on. But it was dark, and when I looked out on the lake and saw the Fire glow . . . I got back on. I don't know what would have happened if it had been daytime."

Danny told her about the old man at the truck stop, with his box of Bibles. "Maybe . . . there's always a last chance to change your mind." He wasn't at all sure he believed yet in a call, but he couldn't deny that it made sense.

"Turn back, O man," Katie sang without much of a tune, "forswear thy foolish ways."

Danny said, "Do you still hear from your folks?"

"Mama writes every month. Dad's not much of a writer, but he always puts a line or two in. Sends a photo, sometimes. You know what a bloodstopper is?"

"No."

"Some people can stop bleeding, with a word, sometimes just by willing it. This is old, long before the elves came back. All the loggers know about it; somebody'd take an ax in the foot, or a bucksaw right through the hand, and they'd call the bloodstopper. Even if he was on the phone, he'd work the charm, and the bleeding would just quit."

"You've seen that?"

"Yes. My dad can do it, and on the drive to Green Bay he taught me. A man can only teach a woman, and a woman has to teach a man." She paused, put her hands together. "I haven't worked it. Shade medicine's strange—the elves' and ours both. I'm not sure of it. Not like Tommy." She touched the gun. "The Ojibwa say that everything you are is a gift from the spirit world, and until you have those gifts inside you, you aren't really anything."

Katie smiled crookedly at Danny, as if she wanted him to answer that.

He smiled back, and nodded. He didn't have an answer.

Over a late lunch Monday, Stagger Lee said, "How long has it been since you went to a movie?"

"A while." It had actually been two years. There was no theater in Adair; every chance they could, Danny and Robin had hitched to the drive-in a county over. Rob usually talked them in for half price, since they wouldn't be taking up a car slot: the guy at the gate looked dubious, but Rob had always been good at getting his point across.

Danny couldn't remember what the movie had been.

Stagger Lee said, "The Biograph's showing *The Train* with Burt Lancaster. That's supposed to be first-rate, and even if it isn't, it's Lancaster. And it's Monday, so Laughs Lost will be running Chaplin all afternoon."

"I don't care."

"Biograph, then. I'm not that big on Charlie. Keaton's on Tuesday: that's different."

The theater was only a few blocks away. No prices were posted at the box office, which was manned by a halfie in a brass-buttoned jacket and an odd round cap. Danny saw people in line pay with silver coins, little scrolls of brown paper, a bundle of exotic weeds. Stagger insisted on paying for both of them, with a tarnished quarter. He scooped up the tickets and waited.

"Change, Johnny," he said finally.

The boy behind the glass said, "What, Mr. Lee?"

"There's only two of us for one show. Besides, I saw you palm the dime the World lady gave you."

The boy pushed it across.

As they walked through the doors, Danny said, "How could he do that?"

"What? Cut a deal? Same way I did. Down on the Levee, *nothing* has a fixed price, and *nobody* pays retail. Allow me to demonstrate further." He went to the snack counter, waved at the young man behind it.

"Afternoon, Mr. Lee. What can I get for you?"

"Your neon box is stuttering. How about two giant double-butter popcorns for a recharge?"

"Just a moment, Mr. Lee."

The counterman tapped on a side door, spoke with someone within. "Manager says sure thing, Mr. Lee. You know the way?"

Stagger Lee waved a reply and led Danny to a door marked EMPLOYEES ONLY. Beyond it was a service room lit by a steel-shaded bulb, meters and junction boxes around the walls. Some of the boxes had red-lightning warning labels, others a tilted-spiral mark and the words CAUTION SPELLS ACTIVE.

Stagger Lee rapped his knuckles on one of the spell boxes, cocked his head as if listening for something. Danny couldn't detect any change in the room's overall hum.

Danny said, "Should I—you know, watch this?"

"Nothing secret about it. You don't need hocus-pocus when the trick really works."

Stagger opened the box. Inside was a flat brass ring ten inches across, surrounded by other bits of shiny metal and glass. The ring rotated about a turn to the right, then back as far to the left. At each reversal the rest of the machinery ticked and flashed. The big ring didn't seem to be physically connected to anything else; the devices made no obvious sense at all.

Danny wondered how he would explain a fuse box to someone who'd never heard of electricity: *You mean the little wires are sup-posed to burn up?*

Stagger brought the silver dime out of his pocket.

"Does that—"

"Just a second, please. Gotta concentrate."

Carefully, Stagger held the coin in the center of the brass ring. He put two fingers of his other hand on a flattened sphere of red glass, and muttered something Danny couldn't hear.

A blob of darkness appeared around the coin, and Stagger pulled his fingertips away. The red glass glowed, not very brightly, and Stagger let it go as well.

The darkness filled the ring, and the coin vanished into it. The blob was like a blind spot in the eyes after staring at the sun; Danny looked away. Stagger exhaled loudly and shut the box.

Danny said, "The coin's fuel?"

"Not really, though it'll get used up. Magic doesn't just happen, abracadabra poof. It runs on energy, like everything else. Can you get your head around the idea of multiple universes?"

"Like Elfland."

"Like that. Some people always thought there were other universes; it helps a lot to have one we can point to. Elfland's a parallel universe, and the magic source is another. There may be more, maybe an infinite number.

"Anyway, Elfland's got a wide-open channel to the magic source. They're bathed in it, like we get sunshine and cosmic rays, while we're insulated. Sometimes, though—at least since Elfland punched the big holes—we can get into contact with the power."

"The Touch."

"You got it. If you're good, you can pull in power without props. But spellboxes need something to drop the resistance. Some metals can do it, especially silver." He tapped the box. "The flow will eventually wear the dime away. Nobody rides for free."

"You said people didn't need props," Danny said. "What if you're the dime?"

Stagger Lee said quietly, "Doc, you are no more than the third person I know who's ever asked that. The answer is that we haven't been doing this long enough to know. It's going to be interesting finding out. Come on, let's go collect our popcorn and some good seats."

The movie was exciting, a World War Two adventure with evil Nazis and brave Resistance fighters and a long railroad chase. It was in black and white; Stagger explained that movies were still made that way even after color was available. "Artistic choice," he said. "The sort of image you want in the viewer's mind."

"Well, sure, but isn't it—"

"Not what's on the screen. In the *mind*. Like any magic trick, it's what the audience remembers that counts."

They went back to the house and collected Danny's car. This time they drove north, to a place called the Rush Street Grill. It had large round tables, a short but busy bar, a small bandstand with drums and an amp set up. Lucius Birdsong was there, alone at a big round table, eating a huge sloppy cheeseburger. He was wearing a sweatshirt with what looked like a college seal, with the school name and motto in neat lettering. It actually read J-SCHOOL *is for the other guys*.

"Glad you could make it, Doc," Birdsong said. "I trust you have brought all you hold dear, intent on bidding it farewell?"

"Listen to this guy," Stagger Lee said. "I've seen him shove in his last typewriter on a pair of fours."

Carmen Mirage came in. Heads turned. She was wearing a bronze shirtwaist blouse with a deep-cut neck, and a long black leather skirt. Her hair glowed with fairy dust. She sat down with Danny and the others. "Deka won't be here tonight. She's got a gig way uptown."

"Neither will Spoke," Stagger Lee said. "He's got a date . . . some distance downtown." Carmen laughed musically.

A woman sat down behind the drum kit, and a man in a vest and black T-shirt stepped up next to her, carrying an electric guitar. The woman began with a stately beat, the man joined it, and then they launched into an instrumental of "Wall of Death."

During "Valentine's Day (is Over)" the Tokyo Fox came in. Under her coat she was wearing a brilliant red dress, one of those Oriental silk dresses with a high collar and a slit halfway up her thigh that showed black stockings and red high heels.

She looked straight at Danny. "Good evening, Doc."

Danny had the impression that the others were looking at him as well. He didn't turn his head to check. He had a feeling that his response was important. "Hello, Miss Kitsune. Pleased to see you. Are you joining us?"

"Wouldn't miss it," she said as she sat down.

A couple of songs later, the waiter whispered into Carmen's ear. "Well, of course, *cara mia*," she said, excused herself, and went up to the bandstand.

The drummer began a quick four-beat; the guitarist launched into a twanging riff. Danny hadn't expected country music here. It wasn't that he didn't like country. He was just, well, tired of songs about guns and trucks and the love of good women, dogs, and Jesus in no particular order.

What Carmen sang, though, was jazzy and very quick, not danceable at all:

> *Black iron through the hard red wheat*
> *Blue crocuses around her feet*
> *North prairie house that stands alone*
> *And the light goes down behind the painted shutters*
> *In the early dark*
> *And Persephone's daughters are home*

Danny had read the Persephone story: she had been taken away from her mother for part of the year, and the separation made winter. But her daughters . . . ?

> *Hard benches in the emigrant cars*
> *Straight horizon under strange new stars*
> *Railroad passage to a dream of land*
> *Until the wheels stop turning*
> *And the milk needs churning*
> *And the chaff wants burning*
> *And the days get over too soon*
> *To quite understand*

White crosses in a pale green plot
Time passes but the heart moves not
Take comfort that it's Someone's will
As the storm wind's rising and the beech tree shudders
In the golden haze
And Persephone's daughters are still

Long shadows from the great white mills
Thunder echoes from the unseen hills
Somewhere surely there are welcome lights
But this is where you're dwelling
And the crop needs weeding
And the children feeding
And there's never time for a word
To soften her nights

Danny glanced around the room, wondering if there was anyone here who hadn't left home for the Shade. Did *anyone* get born
here? He hadn't seen any children at all. He turned his head away,
looked out the window at the empty street. He didn't stop listening.

Gray geese across the diamond sky
How long the wings have passed her by
Good children ought to carry on
But the clouds shine doubled on the clear blue waters
In the silver night
And Persephone's daughters are gone

Carmen took her bow and came back to the table. Around the
room, the other diners were rising from their seats. "Guess we
should start?"

"Guess we should," Lucius said.

The crowd was moving to a large back room. The tables here
were covered with green felt. Behind a brass teller's cage Danny
could see racked chips, cased decks of cards in neat stacks. There
were already people around a craps table, and a roulette wheel was
turning.

A slightly plump blond woman in a green velvet tuxedo was

greeting people, shaking hands. "Hello, Lucius, Fox. Nice number, Carmen; thanks. Or do I owe you?"

"Owe Alvah next time you see him. It's his lyric."

Lucius said, "Doc, this is Flats Montoya. She owns this joint. Flats, meet Doc Hallownight. He's giving us a try tonight."

"Good evening, Doc. Didn't I read about you in Lucius's column the other night?"

"She can cook a rare burger and she reads my column," Lucius said. "Will you marry me? Or at least let me leave teeth marks on your ankles?"

"Let's hear it for journalistic ethics. Welcome to the game, Doc. Good luck."

They sat down at one of the round tables. Stagger Lee said, "Our game is even buy-in, table stakes, dealer's choice. You can sit out any game you don't like; we're all friends here, but the game's still poker. Is that all right?"

"Sure."

"I'll get the box," the Tokyo Fox said. "Hundred chips each?"

"Make it a hundred fifty," Stagger said. "Keep us going longer."

Kitsune nodded and went to the teller's cage. Danny saw the others putting coins on the table, and did likewise. Stagger helped him work out the value of his stake, since the original denominations of the coins didn't seem to mean much here. The Fox returned with several racks of chips and a black wooden box. "The cash goes in here," she said to Danny, "and the house holds the box until we're finished and divide up. They also get a cut of the box for the use of the table. Got it?"

"Yeah. But why does the money all go up there?"

"Two reasons," the Fox said. "One, a lot of things get used for money in the Shadow; this establishes that everybody put her stake up, whether it's gold or shamrocks." She herself had put in a small pouch full of beautifully cut stones. "Two, it avoids confusion if someone isn't paying attention, or takes a long piss break, or whatever. Oh, and there's bar service back here too, just in case you think you're playing too well."

So they played poker. It was, as Stagger Lee had said, a friendly game, but there was nothing loose about it; a dropped card meant a redeal, as Danny found out early on. Stagger Lee never dealt anything but seven-card stud, no wilds. Kitsune liked draw games, with occasional variations. Lucius alternated seven-stud and five-draw. Carmen changed games every deal, but always called for high-low; it seemed to pay off for her. Danny stuck mostly to five-card draw, what he knew best; he won a couple of big pots but mostly lost slowly.

There was one thing Danny had never seen before: the buck to show last dealer was a waiter's green order pad, and part of the deal was noting each player's total of chips. All the tables seemed to be doing it.

It was nearly eleven when the lights flashed red, and a low chime sounded through the room.

Immediately everyone shoved his and her chips into the center of the table. Every table. Danny stared for a moment, and Lucius shoved Danny's chips in. The Fox slipped the green pad into the flap of her dress. There was a buzz, and the centers of the tables just opened up; the chips dropped out of sight, and the green felt sealed up again.

Meanwhile, the craps players snapped their chips into racks on the table edge, and the table slid like a drawer into the wall. Two croupiers pulled a false tabletop away from the wainscoting and dropped it over the roulette table; a moment later, waiters were setting salad and hors d'oeuvre dishes out on the "buffet." The teller's cage retracted a foot into the wall, and a panel slid down and faced out flush.

Another set of waiters came in with trays, and dealt out tea cups, pie, and brandy to all the seated patrons. The standing players were handed drinks; some lit cigarettes, some lounged against the walls.

A few moments later four police officers came barrelling through the door. Copper buttons glittered on their blue uniforms. "All right," the man in the lead bellowed, "this place is—" He paused, looked around.

Flats came in, her tuxedo jacket off, a bib-front apron tied over her ruffled shirt and velvet trousers. It read KISS THE COOK. "Hello, O'Gara," she said pleasantly.

"What's been going on back here, citizen Montoya?" the policeman said.

"Looks like dessert, O'Gara. Want some tea? I'm all out of doughnuts, and you know I can't afford coffee these days."

The show went on for fifteen minutes or so; finally the cops filed back out.

"We always give them fifteen minutes' departure grace," Lucius said to Danny. "Drink your brandy: when there's a raid it's on the house."

"Which is to say, the house take covers it," Carmen said merrily.

After fifteen minutes, the table service was removed, order was restored to the craps and roulette players, and the panel covering the chip bucket opened up. The Fox took out the green pad and they reclaimed their stacks.

"What if they raid us again?" Danny said.

"Never happen," the Fox said. "It'd be bad art."

There were no further interruptions. Shortly after one AM, a different chime rang, and Flats came out to say, "Closing down, ladies and gentlemen, closing down. Have you no homes to go to? Last Deal coming up next, ladies and gentlemen, thank you all."

They finished the hand they were playing—Stagger Lee won with a completely hidden straight—and Kitsune went to retrieve the cash box.

Danny said, "What about the last deal?" Stagger raised an eyebrow and turned to Lucius, with an odd expression; Lucius touched Danny's elbow and shook his head slightly, conspiratorially.

Danny followed Lucius out of the back room. The musicians had closed down in the front, but there were still several diners. Danny turned; Kitsune had followed him, but not the others.

"Sit down a minute, Doc. No more for you, you're driving. Al, burnt beans black for the Doctor here, will you?"

Danny looked around. Some of the other back room patrons were gathering their coats to leave, a few were ordering desserts. In the corner two police officers were talking over beer mugs and ravaged hamburger platters. Danny was absolutely certain they had been in the raid.

"Stagger Lee'll find his own way home," Lucius said. "Let me explain about Last Deal. Everybody still back there gets fifty chips, and they play five-card draw until half of 'em are tapped. Then everybody goes home. First player out with the biggest winner, second with second, and so on. Odd number makes a threesome in the middle. Clear on the concept?"

Danny tossed it around in his mind for a moment, then nodded.

Lucius said, "We're just here for the poker. Figured you were, too."

"Don't blame Stagger," Kitsune said. "He'd have told you if he expected you to play. He made sure you had a ride home, right?"

Danny drank his black coffee, looked from one of them to the other. "And you—and Lucius—are you—"

Lucius's eyebrows went up, and he showed a lopsided smile. Kitsune was smiling too. She touched her knee, exposed as she perched on the bar stool. "Don't let the red roses fool you, kid. Lucius only chases girls, and so do I."

It was all happening too fast. Danny thought hard about what the Fox had said. His mother would have left the room. His grandmother would have come back with a shotgun.

He thought about—a great number of things. He said, "Can I give either one of you a lift home?"

Kitsune said, "I'm covered. Lucius would probably appreciate it, though."

"Yes, I would."

In the car, driving through the uncertain streets, Danny said, "It's not like I expected. The Shade, I mean."

"Very little in the world is. I myself find that uncertainty to be one of the few things that makes the prospect of another morning endurable."

Danny looked at him. Lucius said, "Excuse me, Doc. I was talking like my typewriter."

"It's all right."

"Is it? It matters, you know."

"Well . . . the other night—"

"No. Wait. Hold it. I am a journalist, Doc. Anything you tell me is liable to wind up on the opinion pages of a hundred and twenty-seven newspapers syndicated through Global. If you give me your trust, I will value it. I will brood over my ethics, I will agonize, and I will use your secrets, just to get through one more column."

"I saw somebody get killed the other night."

"Friend of yours?"

"No." Danny thought about telling Robin's story. No, that was really out. "I just wondered if—a lot's happened since I got here, and I don't know what to think about most of it."

"Stop here," Lucius said. They were in the middle of an empty, half-ruined block.

"You don't live here."

"Just the fringes of my palatial estate. I want to walk the rest of it. Muse upon a couple of things. Good night, Doc. Thanks for the ride."

"Yeah. Good night, Lucius."

Danny drove the rest of the way back wondering what he had said, what he could have said.

When Danny woke late Tuesday morning there was a pot of coffee outside his door, and the *Centurion*.

THE CONTRARIAN FLOW

by Lucius Birdsong

What times we are living in, loyal readers, what times. Not since the days when the Powers That Clout feared the wholesale dumping of LSD into Our Fair Levee's reservoirs (for late arrivals, LSD refers to a drug of whoopee, not that road on the waterfront) has there been such a to-do over a non-alcoholic beverage.

Mere days ago one could walk into any flop, crash, or unlit basement in Our Fair Levee and crack open a bottle of the Drink that Keeps on Soaking. No grubby expeditions up to the source, no hoping the source wouldn't laugh in your slack jaws. Why, it was said that in some of the finest wicker hampers of the Gold Coast and the Way Outer Drive, tucked in among the Nehi and the Canfield's, was the odd bonded flagon of Sucker Punch.

And now? Now you not only have to know to knock two longs and a short, that Louie sent you, and that the password is swordfish, you have to have brought your own, because they ain't got any. Friends, of all the un-Levee-like phrases this correspondent has ever heard, "ain't got any" is by far the un-Levee-est.

Now, I submit that Our Fair is founded on the principles of personal liberty, free enterprise, and entrepreneurship. If you want to refresh yourself from a noble friend, that is personal liberty. If you prefer to pay someone else to draw one, draw two, draw three-four units of red, that is free enterprise. And if somebody taps, and somebody tipples, and somebody in between collects from both ends, why then, one of you is an entrepreneur and Devil take the hindmost.

But does it seem, despite all that, that for the last few days Our Fair Levee has had just a little bit less Hell to pay?

Okay, Danny thought, *maybe it makes sense, maybe we did something good. Thanks, Lucius.*

He let out a breath. His chest had been drum-tight without his even noticing. Suddenly, a little relaxed, a little relieved, he had an idea.

Danny picked up the phone and asked the operator for Ginevra Benci's number. She made the connection for him.

"Hello?" She sounded sleepy. Danny started to apologize, then caught himself: if he didn't go straight into this he would never manage it at all.

"It's Doc, Ginny."

"Hi, Doc." A yawn. "What's going on?"

"Are you working tonight?"

"Yeah. Tuesdays to Thursdays, usually, eight at night to two."

"Would you like to . . ." Okay, *what?* ". . . see a movie this afternoon? Maybe have some dinner, before you go to work?"

"This afternoon? Oh! Sure, yeah, that'd be great. What movie?"

"I heard that there's a Buster Keaton show, all afternoon."

"Okay. At Laughs Lost, right? Should I just meet you there?"

"No, I'll come get you."

"Great. Give me an hour or so, okay?"

"Yeah. Yeah." He looked around wildly for the clock. "Two o'clock?"

"See you then."

The phone nearly slipped out of his hands as he hung it up. He cleaned up, dressed, went downstairs. Fay and McCain were in the dining room.

Danny said, "Does Mr. Patrise need me this afternoon?"

McCain said, "No, I don't think so. He'll be going to the club tonight, and I think he'd like to have you there."

"I'll meet you there at eight, if that's okay."

"Just so. Mind telling me where you'll be till then? Just in case."

"I'm going to the movies. Laughs Lost. We'll probably go out to dinner after—but I don't know where. We, that is—"

"You needn't say," McCain said easily. "Your time's yours."

Fay said, "Radiant speak connect? Trupsever glow, carol, abundaniel."

She knew, Danny thought. She had sensed something, seen something—or was it obvious? Was McCain grinning, secretly?

He nodded to her. She nodded back. He turned to McCain, whose eyes were suddenly flat and cool and empty. "Enjoy yourself, Doc," he said.

When Danny got to Ginny's building, she was waiting, dashing down the steps in a bright red cloth coat, a bag slung over her shoulder. "My work stuff," she said, tossing the bag behind the seats. "I can change at the club. So we can have a nice, slow dinner."

Laughs Lost had a big marquee out front, with half an acre of electric bulbs, and spell-fired neon tubing bent into smiling masks. The lobby was full of framed photos of movie stars; all the pictures seemed to be in black and white, and most had a kind of foggy glow—that was glamour, Danny thought. The seats were worn, and a little creaky. As the lights started to dim, someone dressed as Chaplin's Tramp pushed a broom down the aisle. He tipped his hat and disappeared into the darkness.

First there was a cartoon, a Red Riding Hood and the Wolf

story set in a world of nightclubs and big cars. When Little Red threw off her cloak, revealing a tiny white dress and a lot of herself, and went into a swing dance, the Wolf's eyes popped yards out of his head. He bashed himself with a mallet. Danny stared. When had they made this? It couldn't have been for kids.

The cartoon ended, and in the minute of silence Danny felt his heart banging. He looked straight ahead. The screen flickered again.

Danny had heard of Buster Keaton, but never seen any of his films. He was hardly ready for the little man with the sad eyes, who never seemed able to smile. Keaton walked onto the screen, in his flat hat and rumpled clothes, and Danny thought, we're supposed to laugh at *him*?

Whatever they were supposed to do, they laughed.

There was a short movie about a moving man with a horse-drawn wagon, slogging on against what seemed like all the powers of nature. And another where Keaton was mistaken for a criminal, ridiculous on the face of it, yet his every action only got more police chasing him. And then a long film about the Civil War, with locomotives chasing one another, burning bridges, cavalry charges—Danny kept thinking of the tight-lipped thriller he had seen the other day, with its spies and trains and war, and somehow it only made this one funnier. The last image was of Buster triumphant (though hardly seeming to notice it), finding a way to salute his fellow soldiers and still kiss his girl.

Ginny's hand, Danny realized, had slipped easily into his. He started to turn, saw her face white in the glow of the screen. Then, with really rotten timing, the lights came up.

Stagger Lee was in the lobby, popping chocolate-covered raisins from the jumbo box. "Good afternoon, Doc, Miss Benci. Haven't seen you here before."

"No," she said. "I've been to some of the late shows, but not this."

"First time," Stagger said. "What an enviable position. Wish I'd known. It's an addiction, you know: you try the really hard stuff and you'll never kick it." Danny wasn't sure he liked the sound of that. But Stagger Lee just smiled, said, "There's a matinee every weekday. Tomorrow's Laurel and Hardy: I think they figure that's midweek, better bring out the heavy artillery. Thursday rotates: Snub Pollard, Charley Chase, Harold Lloyd, lots of other people you never heard of." He pointed a thumb at the pictures on the lobby wall. Stagger Lee had a striking resemblance to Lloyd. "Friday's sound shorts. Fields, the Stooges, Andy Clyde. And the Little Rascals, which is good, because those days I can get some work done. Did you like the cartoon?"

"It was great," Ginny said, laughing. "That crazy wolf—and the dancer! How did they do that?"

"Magic," Stagger Lee said. "The old kind. Weekends there are cartoon matinees. Do they still remember Superman, out in the heartland?"

Danny realized Stagger was asking him. "Sure. 'Truth, Justice, and—' "

"The American Way, right. But come by in two weeks and you'll see him like you never have. And more too. The greatest heroes of American fiction are Huckleberry Finn and Bugs Bunny."

The lobby lights blinked. "You'd better get back to your seats," Stagger said.

Ginny said, "How about you?"

"Oh, I've got a spot in the back. I like to watch the audience, you see. Almost more than the movies." Quietly, just to the two of them, he said, "Have you noticed how many Ellyllon are here today?"

Danny hadn't, but now he looked: the crowd was maybe a third elves, more than he had ever seen in one place.

"They like Buster," Stagger said. "I've overheard them claiming that he must have had some of their ancestry, which is the funniest thing I've ever heard an elf say."

Danny noticed the Truebloods after that. Sometimes they laughed at different spots, or a little before or after the humans, but mostly it all came together, elvish laughter and human, silver and gold.

When the second matinee ended, they paused to look over the coming-attractions posters in the lobby. Danny turned to find Stagger Lee standing quietly behind him. "Ask you something?" Danny said.

"Just my specialty."

"Why are so many of the movies here in black and white? I know the silent ones are from before there was color, but . . ."

"Ah." Stagger looked around; the lobby was mostly empty. "It has to do with Trueblood vision. They don't see colors in the same way we do; subtle combinations turn muddy, can even give them headaches. You ever see an elf wearing more than one color, plus black and white?

"They can get through some of the really vivid Technicolor pictures, and cartoons—and I think they'd watch *The Wizard of Oz* and the Errol Flynn *Robin Hood* if they got nosebleeds—but black and white is just naturally more popular." He lowered his voice. "I assume you know the story of Joseph and the many-colored coat? I have a friend at the University of Chicago who believes that's a mythified version of a changeling narrative—elves abducting a human child."

Danny said, "You're kidding."

"My friend isn't. You should see her research. And it's more important than just one story. A lot of people would like to know just when Elfland went away the last time. The Truebloods aren't very forthcoming, so we're hunting for events that indicate the gates were open."

"Mr. Lee?" the woman behind the candy counter said.

Stagger Lee threw up his hands. "The things I do for free popcorn. Th-th-th-that's all, folks." He went into the manager's office.

It was dark outside, and the masks on the marquee were bouncing and spinning with light. Danny and Ginevra went to dinner at a little Italian restaurant a few blocks from the theater. Several people said hello to them, calling Danny by his Levee handle, tipping hats to Ginny.

"It's like I'm somebody famous," Danny said, embarrassed.

"You are," Ginny said. "You're close to Mr. Patrise. Mr. Birdsong wrote about you in the paper. That's what famous is, right?"

"But I haven't done anything."

"You saved Norma Jean's life, and someone said you took care of Cloudhunter. I think that's something." Much more softly, she said, "You're taking me out to dinner, and I think *that's* something."

After dinner they drove to La Mirada. Ginny disappeared into the back to change.

"Hallow, good evening," Patrise said. "I trust you had a pleasant afternoon?"

"Very pleasant," Danny said.

"Good. Good. We've got a place at the table for you."

There were two elves at a nearby table, Ruthins in bright red leather jackets. White silk scarves, that sparkled in the light, wrapped their throats; with their mirrored sunglasses, whipcord pants, and boots, they looked like pictures Danny had seen of World War One aviators. With them were a couple of human kids, not badly dressed for Vamps. Danny could see the butt of a pistol inside one of the Vamps' jackets, but there didn't seem to be any hostility or tension in their look, just the usual moony sucker stare.

Something felt wrong, though. Danny couldn't tell just what. Not the Ruthins, not Patrise's company . . .

Carmen came out, in a loose gold metallic shirt over a short, tight leather skirt, black sandals laced up her calves. Alvah banged out hard fast chords, and Carmen sang clear and uptempo:

> *Here I go again into the valley of sublimation*
> *Flashin' syncopation says there's trouble ahead*
> *I don't intend to swerve*
> *Waitin' for a washout or a bridge to freeze*
> *Playin' metal music on the Corvette keys*
> *Nothin' could be easier than slidin' into Dead Man's*
> *   Curve*
>
> *Tell me do you think this is a suitable case for treatment*
> *Are you gonna take me to that beautiful place*
> *Shelter me from the cold*
> *Nobody believes in a one-night stand*
> *Nothing lasts forever on the other hand*
> *Meet me in that faraway land where the good die old*

Danny knew what the problem was. It was with him. Or Ginny, or both of them. He was over here at the table, sipping dark beer, and she was over there pouring it.

This was part of his job, he thought—he had his bag, and was supposed to stay ready and sober enough to use it—and she was doing hers, just as Carmen was singing and McCain and Cloudhunter were on watch.

Fay gave the last performance, as usual. Danny stayed on through the empty hour after that, when the Ruthin elves led their followers away, and Patrise bid all good night. He played a quiet game of penny poker with Lucius and the Tokyo Fox until two, so he could drive Ginny home. He tried to tell her what he'd been thinking. She said, "I like what I do. The crowd at the Mirada doesn't treat us badly: they know Mr. Patrise can lock anyone out he wants to. And I like seeing you there, having a good time." She touched his arm. "You do have a good time there, don't you?"

"Yes."

"Then so do I."

Once or twice a week after that, Danny met Ginny for a movie. They saw the cartoons Stagger Lee had so insisted on, and *Adventures of Robin Hood* with Errol Flynn at the Biograph—which indeed had a large audience of Ellyllon, who cheered at all the right places. One evening she called, insisting that he must go with her to see somebody called Danny Kaye; the picture was *The Court Jester*, and over coffee and pie afterward she got him and half the restaurant letter-perfect on where the pellet with the poison was.

They went to *The Magnificent Ambersons*, because Orson Welles was supposed to be good. Danny watched it all, but he couldn't enjoy it. The small-minded people who couldn't see or think of a world different from their own, wearing their fears and self-righteousness like jewelry, were too much like people he had grown up with. He didn't believe the happy ending at all. Ginny seemed uncomfortable too. He wondered if she felt the same way; but he didn't ask.

Danny spent most of his evenings at La Mirada, watching, listening, learning to hold his drinks, bandaging the occasional kitchen accident. Sometimes there was a worse wound, gunshot or knife, someone he didn't know or had seen only in passing.

By now he was an expert in isolating elf blood—*gwaed ellyll*, he had learned to call it. One afternoon, Cloudhunter complimented him on how much of the Ellytha Danny had learned; Danny hadn't really noticed it happening, but the praise warmed him for days.

It no longer bothered him to see Ginevra behind the bar. The more he watched her, the more it seemed that she really did love her work, and the more he liked to watch her do it.

Every time he left her at the apartment steps, or waved good night to her as he went off to a midnight surgery, he wondered why it was so easy to go. Wasn't his heart supposed to break, or at least sink a little, when he said good-bye?

He wondered if he would know what a heart breaking felt like.

About once a week, late at the house, there were dead elves to be dissected, one or two. He worked alone now, cutting and drawing the lead from the dead white meat, pausing for a swallow of coffee or a bite from a sandwich. He was trying to be neat, even elegant; he would close up the incisions with a few stitches, zip the body bag, and call someone to take them away. The bullets went into an envelope for Stagger Lee. Danny wondered what was being done with them, but he did not ask.

One night at Mirada, a Glasa-gang elf in a green leather sheath dress fell through the front doors, cut all up in front—slashed, as if by an animal. Pavel shuttered the corridor at both ends and steered customers to a side entrance. The Ellyll woman bled maybe a quart into the carpet while Danny packed her in gauze, wound her in yards of tape. Hemlock and pressure finally stopped the flow, but the morphine didn't seem to be taking, and she gasped and moaned and arched her back, calling out in Ellytha. Once she got her hands around Danny's shoulders and pulled; Cloudhunter unwound the hands without speaking.

Mr. Patrise watched for a while, then nodded, patted Danny's shoulder, and went back to the main room. Finally two other elves wearing green took the woman away; up to Division, to heal in Elfland, Danny supposed. But he didn't ask.

He asked Mr. Patrise if he could go home. His shirt was saturated with *gwaed ellyll*; he stripped it off in the Mirada kitchen and buttoned on a clean white cook's jacket. Cloudhunter drove him back, and then followed him to his rooms; Danny was too wound up to offer any objection.

With the door closed, Cloud said, "You followed her words, did you not?"

"Yeah."

"She was unminded. Pain, injury, drugs. She did not know you, nor where she was, nor what she said."

"She called for the Wild Hunt. For me to send the Wild Hunt after her. Does that mean—"

"You are correct. The Hunt is not Death."

Danny nodded. He was shaking. "Cloud," he said, feeling horribly empty, "I cut up the dead ones, and I don't care."

"You saved a lady's life, and you do care," Cloud said simply. "When she crosses the portal, all will be healed. She will not remember what happened, what she said, what you did."

Danny let out a breath, looked up. "Thank you, Cloud."

"Any thanks due are to you, Doc. But if I assisted you, you are welcome." Cloudhunter bowed his head and went out.

Danny stumbled into the bathroom and undressed, checked himself for remaining elf-blood; he turned the shower on hot and collapsed into the sprays.

He knew enough of what the Glasa woman had said. Mr. Patrise probably did too. And Cloudhunter would have heard all of it.

He had tried to think of her as just a set of wounds he was closing up, a combative patient. But no patient had ever howled to be hurt again. And to beg for the Wild Hunt—

Was that what he wanted Ginevra to say to him?

He had the kitchen send up a pot of cocoa, sat in his living room with every light on drinking it until well toward dawn.

The phone woke him. "Hello."

"Happy birthday, to you," Ginny said. "Happy birthday to you, happy birthday, Doc Hallow, happy birthday to you."

"But it's not—"

"Yes, it is, too."

Then he understood. It was two days until Halloween. "Oh. Well, thank you."

"You aren't busy tonight, right?"

"No."

"Then you're busy tonight. See you at six." She hung up.

He stared at the phone for a moment. Then he laughed.

That afternoon, McCain asked to meet Danny in the infirmary.

"What can I help you with, Linc?" Danny said, absurdly aware that he was playing the old country doctor.

"It's about not getting—a girl pregnant."

"Well, there's condoms." This was getting more ridiculous by the second.

"I know about rubbers. I have to know if there's anything better. Something that can't miss."

"There are pills—"

"For the guy?"

"No, the girl. And there are those sponges."

"No. Not something for her. For me." Between the topic and the crazy urgency in McCain's voice, Danny was hopelessly out of his depth.

"I don't think anything's absolutely perfect. But if you cover from a couple of angles . . . There's a cream, too, that kills sperm. If you use that with the rubber, you ought to be all right."

"Okay. I guess that's good. Have you got some of that?"

Danny had to hunt around in the cabinet, but there turned out to be four tubes. "You don't have to tell me, Linc," he said with what he hoped was quiet understatement, "but why—"

McCain said flatly, "I'm a Vamp. Loop Garou, as if you couldn't guess."

Danny managed not to blurt out anything stupid. "But . . . you don't . . ."

"Not anymore. But they say you don't ever get it all out. The idea of a kid born that way . . . couldn't do that, Doc."

The revelation, from McCain, made Danny feel like whistling in the graveyard. He dispensed the meds and what wisdom he could offer with them.

"Thanks, Doc," McCain said. "Wasn't something I could talk about with Stagger Lee. Don't tell him that."

" 'Course not."

When McCain had gone, Danny let out a long breath, and stocked his own pockets.

The movie at Laughs was *The Ghost Breakers*. Danny hadn't much liked the Bob Hope movies he'd seen, but this one wasn't bad, funny and mysterious and even a little scary. Ginny's hand locked onto his during the first thunderstorm scene, and never let go until they were out of the theater and in the restaurant up the street. Then she let him go long enough to get into an inches-deep pizza with half the garden on top.

A bulky figure in a baggy, wrinkled trench coat came up. "Good evening, loyal readers."

"Hi, Lucius."

"Don't stop," Lucius said. "I may be a busybody—in fact, I *am* a busybody, and a highly paid one at that—but I know better than to interfere with serious eye contact."

"It's a birthday party," Ginny said.

"Oh? Oh, I see. Happy birthday, Doc."

Ginny said, "Would you join us for a while, Mr. Birdsong?"

"Oh, Ginny. Have all those long scotches come between me and my first name?"

Danny said, "Sit down, Lucius. Please."

He spread his hands, shrugged his coat off, pulled up a chair.

Ginny said, "We want to go out someplace after dinner. Not one of the usual places. Do you have any suggestions?"

Lucius ordered a beer. He was frowning. It looked strange on him. "Can I tell you a story, by way of answering that? One you'll never read in the column?"

Danny said, "Sure."

"Okay. Wait for the beer. It needs a beer." They talked about nothing in particular until Lucius's drink came. He clicked glasses with them, took a sip.

"Once upon a time," Lucius said, "I got lost on the Levee. Somewhere up around Division and the River. I mean, *I* got lost: the Minstrel of the City Streets. I certainly wasn't going to ask directions. Even if I'd seen anyone to ask, which I didn't. It was a cool night, not cold, good for walking. So I walked. Straight line, keep going. After all, sooner or later I'd hit Elfland, or the lake, or New Orleans, or San Francisco, any of which would do for orientational purposes."

Danny had never heard Lucius *tell* a story before. His voice was soft: he was speaking only to the two of them. He had some of the same manner as the newspaper column, but not so dry, not so distant.

"Eventually there was a neon sign up ahead: not buzzing, wired to a spellbox, so I hadn't crossed the Line without noticing. It was a dance joint, jumping pretty good; in go I, who do not exactly jump with the best. It was Danceland. Ever hear of it?"

Danny said no. Ginny said she'd read a magazine article.

Lucius said, "The immediate point is that Danceland is a Shadow joint, but not *our* Shadow, not the Levee, understand? You can't just turn on Blessing Way and Michigan and get there. But I got there.

"Inside, there were elves in leathers, whole-Worlders in destroyed denim, halfies in anything and all. A bunch of them were slamming, and though he might jitterbug or even Madison if the cause were strong, Birdsong does *not* slam. Two half-naked Ellyllon were doing the lambada—I don't suppose either of you has ever seen a lambada?"

They shook their heads.

"Good for you. Oh, and a werewolf was waltzing with an elf maiden. Waltzing, Jesus Matilda. So I watched for a while, and then went to the bar, because there are some true compasses in the thickest weather.

"I turned around then. Maybe something made me turn. I saw a man: my height, my build, my color. Thinner, but if any of my other parts got the exercise my tongue does I'd be pretty trim too. He was wearing buckskins, moccasins, and eagle feathers in his hair. He looked me dead in the eye, and he started to dance, solo. Slow, not hard to follow, one-two, step-two. And I follow.

"No one looked at us. What's strange enough to stare at in Danceland? Not dancers, surely. I danced all night with my eagle brother, until the spells that drove the neon died, and the loose fairy dust in the air got thick enough to choke on, and the fire we show the World went out. Never did touch a drink."

Lucius reached inside his jacket, took out a flat leather case. He showed them three feathers, black and white and golden. "You're an open-spaces man, Doc: have you ever seen an eagle?"

"No. I thought I did once, but it was just a turkey buzzard."

Lucius turned the feathers over in his fingers. "Reporters have sources. That's like magic, but more expensive. There hasn't been a confirmed sighting of a wild eagle since the return of Elfland. Nor a California condor. And there are rumors about the ravens of Dresden." He put the feathers away.

Danny said, "Are you suggesting we go to Danceland?"

"Oh, no." Lucius finished his beer. "Birdsong on high adventure in one paragraph: Even if it were within my ability to send you, I was just pointing out that you don't really seek places out in the Shades. You find them." Suddenly he reached out, put two fingers against Danny's jaw and turned his head. Ginny had been leaning against Danny's shoulder, and their cheeks touched with something like an electric shock. They both jumped.

"Good night and good hunting," Lucius said, picking up his coat. "See you in the funny papers." He drifted out into the night.

Danny said to Ginny, "Where do you think we should start looking?"

"Do you think you could find my place? I mean, up the stairs and everything?"

"It's worth a try."

Ginevra's apartment was small, and tidy. No, it was austere. Ginny went into the kitchen to make tea, and Danny absorbed the details: a portable CD player and a few dozen discs, classical and old rock and folk; paperbacks on bare wooden bookshelves, plays and poetry and illustrated travel books; cardboard bins of magazines about travel and history. The rather hard chairs were softened a little by throw pillows, and a small orange rug lay precisely in the center of the polished wood floor. The only wall decoration—the only decoration at all, really—was a framed poster of an ornate, domed building with a tower, in the middle of a foreign city. FI-RENZE, it said.

Ginny came out of the kitchen, holding a tea tray. Danny swallowed. She was wearing black cotton pajamas, a high-collared shirt and long trousers.

"You don't mind my getting changed," she said.

"No. 'Course not. It's your house." *Shut up*, he told himself.

She put the tray down, sat in the one comfortable-looking chair; she was scrunched over to the side, leaving room. Danny sat on the floor. She smiled oddly and tucked her feet up beneath herself. "There's nothing in this room really big enough, sorry."

He shrugged, shook his head. It was clear enough what she

meant: there would be only one other furnished room in the apartment, and there was no bed in this one.

But he was happy just to look at her, the curves of her body under the cloth. She handed him a teacup.

Danny said, "Do you think this is what Lucius had in mind?"

"Maybe," she said, with a hint of a laugh. Then she said, "He seems so lonely. He's at the club a lot, but he's never with anyone, unless it's someone he's talking to for a story. Or Kitsune Asa."

"Is there really a typewriter there for him?"

She nodded. "That's part of what I mean. He'll be in really late, sometimes the last person there, typing, like he didn't have anyplace else to go. As if going home were like dying." She rubbed her hands on her teacup. "When he told that story, tonight—I wondered where he was going, when he got lost." She shifted again, looked at her bare feet, looked at him, smiled. "Tell me a story, Doc."

"What about?"

"About you. Tell me something nobody else in the city knows about you."

"Oh—"

"Come on, please. You must have done things before you came here. You must have had friends."

"Robin was my best friend at home," he said, too quickly.

"What was she like?"

"No, Rob was a guy. He was about my size, sort of blond. I'm sure he was a lot better looking. He sure didn't have freckles."

"Hmm."

"But, see, the thing about Rob was that he could really talk to people. You always knew what he meant, know what I mean? See, I can't do it."

"Go on. He was your best friend. You took girls out together, that kind of thing?"

"No. I mean, nobody did, really. We were all a long way apart, and nobody had cars. We had bikes—bicycles, not motorcycles—but where can you go on a bike? The only place close to go, really, was when there was a social at the school, and then everybody's folks went too." He took a swallow of tea, but it didn't stop him: he was started now, and knew he was going to tell it all. The incredible thing was that he hadn't told it before now.

Ginny tucked herself up tighter in the chair. Danny put his cup down so he wouldn't spill it. Quickly he said, "What happened was, we were haying on Danny's folks' place. We—were you ever on a farm?"

"No."

"We all did that. Help's always short, and they don't use the machines too much, now, but—well, there was a mechanical baler. That's a machine that bundles up the hay with wire. Rob got caught in it. I don't know how, nobody saw what happened, but he yelled, and you could see blood. . . .

"A couple of us got him out. He was really messed up bad. I'd read some first aid books—I kind of wanted to be a doctor, I guess, but it wasn't going to happen."

"Why?"

"What?"

"Why couldn't you be a doctor?"

"Because you have to go away to school for a long time," Danny said faster than he could think, "and my folks didn't want that." He paused. "I don't have any brothers or sisters. I had a little sister, but she died of flu when she was four."

"I'm sorry."

"Yeah." How could he explain that he had felt nothing? That she had been there, and then she wasn't, and at six years old Danny had no idea what all the fuss was supposed to be about?

Ginevra said, "Rob got hurt in the baler machine."

"Yeah. Like I said, I knew a little first aid, and I got tourniquets on, so he didn't bleed to death. But he lost his left arm, and most of his left leg.

"Rob's folks were really grateful. His dad was on county council, and he helped me get my EMT card; the county paid for the training, and I worked at the hospital, and then for the fire department after I made paramedic. And, uh, they helped me buy the TR3 from a sheriff's sale. I don't think my mom and dad were too happy about that."

"And then you came up here."

"Yeah. I hauled some stuff downstairs, and we yelled at each other, and I said they could shoot me if they wanted to but they weren't gonna stop me.

"I couldn't stand seeing Rob, see. I'd go visit, because we were friends, right? And I'd see him at school, and church. And he'd just sit there in the chair. I told you, Rob was good at letting you know what he meant. He sure did. He hated me 'cause he hadn't died."

"Did he have a girlfriend?"

"No. Not really. Nobody did, much." He tried to follow the question. "He was okay, wasn't cut up—you know, there."

"Was he gay?"

"*What?*"

"Im sorry," she said, sounding frightened. "I'm really sorry, I shouldn't have said that."

"No, it's okay. Really, really, it's okay." He wanted to hold her, show her it was all right, calm her fear, stop his own. "The thing is, you're right. One day—this was maybe a year before his accident—Rob said, 'Let's go for a ride,' and we got on our bikes and just rode. I don't know how far, five miles at least. That's when he told me." How would she understand? She came from the other side of the earth, and lived here, even farther away. "We didn't *have* 'gay people.' Sometimes you heard somebody was a *fag*. You know what decent people do to fags in Iowa?"

"I know what they did in Ohio," she said quietly. "Probably not much difference."

"Probably not," Danny said, and shut himself up for a moment. Suddenly Ginevra seemed much closer to him, maybe close enough to touch.

He said, "I guess that's why he hated me so bad. If he could have gotten out, come here, or anywhere, who would have cared? But now he'll never get out. I didn't let him die, and I sure didn't save his life. Like I say, he knew how to tell you things."

"I think you know how to hear things," Ginny said. Danny, with no answer for that, took a swallow of the tea. It had gotten cool, and bitter. "I think I ought to leave."

"Do you?" She unfolded, arching her feet on the floor, opening a lap to sit on. "Nothing's found us yet. We could keep looking."

"No, I'll go." She seemed about to say something: would she

ask him, straight out? He shifted uncomfortably. Could she tell he was hard? If she—*begged* him—

He stood up. "I had a really good time tonight, Ginny. Thank you."

"Oh. Hey, it's your birthday." She stood up. "You still have a hug coming."

He nodded. She put her arms around him and pressed. She was naked under the pajamas. His crotch tightened some more.

She pulled him down to the floor. They bumped knees, elbows, scraped ankles. She was on top of him, soft, so soft. He held her; he couldn't stop.

He said, "I just don't—"

"This is your birthday hug," she said, her breath warm against his ear, her hair blinding him. "You say when it stops." Her hands played his ribs like a piano. "Or how tight it gets."

This was good, he thought, relaxing. This was fine, he could do this. He didn't want to let go; he didn't seem strong enough to pull away. They stayed there, just holding, until Danny's head bumped the floor and he realized he was almost asleep.

"I should go."

"Go? *I* think you should—" She stopped, pressed her face against his shoulder. "What should *I* do, Doc? What do you want *me* to do?"

He almost told her. His hands were near enough to pin her shoulders in a moment, to lock around her slim strong wrists. He shook.

He looked down at her, and saw the brutalized elf-woman from the night before, clutching and pleading. He wanted to crawl under a rock, away from his thoughts.

"Doc . . . ?"

He said, "Just . . . don't be angry."

"Is that your safeword, Doc? 'Don't be angry'?" she said, smiling.

"Maybe." It came out a whisper.

"I'll never be angry with you, Doc." She unwound herself, sat up with her hands around her knees.

Danny stood up. "Will I see you at the club on Halloween?"

"No. I'm helping sit some of the little kids in the building, so their parents can go out."

"Oh."

She laughed. "Night of horror and suspense, huh."

He said, "Next Friday's some kind of special show at the Laughs. Stagger Lee keeps talking about it."

"What is it?"

"I forget. Somebody named Corvette."

"Not really."

"It's something like that. Want to go?"

"It's on."

The air outside woke him up, but it did not make him cold.

Late on Halloween afternoon, there was a knock at Danny's door. It was Boris Liczyk, carrying a small leather case and a garment bag. "I've brought your costume, sir."

There were slightly baggy trousers, a high-collared white shirt with a ruffled front, a velvet string tie.

"Shall I manage that for you, sir?"

"That'd be fine, Boris."

Danny faced the mirror; Liczyk stood behind him and effortlessly spun the tie into a shoelace bow. Boris held up the jacket, and Danny slipped his arms in; it was a long coat, nearly to his knees, with a narrow waist. The slightly stiff fabric was deep forest green, the collar of a lighter green velvet. Liczyk did a bit of pinching and the fit was perfect.

Then he brought out a long cloak, dark brown with a golden satin lining, adjusted and tied it around Danny's shoulders. "You might wish to walk about for a while, sir. Men don't wear such things nowadays; moving gracefully requires a bit of practice. Please be quite careful on the stairs—wouldn't do to lose our physician."

"I'll be careful."

Boris held out a pancake of dark green silk. "Observe, sir." He flexed the object, and it sprang into shape as a top hat. "Just like Mr. Astaire," Boris said, smiling. He put it on Danny's head, showed him the proper tilt. "I am to remind you to carry your bag as well, sir."

"To the party? With the costume?"

"Yes, sir. That's all I have for you: is there anything else I can do?"

"No, I don't think so. Uh, Boris?"

"Yes, sir?"

"Shouldn't formal stuff be, you know, black?"

"Not for you, sir. Black isn't a red-haired gentleman's color. Which reminds me, we must fit you for a dinner suit soon. It'll only take an hour or so."

"Sure. Thank you, Boris."

"My job, sir. I enjoy this." He bowed and went out.

Danny looked at himself in the mirror. Okay, what was he supposed to be? The ruffled shirt and tie had a sort of Western look; he'd thought of Doc Holliday. But surely not the top hat and the cloak. And he was supposed to carry his bag. Was he Doctor Jekyll?

Oh. Of course. He got the bag, took out the dissecting knife.

The phone rang.

"Hello, Jack the Ripper here."

There was a burst of laughter. Mr. Patrise's voice said, "Good evening, Jack. Would you join me in the office for a few minutes? Bring your costume things—we'll go straight to the party."

"Certainly, sir."

Danny went up a flight. Boris Liczyk was right: the cloak was dangerous on the stairs.

Patrise's office was a long, high-ceilinged room with geometric carpets, Deco furniture of glass, chrome, and black wood, artwork on the walls. The desk was a spotlit, L-shaped block of white metal with a black marble top. Patrise sat behind it in a leather swivel chair. He was wearing an ornate brocaded jacket, like something from a Shakespeare play, and his hair was combed straight down on to his shoulders all around. It never seemed so long, tied back as he usually wore it. He waved a hand, with rings on all the fingers. "Hello, Hallow. Happy birthday. Drink?"

"Not just now, thanks."

"We'll just be a moment. I was thinking about Ginevra Benci, and I wanted to ask you a question or two."

"Yes?"

"You've spent some time with her. Certainly more than I have lately."

"Well, we're friends—"

"Of course. I'm sorry she couldn't be here tonight. I tried to make arrangements, but . . ."

"I'm sure she'd have been here if she could."

"Oh, it isn't her fault. Almost anything can be purchased in the Shade, but a trustworthy babysitter is beyond an elf-lord's ransom. Perhaps I should enter the business." He played with one of his rings. "Ginevra is a talented woman; obviously bartending doesn't begin to challenge her." He looked at Danny's bag. "I imagine she could learn first-aid nursing in not much time at all. I'm sure Lucy Estevez at the hospital could arrange something."

"It'd be up to Ginny."

"I'm perfectly aware of that. But she isn't here, and I wanted your opinion."

"I think she likes her job," Danny said carefully, "a-a-and I wouldn't want her to think she was being moved around. Certainly not on my account."

"Yes. That's a very considerate response. Thank you, Hallow. Now, we'd better get down to the party." He stood up and came around the desk. The "jacket" was actually just the top of an embroidered gown that fell in deep pleats almost to the floor.

"Oh, by the way, Hallow . . . you're welcome to play your part as Saucy Jack if you wish, but he wasn't the original idea."

"Oh?"

"Boris never remembers these things. If it isn't cut on the bias, it might as well be made of air to him. You were meant to be H. H. Holmes. Local fellow of the same era. He put away a dozen times Jack the Ripper's total. Which shows you how fleeting fame is."

"And you, sir?"

"I'm Cesare Borgia. Do you know what I could have done to you for not knowing that? Come along."

All the rooms on the ground floor had been rearranged to make party space. There were at least a hundred people there, all in costume, none alike. Danny thought of the Halloween socials at home—half a dozen pointy-hatted witches, as many ghosts in percale, here and there a Frankenstein ragbag or a pumpkinhead. One year two kids had shown up as Dorothy and the Scarecrow from Oz, and been sent home by a couple of parents. Witches were okay, at least if they were warty and toothless, but subversive literature was something else. He wondered how many of these costumes Patrise had provided. Boris Liczyk had been looking a bit worn for the last few days, and McCain told Danny later that the tailor had the night and weekend off.

McCain wore the flour-sack face of a scarecrow, a wooden beam across his already broad shoulders. From time to time he would laugh. It was scary. Cloudhunter was some kind of fantastical warrior, with leather armor and a black two-handed sword carved with mysterious figures. Another elf was Poe's Red Death, in a cloak the color of an arterial spurt, with bleeding gravewrappings beneath.

The Tokyo Fox was dressed in a tweed Inverness cape and deerstalker hat. She hardly needed to produce a huge round magnifier and examine the mantelpiece and the other guests—or maybe she did, because somehow it worked, despite gender and height.

She examined Doc's left sleeve. "Ingenious, Doctor," she said, with a curious Eurasian accent.

Danny caught the cue. "Why, thank you, Holmes."

"Indeed. I ask you to disguise yourself so as to divert suspicion, and you arrive in the guise of the most wanted murderer in London."

There was a laugh. But Danny had this one. "Egad, Holmes, I'd hoped to follow your own advice on the subject of disguise, but do you know how difficult it can be for a naked man to hail a cab in Mayfair?"

The crowd applauded. Patrise stared for a moment, face open with wonder, and then laughed out loud.

Matt Black had a slouch hat and cloak, a scarf across his face, and two Colt pistols. Gloss White was wrapped all up in gauze, her features barely visible; someone told Danny that she was Resurrection Mary, the Archer Street ghost. Danny thought back to the night of the blood raid, and was glad not to see any close resemblance.

Phasia was dressed as a spectral Marie Antoinette: a red cicatrice circled her throat, a thin trickle of blood seeping down. She did not speak, of course, but waved her fan with cool authority.

Carmen Mirage was wearing a black silk cheongsam embroidered with a golden dragon; she had sheer black stockings, wildly high heels. Her hair was pulled back into a knot pierced with two lacquered pins, and makeup gave her eyes an almond shape. A narrow black scarf was around her shoulders: it was full of points of light, like a strip of the night sky.

"And who might you be?" Danny said, trying to sound genially sinister.

"Fah Lo Suee," she said coolly. "Perhaps you are acquainted with my venerable father, the Doctor Fu Manchu."

Not much really happened during the evening; people played at their characters, occasionally danced a bit without music, ate, drank, and generally seemed to be having a good silly time. Now and then someone—or more often two someones—vanished. Now and then they came back.

About ten o'clock the wind could be heard rising outside. That was strange: the house was built like a bank vault, and didn't let wind noise through. Then the lights went out. Someone shrieked. People collided; elf voices muttered in English and Ellytha.

Lit candles appeared then, and the hurricane lamps were lit. The dining room and ballroom chandeliers were lowered, and candles set in place on them. In fifteen minutes it was as if nothing had happened.

No, not quite. People seemed merrier now, as if they had been waiting for this.

It was well after midnight when things began to wind down. Danny found Patrise seated next to Fay, holding her hand. "I think I'll go upstairs now, Mr.—my lord Cesare."

The candlelight made something strange and deep of Patrise's smile. "Yes," he said. "Rest well."

A candle was waiting on the foyer table. Danny lit lamps in the living room, the bedroom, the bath. He had just hung up the cloak and the coat, and gotten the string tie loosened, when there was a knock at the door.

It was Carmen.

"Hi," she said. "Could I borrow your bathroom for a little bit, to get out of this stuff?"

"Oh. Sure."

"Thanks, Doc." She came in, shut the door, took a look around. "How was your evening?"

"Good. Yours?"

"Oh, I'm great." There was something in the way she said it that denied it. "Which way . . . ?"

He led her to the bathroom. "Stay there," she said, running water into the sink, "talk to me."

"What about?"

"Anything. You, for instance."

He felt odd, suddenly. This was too much an echo of two nights back. "I haven't ever been to a really big party like this."

"Halloween's special," she said above the rush of the faucet. "We all get to play being something else." She leaned into the doorway. A strip of flesh-colored adhesive tape hung off her fingertips, and one of her eyes had lost its tilt. "Big change."

Danny sat still on the edge of the bed. Carmen came out, toweling her face. "Whee, that's better. Just call me Blinky." She sat down on the bed, right next to him. "So I hear it's your birthday."

Oh, God, he thought.

"What's the matter?" she said, "What's the matter?" and her voice was aching so that he looked her in the face, and saw—

Oh, God.

He said, "Look, you know I—"

"Yeah, I know you. And her. And I know you're not."

He stared.

"No, she didn't tell me. She didn't have to. That's one—well, let's say *wistful* girlfriend you've got there, kid."

"I'm not . . . a kid."

"You're twenty by one day. I'm twenty-seven. And you're a virgin, which I sure the hell am not."

"Well, so what?"

She spoke softly. "So you're probably scared—*take it easy*, Doc. And I'm a horny old lady who can't hold on to a guy with handcuffs."

He flinched.

She didn't seem to notice. "So, how'd you like to lose it to No-Tell Daisy, up here where nobody's gonna notice? It'll make you feel good. It'll sure make me feel good. And in the not-so-long run, it'll make her feel good too."

"That doesn't make any sense."

"Sure it does. Watch." She wrapped her arms around him and kissed him hard on the mouth, shoving her tongue between his lips. He sucked in a breath, pulled away. "See?" she said. "Everything south of your eyeballs knows it makes sense."

He stared at the floor.

"I'm sorry," she said, and the hurt in her voice made him look at her again. "What you do is, you say yes, or you say no. That's all."

"Yes," he said, though he wasn't sure the voice was his.

"Okay."

He stood up, dizzy. "Do you want me to wear a . . . the . . ."

"A condom?" she said, very gently.

"Yeah."

"Up to you. I've been tied."

"Wha . . . at?"

She looked straight at him. "Tubes. You know." She made a knotting gesture. "When I was sixteen, I figured I might not know what I wanted to do with my life, but I sure knew what I wanted to do with my personal equipment."

Danny nodded. He knew, in a book-learned way, what a tubal ligation was. He'd never heard of anyone at home with one, or for that matter a doctor who would admit to doing them. Here, apparently, the patient didn't even have to be twenty-one. He supposed it would be stupid to ask about parental consent. . . .

He thought about some other things he knew only in the abstract. Like how to put a rubber on. Nothing he'd heard had been particularly precise.

He sat down next to her, put a hand on her hands, reached experimentally around her shoulders, feeling softness, the smooth movement of the shoulder blades. There was hardly any fabric between. The lamp flickered highlights in her hair.

She said, "I'm glad you asked, though. Guys don't, usually. Truebloods never do. And afterward they think there's something dirty about halfies."

"I can still get a—"

"Uh-huh. You know how? Don't fib."

"Well, I—"

"Right. Go get it. It'll take five minutes to demonstrate, and make your whole life better." She kissed him, on the mouth. It was just as startling the second time. He pulled her closer. Her tongue wet his lips. His hand slipped to her thigh, through the slit in her dress, closed involuntarily on something hard. It was a garter strap.

"Good place to start," she said in a thick voice.

He tried. It wouldn't give. Her hand closed on his, and she led him to the chair across from the bed. "Sit there, and watch."

Danny felt himself flush.

"No, really. Just watch. It'll be fun." She pressed down on both his wrists. "And you can't get up until I say so, all right?"

"All right."

She slipped off her shoes, tossed them aside. She stretched, then flicked open a garter strap with two fingers, reached around her thigh and did it again, and again. She sat back on the bed and began rolling down her stocking. Slowly.

Was the game that he was supposed to sit still? Soon enough he knew it was, and why it was a game, and that he was losing it fast. What was the elf word?

The Wild Hunt. Right. He tried not to think about that.

Now she was wearing some underthing of gold lace, no shoulder straps, barely over her hips. It had white pearl buttons down the side; it might as well have had printed instructions.

He started to get up, but suddenly she knelt in front of him, leaned on his lap. He gasped.

"Did I say you could get up?" She unfastened the first of his fly buttons.

He said, "Don't."

"One of us has to." Another button. "Jesus, Doc, you've gotta be hurting."

He was. "I'll do it."

Her fingers moved again, and one of Danny's braces flew free. "If you really want me to stop," she whispered, "*make* me stop."

He grasped both her wrists. Her eyes closed. "*Now* you got it, Doctor."

The Wild Hunt howled in the thickets.

She opened her eyes, all black. "You don't want to just *hold* me like that all night."

"I don't want—" He stopped. He was going to lie. He was scared to death and had the heartbeat to prove it. "—to hurt you," he said, which was the truth, or at least he hoped it still was.

"I didn't think you did. *That* I can get anywhere." She pulled easily out of his grip, picked up the long, thin black scarf with the starpoints in the silk. She draped it across her wrists, dropped to her knees again.

"There aren't a lot of girls who'll tell you what they really want, Doc. And damn few who'll trust you this far." With an improbable kindness she said, "Are you gonna abuse a girl's trust?"

He felt the silk. "I'll ruin this."

"That's Nancy silk. If you can tear that, I'd better send for the Kryptonite." She laughed. "You can't even *take* it . . . and I haven't got anything else you *can* take." She lowered her left wrist. "Meet me halfway. One hand, to the bedpost."

When he hesitated again, she reached out, put a finger on his hand. "Listen. My safeword's 'tortilla.' Sounds dumb, right, but I'm not gonna yell it by mistake. You hear that, you stop. No guilt, no hard feelings, we just stop. Is that good enough?"

"I guess so."

"What's the word again?"

"Tortilla."

"Good man." She leaned back, held very still as he tied her right wrist. He tried to hide the sudden heaviness of his breathing. He started to unfasten his shirt.

"Move back a little," she said softly, "let me see you."

He got undressed. He wasn't sure how; there was no sensation in his fingers, and she was watching the whole time. Then he crawled onto the bed and started on the pearl buttons. She moaned, and he was sure he must be crushing her. He shifted at once, but she just smiled, eyes closed.

He unfolded the gilt lace; she arched her back and he slipped it free, let it fall to the floor. There wasn't anything else in the way. In the lamplight she was all gold and darkness.

She tugged hard with her bound wrist. It was quite secure.

"See, Doc? You can't tear it, or stretch it. It's hard. It's got *no* mercy."

You're not at home anymore, he thought, what little of him could still think, nobody here cares. And he had to know. Maybe even for Ginny's sake. At least next time, he'd have some idea of how.

He moved, and groaned. Her left hand brushed him—he nearly screamed—and then practically pulled him in; after that, it actually started to seem easy, something you could do again, almost without effort.

Like going down the stairs into the darkened cellar, and wondering what it could have been that you had been so afraid of.

And then, in the middle of the night, waking with the fear fresh again, all around you.

Carmen looked asleep. Carefully, trying not to wake her, he unfastened the loop around her wrist. He stroked the silk: it was, indeed, undamaged.

She wrapped both arms around him. "Hello, Doctor Hallownight."

"Are you okay?"

"Great. You wanna continue the therapy anyway?"

"I, uh—"

"Uh-huh. I'd better fly."

"What time is it?"

"Almost five. Same morning." She stood up, wound the black scarf around her throat, picked up her gold slip. "I should go. Really."

"Well, do you—shall I drive you?"

"No. Jesse'll get me a ride back. Or I might just walk." She began dressing. "Safest night of all for it: all the mortals are afraid of the haunts, and who fears the devil? Not I. Not I, says Carmen alone."

He sat up, pulling the sheet to cover himself. "Well, shall I at least—"

"Don't do anything," she said. "I want to remember you just like that."

"Will I see you again?"

She laughed. "You see me all the time; figure that'll change?"

"I mean—"

"I know what you mean. No, I don't think like this. Not for a while, anyway." Quickly, she said, "It wasn't anything you did, okay? You were fine. You were good. I'm just kind of ... well. My birthday's in June. Maybe you can wrap me up a present. But I'll bet two silver Georges and a Trueblood's lock you're in love by then."

The same pain in her voice, still there as before. Nothing at all might have happened. "Maybe *you'll* be in love by then."

"You're very kind, Doc." She came over, bent down and kissed him on the forehead. "You *are* kind. I mean that."

"Maybe," he said, his mind's bearings grinding off-balance, "at the poker game—"

"No. Please, don't do that. It wouldn't make you happy. Even if you got me." She leaned very close. "Remember: no guilt. I made you do it. You were helpless." Then she tossed her coat over her shoulders, snatched up her shoes and stockings and walked out of the bedroom without stopping to put them on. He heard the hall door close.

He sat there for a while, wrapped naked in the damp bed-clothes, all that had happened lingering thick in his senses. No guilt, Carmen had said. He had been—

Then he thought of the one other time he had said *Will I see you again?* and his heart fell, and fell, and fell.

NOVEMBER

At midday Doc found Cloudhunter in the walled garden, wearing black glasses against the bright, cold November sun, sketching the branches of a small fir tree.

"Cloud, what's Nancy silk?"

Without looking up, Cloudhunter said, "It comes from our side of Division. 'Nancy' is a mortal kenning; we have others."

"Is it true that it can't be torn?"

"Not by hands. Nor cut by any dark edge."

"What does it mean that it can't be taken?"

Cloudhunter put down his pad and charcoal. He reached inside his jacket, drew out the end of his starry blue scarf. With complete patience, he said, "It may only change hands as a free-willed gift; if stolen, or sold for dross, it always returns, and leaves bad fortune behind. The Weavers give it to some of the *gwaed gwir*; sometimes we give it to yours."

Cloudhunter ran the scarf through his fingers. "These, and shawls, are the commonest gifts, simple flat pieces. There is a story of a shirt, woven all of a piece, since needle will not pierce it. I do not know if the story is true. If it is, all Elfland would not ransom it."

"I see. Thank you, Cloud." Doc tried to imagine that: at home he had known people who wove cloth, and all the women sewed, of course. A fragment of a song floated through his head: *without a seam, or needlework* ... "How could you weave a whole shirt in one piece?" He thought of the drape of a shoulder, joining a sleeve. "What kind of loom?"

Cloud looked up at Doc. He pressed the heels of his hands together, arched the fingers. "Eight legs, same as spin it."

"Oh." Suddenly the beautiful cloth made him uneasy. "Thanks, Cloud."

"Always." He tucked the scarf around his throat. "May I ask you a favor, Doc? In return, if you please?"

"Of course."

"There is a hall of relics—a museum—in the city, just beyond the Shadow line. It is called the Field, though I believe that is a person's name."

"Yeah. The natural history museum. I've heard of it."

"Have you ever visited it?"

"No."

"Then would you like to do so with me?"

"Now?"

"If you have no other obligations."

Mr. Patrise assured Doc that he was free for the day. "Render unto Caesar," Patrise said.

"Sorry, sir?"

"Have Lisa give you some honest American folding money from the safe. The World has its ways."

Cloudhunter proposed that they walk, but after consulting a map and guidebook they decided that the museum would be exercise enough. When Cloud stood by Doc's Triumph, it never seemed possible that the Ellyll could fit into the little car, but he folded himself in without apparent effort. Doc drove them south, over the river and into the World. The transition was barely visible in clear daylight, and Doc felt nothing; if Cloud did, he didn't show it. "I appreciate this," he said to Doc. "I have gone with Stagger Lee to the science museum, farther down the coast, but he has never shown much interest in this one."

"I always figured Stagger was interested in everything," Doc said idly.

"Oh, he is by no means impolite. But one sees."

Doc glanced at Cloudhunter. The silver elf eyes were hidden by the sunglasses.

The museum's columned, white marble front stretched for a block and a half. Broad stairs led up to the doorway. Doc reached for his wallet, but Cloudhunter waved a finger and paid both admissions. The ticket seller loudly and elaborately counted back the change, as if to a small child. Cloud jingled the coins in his hand as they walked past the booth; a few steps on, he showed them to Doc. "Nickel and tin," he said, vaguely smiling, and shoved them into a pouch.

They were in a high-ceilinged hall that ran from one side of the building to the other, display halls opening off to either side. "So," Doc said, "what shall we see first?"

Cloud examined a floor-plan brochure. "Upstairs, I think." He led the way up a massive staircase. The sign ahead of them read DINOSAURS.

As they entered the hall, Cloudhunter's eyes blazed—not a twinkle, but a flash like close lightning. "Dragons," he said softly.

They were surrounded by the bones of giants. Doc knew *Tyrannosaurus* and *Stegosaurus* by sight, but the variety of shapes and sizes on display here was a surprise. Some stood, some crawled, some ran; one dove on them from above, having apparently leapt from a tall glass case. They were all only bones, of course, except in the paintings that accompanied the displays, and a few surprisingly live-looking clay models. Looking at the skeletons, Doc was suddenly reminded of a fire he'd been to, in the hours before dawn: the sun came up on a blackened stick model of the buildings they'd tried and failed so save. He felt the same sense of *Gone, won't come back*.

Cloud was moving from display to display, case to case, quiet as a shadow. Across the hall, someone pointed at him. Doc tried to keep up with the tall elf.

Cloud said, "It isn't allowed to touch . . . ?"

"This one says you can," Doc said. There was a brown bone, more than a yard long, set in sand-colored concrete. "I *think* it's real."

Cloud put his fingertips delicately on the surface. "It is genuine, Doc. Touch it."

Doc put a hand on the bone. It felt cold, smoothed by who knew how many hands before.

"Now take my other hand."

Abruptly the light was slanting and fierce, yellowed by dust in the air. Doc's vision was tilted to the right. His head hurt; so did his back and right hip. There was a heavy, sweetish, boggy stink. Just before his eyes was a clump of fat-stalked plants, bristling with fine green shoots: the fresh scent made his mouth water, and he pressed his head forward, but his body wouldn't follow. He stuck out his tongue, but it did no good. His ... tail? ... stirred heavily, making his hip hurt even more.

Beyond the plants, blurry in the distance and haze, a mottled tan shape moved. Teeth inches long flashed in an enormous mouth, and the shape stumbled closer. Alarms rang somewhere in Doc's consciousness, pulling at his muscles to move.

Doc knew what was about to happen, and that he couldn't do a thing to stop it. *This is bad,* he thought idiotically, but could not clearly identify just what was Bad about it, why it filled him with such urgency and rage. The one obvious and understandable thing in his mind was the sight and smell of those green shoots: if he could get a mouthful of those, things would be much better. Everything else would pass.

The allosaur stomped closer.

There was a pop inside Doc's head, and he was back in the museum hall, Cloudhunter's hand on his shoulder, Doc's fingers tingling against the dinosaur bone.

"I thought the sight would be interesting," Cloud said, his voice a soft, plaintive rumble. "I am very sorry if I displeased you."

"No ... I ..." He shook his head to clear it. "The dino died."

"Not then. Memory needs time to dwell in the bone. It never knows its death." Cloud took his hand away slowly. "I would never hazard you, Doc. Still ..."

"Don't be sorry, please, Cloud. It was wonderful. I didn't have any idea you could do things like that."

"Oh," Cloudhunter said, and turned to the text panel next to the bone. "Seventy million years. The depth of it ..."

"How old are you, Cloud?"

"I?" Cloud seemed startled by the question, and Doc worried that he had violated some Trueblood rule. "I couldn't tell you in years. I was not there to see the gates closed. Some of the Ellyllon were, and all of the Urthas—the Highborn." He put his fingers on the dinosaur bone again. "Seventy million years . . . I don't know if even Urthas live so long." He gave Doc a sidewise grin. "Though I shouldn't say such things. Come on, let's see more."

The next hall was lined with totem poles, painted headdresses of wood, pottery and spears.

"These are American native, I think?" Cloud said. "From nearby?"

Doc read the labels. "These are from the Pacific Northwest. Seattle—that's more than a thousand miles. Alaska's at least twice as far."

Cloud absorbed this, looked around again. "Are your people somewhere here, Doc?"

"Uh . . . I don't think so. Just a moment." He found a wall-mounted building plan, scanned the listings. What was he looking for, exactly? Midwestern Tribes of Uncertain European Ancestry?

When he turned back, Cloud was crouching by a little girl, showing her the silver bracelet on his left wrist. Doc had a sudden hollow feeling in his stomach. He looked around for worried parents. There they were, closing in quick. He'd never beat them to Cloudhunter unless he sprinted. Maybe that was the best idea, he thought: create a diversion. But he just walked as quickly as he felt he could, and tried to work out the soft answer that turneth away wrath.

". . . and these are the names of my sisters. They are very long names in English, but we also call them First Star, and Lilac, and Cools as Rain."

"Those are pretty names," the child said.

The father said, "Does the blue stone have a meaning?"

"There are four like this, cut from the same large stone," Cloud said. "Each of us has one in a band like this. There is no meaning beyond that."

The girl said, "Momma, if I have a brother, could we have bracelets like that?"

The woman laughed. "If you ever do, my dear, we'll see."

The man said, "Would there be any offense if we did that?"

"It would be your choice, and the jewelry of your making. There could be no offense to take. But I am being rude. This is my friend Hallownight. He has been explaining the museum to me."

Doc shook hands with the father.

The woman said to her husband, "I was thinking—what about that piece of rock crystal your grandmother brought with her from Greece? We wouldn't need to use it all, just have a few pieces cut."

The man looked thoughtful, then smiled broadly. "Just the thing." He held out his hand to Cloudhunter again. "That's a wonderful idea. Thank you so much."

"I am glad that it pleased you."

The family moved on. Cloudhunter watched them go, then said quietly to Doc, "The girl will have a brother, the summer of next year."

"You know that?"

"I believe the parents do as well. Are human children troubled by their brothers and sisters?"

"Sometimes. They get upset that their folks seem to like the new baby better."

"Is that true?" Cloud asked. The question was perfectly innocent—as a child would ask it, with no prior knowledge.

"I suppose it is sometimes. I don't have any brothers or sisters."

Cloud was silent. Somehow his silence seemed to echo in the long hall.

Doc said, "I mean . . . I had a little sister, but she died when we were both small."

"Oh," Cloudhunter said. "I am very sorry." He looked in the direction the family had gone. "Their fear is, I think, of some old pain, some loss they fear to come again."

Doc considered this. Cloudhunter had used the Touch, of course, but it was apparent he was also interpreting what the magic had shown him. Maybe guessing as well. He wondered how Cloud had known he was lying—well, not telling all the truth—about his sister.

For the first time since he had crossed into Shadow, Doc felt a desire for magic, a Touch of his own. To be able to read a patient's history from the bones and flesh themselves, know without being told where the worst pain was. . . . He glanced at Cloudhunter, who was examining an eagle-headed totem pole and showed no sign of hearing Doc's thought.

How did the Touch show itself?

This wasn't the time to ask. Stagger Lee had said that elves lived their whole lives with magic: there was no reason to suppose Cloudhunter knew what it was like for humans. And there were halls and halls left to explore, a whole world inside walls.

Thirty-five points," Stagger Lee said, examining Doc's cards. "Good thing for you we're not playing Hollywood."

Doc nodded and took a long swallow of beer. They were playing in his apartment, to kill a slow afternoon. He was down a substantial number of points—gin rummy didn't seem to be his game— but he couldn't remember how much they'd agreed the points were worth. "Sure you wouldn't rather play poker?"

"What can you do in poker for two? 'Here's your cards. Yup, that pair wins. Next deal.' Now, two players left out of a table full, that's interesting." He scooped up the cards and began shuffling. "Hey, it's not that long till Monday."

"Yeah. Another beer?"

"Much obliged."

Doc refilled Stagger Lee's glass from the keg. As he set the beer on the table, Stagger fanned and interleaved the cards in an elaborate shuffle, and said, "Last Deal still bothers you, doesn't it?"

Doc sat down slowly. "You've got a right to do what you want with yourself."

"Cool. Now say that again like you believe it."

"Look, have I ever said a word to you about it? To anybody?"

"No," Stagger said seriously, "and I appreciate that. But you act like the word's stuck right there north of your xiphoid, and a good Heimlich would pop it right out. More to the point, about half an hour before Last Deal, the fun content of poker seems to take a serious drop for you.

"It's poker. It's not about fun."

"Nice sidestep."

"I . . . just don't think I get the idea of never knowing who you're going to sleep with."

"We always know who. There aren't any strangers at Flats's place. *Which* is the question." He took a long swallow of his beer. "Don't be offended, but a big reason I didn't warn you about it the first time you were there is that you were a stranger, and you wouldn't have been allowed in anyway."

"Stagger, what's this about?"

"Oh, well, the game wasn't going anywhere, cards made me think of Monday night, one thing led to another. I also thought it was about time to make sure of the situation. I take it you haven't just been politely waiting for an invitation to join the game?"

"No."

"Fair enough. The other thing that you might as well know is that, on any given night, as many of those couples are going to spend the evening listening to Dave Brubeck, cooking an elaborate late dinner, reading comics, or whatever as end up playing sixty-nine pickup. Don't get me wrong: much as I like Brubeck, I am nonetheless bisexual as I ever was."

Stagger finished his shuffling. "Now, if you won't misunderstand, how about I teach you honeymoon bridge?"

Doc and Ginny went to the Laughs show the following Friday. The films had an odd, flat, gray quality, with black halos around any bright light; Stagger Lee explained that they were "kinescopes," films made from early television.

The shows had little comedy sketches, musical numbers, blackout jokes that lasted only seconds. Some of the longer playlets had no characters at all, just kitchen utensils or office machines moving to music; not really funny, past the first surprise, but oddly engrossing, watching the machinery dance.

The artist's name was Ernie Kovacs. During an intermission, Stagger said, "If you'd seen a lot of television, this probably wouldn't look like much to you."

Ginny said, "Why?"

"Because ten years later, twenty, thirty, the rest of television started to catch up to Kovacs's ideas. Do you remember what he said in the third program, about 'the first rule of television is, if something works, beat it to death'? Forty years after he said that, thirty after he died, TV was still following that law." Stagger looked past them, into an unseen distance. "If television is ever allowed to function again, I think we could reconstruct everything good about it from Ernie."

Doc said, joking, "Is the world ready for that?"

"No," Stagger said seriously. "The world is never ready for anything until it's too late. By which time something else has arrived."

They watched a sketch of people getting ready for something special, a party or a night out. There was no dialogue, just music, as the men in one apartment and the women in another showered, shaved, made up, dressed (Doc found himself staring hard at the technique of the garter strap in closeup). This tie wouldn't knot; that stocking was torn. The music was driving toward something, some tension that would have to be released.

A doorbell rang; the women dashed to answer it. Then, abruptly, Doc knew. There were three women in the apartment. There were two men at the door.

Two left with two, and the third woman, her hair and dress perfect, turned away. The camera was looking down on her from above, above the walls of the apartment. Doc did not think anyone in the theater was breathing, all waiting for a doorbell, a telephone. The woman wandered from one room to the other, small in the depths of the shot.

The walls of the apartment collapsed outward, the break of the chambered heart. The music crashed to a stop.

He found Ginny's arm, wrapped his fingers around it.

One of the ushers was leaning over Doc. "Mr. Hallownight, you're needed outside, sir."

He and Ginny went to the lobby. Stagger Lee was pulling on a long wool coat and scarf. He looked worried. "Doc, Patrise wants us. Now."

"What is it? Somebody hurt?"

"Not yet. Ginny, I'm sorry. We didn't know—Mr. Patrise didn't know, it came up suddenly and we've got *no* time. Will you get home okay?"

"Sure," she said. "Unless I can help."

"Patrise didn't ask for you. Good of you to offer, but you'd better not get involved. Take notes on the good bits, will you?"

She nodded, caught Doc's sleeve. "Call me when you get home, okay?"

"Oh. Yeah, I will."

Doc and Stagger slid into the TR3. "So where are we going?"

"Down by the river." He reached inside his coat, brought out a large, odd-looking pistol with a cylindrical wooden grip. "Nice night for a drive," he said. "But what the hell."

Doc drove into the iron tunnel under the L tracks. "Magic's weaker down here than near Division, right? Does all this iron have something to do with that?"

"Heard about cold iron, have you?"

"Yeah. Did it keep the Truebloods out of the Loop? When they first came back, I mean?"

"No. As an antidote to magic in general and elves in particular, cold iron is way overrated. Some people suspect all it ever did mean was that iron weapons gave us a slightly better chance against the fair folks than bronze ones. Not to mention rocks and sticks."

Doc slowed down, swung the Triumph around a wrecked car and a half-collapsed wall. Above, among the dark girders, there was a flash of bright metal. It moved. "Stagger! You see that?"

"*Shit!* Don't slow down!"

A figure dropped from above. A flash of purplish light appeared near it, and a brilliant little comet flew past the car. Doc felt his hair prickle as it went by, and there was a sharp bang behind them.

"Maybe I should give the iron more credit," Stagger Lee said.

Doc looked in the rear-view and saw two motorcycles swing out of an alley, figures in long coats gunning them. From under wide-brimmed hats, elf hair streamed long and white. Before Doc pulled his eyes back to the road ahead, he registered that the bikes didn't have any wheels in their forks: they were gliding an arm's length above the pavement.

Stagger leaned out and fired three times. One of the bikes laid down hard and skidded into an L stanchion.

Doc said, "Where do I go up here?"

"Right, next chance."

Doc slowed just enough to make the turn on all wheels, and

saw another floating bike straight in the headlights. "Hey, chicken," he said under his breath, and floored it. The bike reared up on its rear non-wheel and came for them. Stagger fired another round, then swore and began working at the jammed gun.

The bike's headlight shone full-moon blue into Doc's eyes as they came together. There was a scraping noise, and the bike jumped the car, an empty fork ripping the canvas top as it went over. The Triumph wavered. Stagger had pulled something out of his coat. "When I say now, punch for the next left!" He leaned out, threw the object. *"Now!"*

Doc threw the bar down, heel-and-toed around the corner, seeing a ball of yellow and black fire erupt in the back corner of his eye. Then the two flying bikes plunged out of the light, just black streaks in the moment of vision but still running.

"Go! Go!"

Doc checked the rear-view. Yes, they were still back there. After a moment, two bikes with wheels swung in to join them: two white lights, two blue. Ahead was one of the river bridges, a steep arched one, unlighted, barely visible except as a black gap in the shimmering water. It looked scratchy, like a worn old film.

Stagger said, "After the bridge, turn—"

"Look." Doc flashed his brights, making the coiled wire blocking the crest of the bridge sparkle like dew on a spider's web. As they started up the slope, he pulled the handbrake, threw the little car into a four-wheel drift, praying they wouldn't roll. The suspension ran out of travel, and metal threw sparks. They came to a stop turned one-eighty, pointing straight at the bikes.

Stagger thumbed something on his pistol. It spat a long flame and played a bull-fiddle note. Two bikes went down, the others scattered. Doc drove. Loose bits of motorcycles sputtered and banged beneath the car. A body went *whump* against his door and was gone, all unseen.

There were no more lights behind them. They were alone.

"Where to now?"

"Let me think."

"Should we just go back to—"

"No. We need to tell Patrise." They were both gasping. "It may have just been a random ambush."

"You think so?"

"No." Stagger started to put his head down, then jerked upright, looking around, behind, for more targets. "Not with the bridge blocked. That took some work. So we really have to see Patrise. Turn right up here."

A couple of blocks on, Doc felt himself relax, just a little, and then he laughed. Stagger Lee turned to look at him.

"We beat 'em, didn't we?" Doc said.

"Yeah," Stagger said, and then he was laughing too. "Guess we did at that."

"It feels like . . ." He tried to compare it to an ambulance run, but it wasn't the same thing. It felt good to beat bleeding, or shock, or a stopped heart, but this—

Stagger's voice was suddenly distant. "Next time I'll drive and you shoot. Then tell me what it's like. Second right here."

"The cave thing?"

"That's it."

There was a metal tunnel ahead: streets elevated a full level above them, and a void below. Patrise's big violet car was parked near the entrance. Doc parked behind it.

Stagger said, "Get out slowly. And don't show a gun."

"I don't have a gun."

"Good. Try to look like you don't."

Two elves stepped out of the shadows, and Doc felt his heart skip; but one of them was Cloudhunter. Cloud had a sword out, a long white flare of metal in the dark. The other elf wore a black leather jacket with throwing knives in chest pockets, a black baton and handcuffs hanging from his belt. Then Doc noticed the copper buttons and the badge.

"There are elf cops?" he said.

"Pride, Integrity, *Gwaed Ellyll*," Stagger Lee muttered.

Cloudhunter raised a hand. "What happened to you?"

"We got hit," Stagger said. "Set up, I think. Is it okay down there?"

"Getting no worse," Cloud said calmly. "Patrise will want you both right away." Doc reached for his bag: he saw, then, the rip in the car top, eighteen inches long and straight as a steel rule. He put a hand to his temple, just exploring. Nothing there. He looked up, saw a dark streak against Cloud's white cheek.

"You're hurt."

"Not at all. You are needed." Cloud said "Sergeant Aquila," and the Ellyll officer nodded. Cloud led Doc and Stagger beneath the street. Stagger flipped on a flashlight.

"There's a whole level down here," Doc said, as they walked past riveted iron columns, broken traffic signals, signs corroded past reading, clouds of dust rising and falling in the light beam. He reached into his bag for a tube of goldenrod salve and an adhesive bandage for Cloud's cheek.

"Two levels, at one point," Stagger said.

"Why?"

"It was supposed to solve a traffic problem." He swung the light to this side and that. "Before my time, Doc. City planning's a lost sorcery."

A car's headlights cut a slant across the street. Four, maybe five bodies were on the pavement, a Ruthin Ellyll in a short red leather cape and some humans dressed in Ruthin colors. The headlight beams ended at a door, and next to the door stood McCain, holding a Thompson with the big round magazine. He touched a finger to the brim of his hat, pushed the door open. From within, red light spilled out into the cold dusty underground, as from an entrance to Hell.

They went in.

It was Hell.

There was a large room with an iron-beamed ceiling, and a freight door into another one. The light was deep red, threaded with paler shafts from flashlights. The rooms were furnished with tables and cages and racks. There were people in the cages, people on the racks and tables: strapped to them, roped to them, bolted and nailed to them. There was a heavy smell of blood and urine and shit. The people looked like drawings in anatomy books, though the light was so red it was hard for Doc to tell what he was seeing, what only imagining. Some of them moved, with the scrape of metal, the crunch of bone.

There was a soft, wavering moaning through the room, a sound that pierced straight from the ears to the base of the spine; more horrible than screaming, because it should have been screaming. This was Hell as Doc had always understood it: a mass-production pain factory with everybody suffering at maximum efficiency and nobody dying on the job.

Doc pushed the salve and bandage into Cloud's hand, no longer seeing them.

Mr. Patrise came out of the next room. He was walking stiffly, his face shadowed by his wide flat hat. "Hallow," he said, quite clearly, "I'm glad you're here. I hope you have morphine. Shall we send for more?"

Most of Doc's brain wanted to yell out loud that giving pain shots here was plowing up Iowa with a nail file, but he didn't. He put his bag on a narrow, empty table and got out all the stuff he had, loaded up with meperidine. He looked at Stagger Lee, said with a calm he couldn't quite understand, "Did you know about this?"

"*This?* No. No. I thought maybe, a couple of animals—but this, holy clockwork angels, no."

"Give me a hand, will you?"

Stagger nodded unsteadily. They went to one of the occupied tables, Mr. Patrise following a few steps behind. The body on the rack might have been female, but that was just a guess. It was tough enough to be sure it was human.

Doc shook his head. He wasn't thinking hard enough. "Mr. Patrise, is Cloudhunter busy?"

"Not if you require him."

"Well—" He looked around. "We can save some effort if any Ellyllon here go straight home to Elfland. Probably save some of their lives, too. But I'm not sure I'd know which is which. I thought maybe another elf would."

"An excellent thought, Hallow. But there are no Ellyllon here. That is quite certain."

"All right. Stagger, can you give me a hand with this one?"

Stagger Lee nodded. He fingered the clamps holding down the victim's ankles, unfolded a pocket tool and spun off the bolts.

The body gave an airless howl and the legs bent up, trying to curl into a fetal position, hard as cramp could pull them. Doc pushed the drug in, grabbed an ampule of haloperidol and gave that as well. The body sagged. The lidless eyes rolled over. Doc forced himself to touch the body. There wasn't any pulse or breathing. Raw meat, Doc thought, and it didn't put an inch of distance between him and the body.

"Tell you what, Doc," Stagger said, "let's go toss now, get the suspense over with."

They went outside and vomited into a dark corner. Doc wiped his tongue on a gauze pad; Stagger pushed a flask into his hand, and he swallowed the whiskey straight.

At the red-lit door, they both slowed down, not ready at all to go back in. A black shape, humped and broad, crossed the light, and Doc's chest seized up; but it was only the combined silhouettes of McCain and Mr. Patrise.

Patrise said to Stagger Lee, "We got some of the equipment. They were in the process of removing it. I would like to believe that our information was simply late, and not someone else's early." He stopped suddenly, said, "That startled you. Why?"

Stagger told Patrise about the ambush.

"I see," Patrise said. "For a while we will act as if this all was just unfortunate timing. Find Wolfpond; he'll take you around to the loading area. Give me your assessment tomorrow."

"Hallow, we still need you inside. If you would, please."

"Stagger?" Doc said.

"Yeah," Stagger said, but didn't move.

"Got a deck of cards?"

Stagger blinked once, then pulled a battered pack of steamboats from his pocket.

"Thanks," Doc said. "I'll replace 'em."

Doc and Mr. Patrise went in. It was worse the second time. The shock was over, and the details showed more clearly. Hands, faces, what was left of them.

Mr. Patrise said, "The cards are for what?"

"Triage markers. Dead get a spade. Too bad to spend time saving, a club. Anybody who just needs first aid, not that I expect many, gets a diamond. The hearts are the ones we focus on."

"Very good, Hallow. I will pass the word."

Doc started walking the tables, stopping to look for responsive pupils, check for breathing and blood pressure, poke at exposed viscera and bone. He didn't lay down any diamonds; no surprise there. What surprised him was how few drew spades. Despite the damage, most of the victims were holding on by their splintered fingertips.

Once, at home, his crew had been called a hundred miles out to help with a town a twister had chainsawed through. There had been this much mess, then, but the sorting was mostly done by the time they'd arrived. "Hey, friend," one of the local paramedics had said to him, "let me show you a card trick."

Doc was aware that as he walked, and made decisions, Mr. Patrise's other people had become very quiet around him. As they did, he could hear the soft hum of moaning from those who couldn't move but weren't yet gone.

Mr. Patrise was standing quite still at one side of the chamber, McCain still his armed shadow. Doc said, "Do we have any backup coming?"

"Everyone here knows some first aid. All will follow your directions. I would not expect anything beyond that."

Doc flipped a heart, more from hope than honesty, and got a couple of people working, just to break the silence and stillness. "Then most of these people are gonna die. Maybe all of them." Doc paused, swallowed hard, fought down the urge to vomit again. "Don't mean to be rude, sir, but that's it."

"Understood, Hallow. What do you propose to do?"

Yea, Doc thought, *though I walk through the valley of the shadow of Death, I shall fear no evil, for somebody put me in charge.* Then he pushed himself to think for real, and he knew what the true decision was.

It was something the fire guys talked about, late on call; always about themselves, because—well, you were allowed to decide for yourself. *Suppose a wall collapses, and I'm rice pudding south of the sternum. You won't make me live like that, right?*

You know, if I was gonna be stuck in a wheelchair. . . . if I lost my eyes . . . my right hand . . . my nuts . . .

Somehow it never got to the last word, the action verb. Now and then somebody'd say "Save th' last bullet for yerself," in a John Wayne drawl. Every ambulance, and most of the fire trucks, had a pistol, against regulations. They were always generic name-brand revolvers, the kind everybody had in a bedroom drawer. Easy to drop in a creek, no hard questions.

"It's like this," Doc said at last. "If we do nothing, they'll die. If we move them, most of them will die anyway. If somehow we manage to patch one or two together—what'll be left of them?"

Quietly, just above the rumble of the dying, Mr. Patrise said, "I asked you what you could do, and I accept your answer."

"Okay." Doc ran a hand over his bag. "Morphine would work, but we'd be wasting it. I don't think they'll even feel bullets."

"You heard, Lincoln?"

"Sir." McCain handed the Tommy gun to Mr. Patrise and drew one of his .45s.

"I can do it, sir," Doc said, and immediately wondered if it sounded as stupid to the others as it did to himself.

"It is not your job to do so," Patrise said, with a lack of intensity that seemed somehow kind. "And you work for me. Go home now." His eyes were just black in the unholy light. "I will see you out. Lincoln, you will wait for me."

Doc followed the small man into the iron-framed street. Patrise said, "You are not to go home alone. Do you understand that? Take Cloudhunter with you."

Doc nodded. "He's hurt a little. I should fix that."

"Very good. Lincoln is slightly hurt as well; if you will wait at your car, I will send him out."

"Sure. I'm not—oh. We left Ginny at the theater—I mean, it wasn't too far from her place, but—"

"If you wish to visit her, by all means do."

"No. No, I'd be—I just—"

"My people are under my protection, Hallow. But I will make certain." He turned, stood silhouetted in the red doorway. "I appreciate the difficulty of what you had to do tonight. You understand that I won't apologize for it."

Quicker than he could think, Doc said, "Will you tell them I'm sorry?"

"I will," Patrise said, and was gone.

Doc forced himself to turn around and walk to the car. It was a relief to patch up Cloud's cheek. McCain had a shallow gash almost the whole length of his left thigh. Doc cut away his trouser leg, dressed and bandaged it with McCain sitting in the Triumph's passenger seat. McCain held a pistol ready all through the operation, then said thanks and went back to the building.

Doc and Cloud piled into the car, drove into the dark.

"Cloud . . . what was that place? What was it *for*?"

"They were drawing power for magic. A great deal of power."

"From the people?"

"Life is a great source."

Doc was quiet a moment. "Do you know who they were?"

"A gang of humans. Whisper would not have dared do such a thing to Ellyllon."

"Whisper?"

"His name is Whisper Who Dares the Word of Words in Darkness. He is quite insane . . . though perhaps that is obvious. I do not say it to separate him from my kind. We are not human, but . . . we are not all like him."

"I know that, Cloud."

Doc drove into the garage. Jesse shook his head over the state of the Triumph's ragtop, and pointed out a spattering of shot scars in the trunk lid. Doc hadn't noticed.

Lisa, in the telephone room, told Doc that Ginny had called, wanting to be called back no matter how late. "I'll put it through to your room," she said.

The phone was ringing when he got there. "Hello."

"Are you all right, Doc? There was a rumor about some big shooting."

"Yeah. We're all okay. Lincoln and Cloud got scratched, but they're fine."

"You're sure?"

"All the noise was over when we got there." He found suddenly that he really did want to see her, hold her close; wanted to—

Then he wondered if he would ever be able to want anything again. "Look, I'm probably going to have to stay in the rest of the weekend, but—could I see you next Friday?"

"Yes."

"We'll do something. Think about what you'd like to do."

She didn't answer at once. Doc wondered how he sounded to her. Finally she said, "I will, Doc. Good night."

He went downstairs and had the kitchen make him a plain hot eggnog—no brandy, no sleeping powder. He didn't want to wake up abruptly, sometime in the dark small hours. He got a book from the library, a Rafael Sabatini swashbuckler with brave, kind heroes and the certain promise of a happy ending.

Sometime after midnight the lights flared and died. He wasn't sleepy yet, so lit the hurricanes and kept reading. Sometime after three he jerked awake from a doze, doused the lights and crawled into bed; it didn't work. He lit a lamp again, picked up the book.

At five-thirty, still as dark as midnight, he went downstairs again in his robe and slippers to get some food. The dining room was candlelit. A silver coffee service was on the table, a blue flame keeping it hot. Fay was there, sitting back with a cup cradled in her hands, her feet propped up on the seat of another chair.

She turned, saw him, started to sit up straight. Doc raised his hands. "No," he said, "it's all right, stay right there," and tried to put it into gestures.

She smiled, resumed her position, pointed at the coffee, an empty chair nearby. He poured, sat.

Fay pointed at him. She held up her index fingers, brought them together, made a cradle-rocking motion with her arms, pointed at him again. Doc thought. She knew who his girlfriend was, certainly—then he got it. *Do you have a family?*

He held up the parent fingers, brought them together, pointed at himself, spread his empty hands. She nodded, tapped her chest. *Same with me.* Then she held up the fingers again, slowly folded them over.

"I'm sorry," Doc said, and shut his mouth.

She shook her head, opened her lips, made a rolling-on motion with her hands.

So he talked: he told her about planting and haying, and silly stuff he'd done with Robin, and the time the twister barely missed the house. He gestured a lot at first, but Fay seemed more interested in just hearing the sound of his voice. So he just talked, with illustrative movements now and then, until he noticed that the sun was up. The poached egg and toast that the butler had brought him more than an hour ago were dead cold, untouched.

He turned away from the window, back to Phasia, and his eyelids dropped like fire curtains. She laughed then. It was a sound somewhere between a baby's laugh, wind chimes, and a silver piccolo. She stood up, put her hands on his cheeks, and kissed him on the forehead. Then she pressed her palms together, put her head down-to-sleep on them, and tapped Doc on the head.

"Yeah, I think you're right," he said, and went upstairs to sleep all day.

The house was quiet that weekend. Everyone seemed to be keeping in. Doc ate in his room, finishing the Sabatini adventure and starting another, then shuttling down to the infirmary to read on shock and trauma.

He passed Stagger Lee once in the dining room. Stagger was staring at a half-eaten roast beef sandwich as if it were a chess problem. "Want to play some poker?" Doc said.

Stagger looked up, his expression lightening. "That's . . . well . . . not now, thank you."

"Give me a call if you change your mind."

"Sure."

"Stagger . . . did any of them make it?"

"None of them."

Doc could nearly convince himself that he couldn't have made any real difference to his patients' survival—not even touching what surviving might have meant. He kept catching himself staring emptily at the wall, the book idle in his lap, thinking, thinking.

Part of it was his old job. People didn't die in the ambulance. Often enough they were dead when you got to the scene, and all you did was haul goods; that was unhappy, but it wasn't bad. If the patient was alive, he stayed alive until you got him to the emergency room. His heart might stop, but you just maintained the compressions and ventilation. The declaration, the time check, the paperwork, were in somebody else's hands.

None of them. Damn.

Sunday evening he picked up the phone three times to call Ginevra. But he didn't.

On Monday Patrise announced early in the day that everyone was to meet for dinner at La Mirada. Doc packed up and went early, just after opening. As he had hoped, Lucius was there, sitting alone.

"Good evening, Doc. Buy a member of the free and unbribable press a drink? Or here's a better one: Tell me what tomorrow's column is about and I'll buy yours."

"You heard about what happened Friday night?" Doc said cautiously.

"Ah. Not an ideal topic, Doc. Meddle not with the preconceptions of audiences, for they are obtuse and quick to switch channels."

"Channels?"

"Newspapers, I should have said. My, how hard some habits die."

"It's—"

"It's Whisper. And yes, Doc, the incident is news. It isn't features. Mark the difference."

"You know about him, then. Whisper."

"I know about Whisper Who Dares. We aren't acquainted."

Doc waited. Lucius didn't say any more. Doc said, "What do you think he was trying to do?"

Lucius said slowly, "You really want to talk about it, don't you?"

Doc pressed his hands on the table.

"Well, you can't," Lucius said, more coldly than Doc had ever heard him speak. "I keep telling you, confidences aren't my beat. Just the opposite."

"Who do you suggest I do talk to?"

"Birdsong on trust in one paragraph: Nobody. You do not live among such people, good people though they are. You do not, in fact, live in such a world, good world though it is. . . . On second thought, you do know someone who can keep a secret."

"Who?"

"Phasia."

"Thanks," Doc said unpleasantly, and then suddenly he began to understand. Something was horribly wrong, locked up inside Lucius, and he couldn't speak it directly; he was telling Doc the only way he could. Doc felt angry with himself for not hearing it sooner.

"Would you mind telling me something, then?"

"Within the bounds of time, knowledge, and the language."

"What do you know about Mr. Patrise? How he got started, I mean."

Lucius looked sad, but no longer cold and angry. "I guess you're buying the drinks, huh."

"Sure."

"There are a lot of stories. I came late to him, so stories are all I know, kapeesh? For something closer you'll have to talk to someone who was there earlier—Stagger Lee, maybe, Cloudhunter. McCain goes the farthest back, but, well. So are stories all right?"

"Yes."

"He was a South Side kid, that's pretty certain. There's a story that when he was, oh, nine, ten, he carried books everywhere he went. If you laughed at the bookworm, you found out how neatly a signature binding could hide a stiletto. I'm not sure I believe that one. Or if it's true, I think Patrise has put it a long way behind himself.

"A reliable tale is that he put together a gang to turn over rare coin shops. Pure burglary, no bodily harm anyone's heard of, though it's your call to believe that part. They were very selective: gold and silver, none of the alloy coins that came later. Some stamps, apparently. And some pennies were made out of shellcase metal after World War Two: they always got those.

"Later, so spools the yarn, they quit that and went on to plumbing suppliers and salvage yards—copper and zinc and lead in quantity."

"Lead?"

"This is a what story, not a why story. Eventually, as most of the smarter gangsters did, he moved legitimate. Like them, he was providing what people wanted, not necessarily what they needed—places like this, the coffee trade."

"I see."

"You say that like you know what it all means. It wasn't Patrise who decided the returning elves were Cuban commies from Mars, and saved Miami from a fate worse than death by turning it into a radioactive lagoon.

"Patrise was made in refiner's fire, out of true metal," Lucius said. "Whereas the Great Spirit made me of sawdust and printer's ink and cheap scotch, and was working under deadline."

"Oh, Lucius, stop it."

"I know what you want to know about." Lucius's voice had a rough edge, partly whiskey. "And I can't help you. If it were a simple matter of betraying a confidence, that would be no trouble at all, just as I say. But it's beyond that. I wish I could help you, Doc, you're a good guy, but I can't."

Patrise came in then, and at once the evening had organization and direction.

McCain and Stagger Lee had come with Patrise, Carmen, and Phasia, but not Ginny or Cloudhunter. Doc wondered if Ginny was alone. He wondered what he would do about it if she were.

Carmen came onstage, in a tight gold blouse that showed one shoulder and a triangle of midriff, a trailing black skirt.

> *Say how you cut it*
> *You'll never get it so thin*
> *An edge of softness*
> *To turn the hardness within*
> *When will your face fall*
> *After the long masquerade*
> *The razor's open*
> *Come out and dance on the blade*
>
> *So here's a tip of the hat*
> *To all the melancholy people*
> *So uncertain what they're ready to feel*
> *(Waitin' all night)*
> *Diamond cut diamond*
> *Silk cut steel*

During the second verse Matt and Gloss came out, doing a sharp turn around the floor timed to the lyrics. It wasn't really interpretive. Doc supposed that might have made people nervous.

> *So here's a tip of the glove*
> *To all the solitary people*
> *Undercover in the world of the real*
> *(Hidin' all night)*

> *Diamond cut diamond*
> *Silk cut steel*

Pavel was standing in the doorway, making a hand signal. Patrise nodded and looked away. Pavel stared, then went back into the foyer.

> *So here's a tip of the shoe*
> *To all the predatory people*
> *Overeager for the whip and the heel*
> *(Playin' all night)*
> *Diamond cut diamond*
> *Silk cut steel*

Carmen and the dancers took their bows, disappeared through the curtains. The room lights came up.

Everybody turned around.

Two new people were standing just inside the door. One was a tall, dark-skinned woman with black-and-white hair. She had mirrored sunglasses above lips like a surgical incision. She was wearing a long trenchcoat of silver-gray leather over a loose white cotton suit; no shirt, a thin strip of metallic silver cloth around her long throat. Her hands were thrust into the coat pockets, not casually.

The other was the shortest elf Doc had ever seen, a man built like a bull, his white hair cut down to fuzz on his skull. He had sunglasses as well, heavy-framed black ones. Doc had to check again that he was really Trueblood, and not an albino human, but the ears were definite, as were the weirdly delicate hands—really weird, on those piston forearms. He wore a black team jacket for the Topanga Toons, heavy gray trousers bloused into cycle boots. His wide belt had a bunch of pouches and clips; a white rod, thin as a pencil and eighteen inches long, rode in a sleeve, and there were handcuffs hanging on the other side.

They were cops. They didn't look like any cops Doc had ever seen before, but he knew anyway.

Someone at another table said, in an awful fake British accent, "I say, Patrise, we're not being bally *raided*, are we?"

"Relax, Nigel," Patrise said, with complete unconcern. "The

Mirada is *not* raided. Have another brandy." He stood up. "Officers. We haven't had the pleasure: my name is Patrise, and this is my establishment. Won't you please share our hospitality?"

The two cops came to the table. The tension level dropped a hairsbreadth.

"I'm Lieutenant Rico," the woman said. "This is my partner, Lieutenant Linn." The words might have been steel blanks rolling out of the mill.

Patrise said, "Newly arrived."

"Special assignment. For the Shadow Cabinet."

"Yes, who else. Do sit down. Is there something I can offer you? Coffee?"

Linn put his fingertips together. Rico said "Coffee would be nice of you." They sat down. Alvah played "A Nightingale Sang," and couples came out to dance. The club settled back.

Lieutenant Rico didn't talk much. Lieutenant Linn made an appreciative gesture when his coffee was served, but didn't talk at all.

Patrise said, "You're on special assignment here, you say."

"I did."

"Not voluntary? I think I should be insulted for my city."

"Is it your city, sir?"

"People make cities theirs. Robert Moses and Richard Daley in their ways, Samuel Johnson and Colette in theirs. Excuse me: and Robert Peel, Eugene Vidocq, and Eliot Ness in theirs."

Rico said, "And Capone and O'Banion and Moran?"

"Bugs or Colonel Sebastian?"

Rico turned her head. The silver glasses hid anything that might have been called expression. She said, "You have a reputation as well, Mr. Patrise."

"You're not looking to change employers."

"The Cabinet wants the situation here dealt with."

"Do you mean Whisper Who Dares?"

"I mean the situation."

"That's an admirable desire of the Cabinet."

"They want to avoid a gang war."

"You didn't say 'at all costs'."

"Should I have?"

"No. The Shadow Cabinet never writes a blank check to anybody."

"That's true. It's also true that it takes two sides to have a war."

"Oh, no, Lieutenant. There you're wrong. It takes far more than two sides. There are all those people behind the lines: the ones who support it, supply it, stand facing the walls when the colors pass, and generally say Why Not, all making their particular contributions. All the really good trades are triangle-plus."

Patrise went on, his tone light, friendly, even merry. "You're an officer of some experience, Lieutenant, you and your partner; your reputation has been here before you. How many Ruthins and Silverlords have you hauled off how many pinkies? How many Vamps and Snaketooths and miscellaneous starving freelance shiv artists have you scraped off the sidewalk, only to see them returned or replaced by your next turn around the beat? And has there ever been an end of shift when you took off your weapons and armor and said to yourself, 'At last the world is safe for law and justice'?"

Lieutenant Rico said pleasantly, "I won't take that as an insult, sir."

"Not meant as one. I am, as I am certain you and your partner are aware, a voting member of the Shadow Cabinet. Which means that the other members were confident I would not be outvoted. So which arch-ironists pulled you off that unending duty to visit my city and, you'll excuse me, *deal with* a gang war?"

He had never raised his voice. If anyone beyond the table had heard him above Alvah's music, they had paid no attention.

Rico said, "Thank you for the coffee, Mr. Patrise." She started to rise.

"There's another act onstage in a moment. I think it would be for the best if you stayed that much longer."

"Is that a threat, sir?"

"I never make threats. It's a promise."

Rico stood quite still, drumming her fingers on the chair back. Then she sat, Linn following. The lights dimmed.

Fay sang.

It was a happy song—upbeat, at least, Doc didn't recognize the lyric—but you could never get up and dance to Fay's music. Something suspended all action deep down. Something about The Voice in joy was nearly unbearable. Doc realized that he had never heard her sing a really sad song. People might die of that.

Or, he thought, of joy.

When she finished, Rico was entirely still; Linn's head was bent, his eyes closed, an ivory Buddha. Finally Rico said, "Thank you for your hospitality, sir."

"You're welcome always."

The detectives left. As always after Phasia's set, others began drifting out as well.

Patrise said, "So what do you think, Stagger?"

"Linn is a dynamics master, no question about it. No indications from Rico; she might have a touch of pure receive, but I doubt it. Pickups tend to be brittle. She didn't strike me as brittle."

"Lincoln?"

"They're serious enough."

Patrise rose, went around the room shaking hands and saying a few words here and there. "Coming, Hallow?"

"I'll be along."

"No hurry. If the Lieutenants should come back, make them welcome, will you?"

"I'll do my best."

"But of course." Patrise waved and went out. Doc looked around for Lucius, who was still sitting at his corner table near the bar.

"This was the place they first called them coppers, do you know, Doctor," Lucius said. "For their uniform buttons. This is the true folklore, accept no substitutes."

Doc nodded. He could sense the pressure going critical inside Lucius, and as much as he wanted to know what was wrong, and to help fix it, Lucius showed no sign of explaining himself, and Doc didn't want to be present at the explosion. "Good night," he said. "I'm sorry I couldn't help with your column."

"You did, though," Lucius said. "I'll have to owe it to you. Have Shaker send over the ol' alphanumeric piano, will you?"

He did, and then he went home. He left word to have the newspaper sent up as soon as it arrived, and slept very badly until it did.

THE CONTRARIAN FLOW

by Lucius Birdsong

Do you hear the horns of Elfland,
    Sounding in the night?
Hear them calling souls from slumber
    At the traffic light.
Can you hear the horns of Elfland,
    Echo 'cross the dell?
Mind, oh mind, your left rear fender
    Parking parallel.
Now you hear the horns of Elfland,
    At the close of day,
Seeking out the vile offender
    Walking like a jay.
Should you hear the horns of Elfland
    Soar and swell and wax,
Copper voices soon shall follow,
    Getting just the facts.
When you hear the horns of Elfland
    Cleave the night in twain,
Just remember, on the Levee
    Law and Order reign.

Just a reminder, gentle readers, that from time to time the moon smiles down upon Our Fair Levee with something really putrid caught between its teeth; and if you have been wondering lately if we are really living in a rational universe, why, others are wondering too. Good night, good night, sleep tight.

"I have a message for you," Patrise said the next day. "Norma Jean's feeling much better, and she'd like to meet the man who saved her life."

"Is she coming here?"

"No," Patrise said slowly, and then, "I think this is best done in the World, if you don't mind a drive. There's a nice place on the North Side, not too far for either of you."

"All right."

"Six tomorrow evening, then."

It was almost sunset Wednesday when Doc drove out through the Shadow fire, and full dark when he reached the restaurant, a small place, dark and quiet. He gave his name, and was taken to an enclosed booth that might have been the only one in the place.

A few minutes later, there was a mechanical whirr. A motorized wheelchair appeared. Norma Jean was in it, working a control with her right hand. A tall man in a dark suit walked a step behind.

Doc stood up. Norma Jean smiled. The man in the suit looked hard at Doc.

Norma Jean said, "I'll see you later, Eddie," and the man vanished. "Oh, come on, sit down." She laughed. "*I* sure am."

She was wearing a navy-blue jacket over a low-necked white blouse, a skirt just to her knees, ankle-strapped high heels with little silver buckles.

"Can I—" He reached for the push handles on the chair.

"Nope. Sit." She drove the chair up to the table, and he sat down. He saw that her left arm was in a sling inside the jacket, the hand pale and limp against her chest.

A waiter slid out of the dark. "Just some tea, please," Norma Jean said. "How about you, Doc?"

"Tea's fine."

"I miss coffee," she said, once the waiter had gone. She settled back in the chair. "I wondered what you'd look like. Anna—you know, on the switchboard—said you were red Irish. Are you really?" Her voice was flat, neither musical nor unpleasant; Doc supposed her wind must be short.

He touched his hair. "Really."

She laughed. "I meant Irish, not red."

"Somewhere way back, I think. Is your family Irish?"

"Polish and German. But that's away back too. Seven generations in the city, I think it's seven. We made it to the Gold Coast in the Twenties. My great-grandfather was in the Dion O'Banion gang."

"Yeah?" he said, and then wondered if it was the wrong topic.

But she grinned and said "The real thing. My granddad, his son, used to tell me stories about it. See, when he was little—Granddad, I mean—his dad wouldn't talk to him about the gang days. He'd only say 'I just drove a car, I never shot nobody,' and that it was all made up for the movies.

"But when the war started—you know, with the Japanese and the Germans?"

"Yeah."

"Well, Granddad was going to sign up, because, you know, *everybody* was. Then his dad said, 'We're gonna go on a trip first.' Granddad said, 'How long?' 'Two weeks oughta do it. Can't win the war in two weeks, can't lose it either.' So they got in the car—it was a big Cadillac, that's what Great-granddad always drove, they called him Cadillac Billy—and they went up to Wisconsin. Granddad thought it was a hunting trip, or maybe ice fishing.

"They got to this lodge in the woods. It belonged to a couple of guys from the mob days. There were pictures and newspaper clippings all over the walls, of everybody—Al Capone, Moran, O'Banion, Torrio. They said John Dillinger was trying to get back there, to hide, when the G-Men shot him.

"And they had this *arsenal*—Tommy guns and shotguns and pistols and *grenades*. And Granddad spent two weeks learning how to use them all. And to fight with a knife; he could scrap okay, any kid could in those days, but this was serious. His dad said, 'Two weeks ain't much, but it's better than you're gonna learn from the Army, 'cause most of them guys never had to do it for real. Unless they were like me.' He even made out a list of guys who'd been in the gangs, who Granddad could trust if he needed help. Granddad said he burned the list after the war, because too many of the men on it were heroes then. You want some more tea?"

"Sure," Doc said. When it came, Norma Jean said, "Could you dump two spoons of sugar into mine, and stir it up? This one-wing stuff is no good."

"Your arm's going to be okay, isn't it?"

"Oh, yeah! I didn't mean that—you know I wouldn't have it at all if it weren't for you. They said it may always be a little weak, but I've got therapy three days a week, and Granddad—well, let me finish that story."

"Please."

"Well," she said, a little more softly, "Granddad says that, when they were up there in the woods, fighting and shooting, it was the first time he really felt like his dad loved him, you know? 'Cause he was teaching him what he knew to stay alive in the war. But then he joined the Marines, and he went off and fought, and after he'd fought for a while . . . he understood that his dad'd loved him all the time before—hadn't wanted his son to grow up with guns and knives and wars all the time."

Doc waited. She didn't say any more. He said, "Your Granddad must be quite a guy. . . . I mean, is he still alive?"

"Oh, yeah," she said. "He saw me every day I was in the hospital, and he helps me with my PT. He says I ought to learn to shoot a bow and arrow—you know, an Amazon." She looked down at herself, where the chest wound was hidden. Then she grinned again. "When I got so I could sit up, he said he was making plans to bust me out of the hospital—you know, go over the wall at midnight, like in the movies. He made me promise that if he was ever in, I'd—" Her voice caught. "—crash him out. Funny thing to say, huh."

Doc flashed on the end of *High Sierra*, with Bogart shot down in the desert, and the girl trying to understand his last words, asking what it meant when a man crashes out.

That's a funny thing to ask, sister, the cop replied. *It means he's free.*

He had a sudden terrible certainty of what Norma Jean's grandfather had meant.

"You could meet him," Norma Jean was saying. "I think he'd like to meet you. I'm sure he would. He's never really been to Town, and keeps saying he should. He calls it Old Town—you know the song? 'There'll be a hot time in Old Town tonight' . . . ?"

"In *the* old town."

"No. That was later, when people weren't singing about this city anymore. When the song was written, it was about Old Town here. Really."

"I didn't know. Sorry."

"Nothing to be sorry about. Even people who grew up here

don't know that. Lucius Birdsong, the reporter, told me. Do you know Lucius?"

"Yes."

"Oh, of course you do—someone said he wrote about you. He's such a swell guy, but, you know, so odd—I mean, you wanna carry a torch, okay, but do it for someone who's at least on your side of the *street.*"

Doc waited, but that seemed to be the end of that discussion. Then she said, quite from nowhere, "You living alone?"

He took her meaning at once, somewhat to his own surprise. "I'm seeing somebody. Pretty regular."

He saw lights fade within her. "I'm glad," she said, earnestly. "Do you ever see Chloe Vadis?"

"Sometimes at the club."

"I heard one of her girls ran away. Jolie-Marie, the little one. I mean, *petite*, you know."

Doc nodded stupidly.

"My mom would die," Norma Jean said, to no one in particular, and then painfully, "No, she'd *die.*"

Then Doc understood. Norma Jean was stuck in the World now, and she wanted back—back with Mr. Patrise, or somebody close to him, like Doc. Even working for Chloe the madam would be a way back to the bright lights.

But there she was, in that chair. Just like Robin had been.

Floundering, he said, "I'll tell Mr. Patrise that you're better. I know he'll be glad to hear it. And—I really would like to meet your grandfather."

She nodded.

Doc tried to think ahead. "Some night we should . . . spring him. Get him to the Mirada, at least. My car won't hold three, but I could borrow one of the others."

"Oh, wouldn't that be *great*?" The light returned to her face, briefly. "Unless he—it might not be like he remembers. Wants to remember. I just don't know."

In that moment Doc knew the meeting was over. In the next moment Norma Jean was telling him how much fun she'd had, how great it had been to meet him. She touched the control and rolled her chair back from the table; Doc stood up hastily.

She was offering him no hand to shake, and even a small kiss on the cheek would have required him to swoop and bend over her in the chair. So he just stood. The man in the dark suit reappeared; he seemed to take no notice at all of Doc.

She stopped, rolled back toward him. "Granddad said I should be good to you," she said unsteadily. "That somebody who does— what you do—was really special. You'll tell everybody I miss them, won't you?"

"Of course."

"And tell your girlfriend you're special," she said then, in a voice full of agony and venom. She turned away and was gone.

As he drove back, a windblown winter rain began to fall, that scattered the ghost fires of the Shade far across the real city.

Friday afternoon, Doc went upstairs to see Patrise. He was sitting behind his silver desk in a long violet dressing gown, feet up, a large book of art reproductions open in his lap.

"I don't expect we'll need you tonight, Hallow," he said. "Have a pleasant evening."

Doc hesitated.

Patrise said, "Was there something else?"

"I was thinking," Doc said, "you know, with all the stuff I carry in my bag, it's a wonder I haven't been jumped before this."

"Do you think so?" Patrise said, sounding interested.

"It makes sense. I mean, I drive a car everybody can recognize, and they probably know I don't carry a gun."

"You haven't wanted to carry a gun."

"I still don't. I just . . . guess I ought to be more careful, from now on."

Patrise's voice cut right across the nonsense. "Who do you think it was that set us up, Hallow? Are you afraid it was Ginevra?"

"No, it couldn't have—she didn't know anything about what was happening, any more than I did."

"You don't know that," Patrise said, calm. "You don't have any way of knowing that."

"No," Doc said, and stopped while he still had his voice.

Patrise put his book on the desk, sat up in his chair facing Doc. "But *I* know, Hallow. And she did not."

"Then . . . do you know—who?"

"Let me tell you something about people, Hallow. If you give people work that makes them feel strong and useful, then they will become strong and useful. Their strength, through you, is power, and astounding things can be done with that power. Impossible things.

"Keep the same people in fear, and you may still get use from them, but never strength. If they find strength despite you, the first thing they will do with it is bring you down. No matter what it costs. Understand that very well, Hallow: any being with a real soul will prize it above anything—certainly above life."

"A soul."

"I am not excluding the Truebloods. If Cloudhunter has no soul, then souls are surely overrated." He leaned back. "Have you thought about where to take Ginevra tonight?"

"Oh . . . the movies, probably."

"Why don't you take her off the Levee?"

"Is something wrong?"

"Not that I know. You should visit the World now and then. The Art Institute is open late tonight. It's not far. Barely past the Shade. Made dinner plans?"

"No."

"The Berghoff should do. Here." He scribbled a note, signed it, folded it. "Please, take it. Let me have my fun."

"Thank you, sir."

Patrise waved. "And think about the Art Institute."

"I'll ask Ginny."

"Yes. Tell me, Hallow, if you don't mind . . . do you make her laugh?"

"Uh . . ." Doc had to turn his thoughts sharply around. "She laughs at the movies. And other times too."

"Good," Mr. Patrise said. "It is an extraordinary thing, that half the human species should need laughter so much from the other half. It is no small gift, you know, Hallow. Magic and Elfland have no substitute for it. Now, the best of nights to both of you, Hallow."

———

It was beginning to snow when they left the Shadow. Suddenly the air was on fire, turning the snowflakes blood-red; Ginny gasped, and Doc stopped the Triumph for several minutes while they watched the silent, heatless firestorm.

Ginny took his hand. Under her winter coat she was wearing a ruffled white blouse with a small string of pearls, a long black skirt. "I'd forgotten the fire," she said, sounding astonished.

The plaque NEW ART INSTITUTE OF CHICAGO was on a gray stone building that must have been a department store before the world shifted. The entrance was flanked by huge bronze lions, one old and green, one looking nearly new. A guard tipped his hat as they came through the door; Ginny scanned a brochure on what to see first, and dragged Doc up a flight of stairs, directly to a huge painting of strolling people: Seurat's *Sunday Afternoon on the Island of La Grande Jatte*. Doc had seen pictures of it in books, but . . .

"Look at it close," Ginny said.

He did. It was made up of thousands upon thousands of dots of color. Close up, they exploded into an atomic-structure diagram; a step back, and they coalesced again into the calm people in the sunny park.

In one of the modern halls, there was a painting of a theater usher, a girl in cap and vest standing in a golden slant of light. She looked weary; she looked terrifyingly alone. When he could look away from the girl, he saw that the pattern of the walls was a precise reproduction of a corner of the Biograph's lobby. Or was it the other way around?

He turned, a little dizzy, and there was another image he had seen any number of times before, but never like this: a long horizontal frame, a night scene somewhere in a big city, a streetcorner diner lit against the gloom. A sign on the brick wall sold nickel cigars to a disbelieving world. Inside, small at the big L-shaped counter, were a handful of people huddled over their coffee and pie, a counterman in white. No reproduction Doc had ever seen captured the electric green of the fluorescent light—it was like spellbox neon, though the artist had died long before things changed.

He looked at that picture for a long time, too, until its loneliness was too much to stand.

Near the museum exit was a room bannered *The Third Fire*.

Third? Doc thought. Just inside the door were two enormous engraved illustrations: the Great Fire of 1871, facing the "White City," the Columbian Exposition of 1892, burning at the turn of the century.

Beyond was an architectural model of the original Art Institute building, and an array of photographs. They showed the old building in flames, and a small army of people moving paintings and sculpture and art objects across littered, flame-lit streets. A glass case held a chunk of verdigris bronze: the distorted face of a lion, like those at the doorway, looked out.

"The building burned when Elfland came back, you see?" Ginny said wonderingly, pointing at a map. "They moved it all—in one night, this says."

"Under cover of firehose and spell," a voice said. A uniformed museum guard was standing a little behind them, a plump woman with a small, secret smile. "We lost a few paintings, and a fair amount of sculpture, sad to tell. And one of the lions, of course. But look here." She led them to a side alcove: it was filled with a painting, a surreal, darkly vivid nightscape laced with flame and streaking energy. Across the center, figures—some human, some Ellyll—formed a chain, carrying paintings that, in contrast with the rest of the picture, were rendered with photographic realism.

"*Picasso Crossing Adams*," the woman said. "The elves knew something, even that first awful night. We hardly ever see one here now, but that night—" She shrugged, and smiled again. "Pleasant evening to you."

The woman left. Ginny said suddenly, directly into Doc's ear, "Shall I ask you now? I want to ask now."

"Ask what?"

"If you're coming home with me tonight. You don't have to, you know that. But there's enough suspense in my life. And if we're going to have a really special dinner, I don't want to be knotted up all through it. So just tell me now, and it'll be over with."

He stared at the painting, the fire and art and sorcery, and said, "Yes."

She let out a breath and hugged his shoulders.

Berghoff's restaurant was a crowded, bustling, jolly place, with fancy wood and stained glass. The maître d' looked coldly at the young couple with no reservation until he saw Mr. Patrise's note, and at once they were given a table, and brought soup and steak and amazing platters of sausage, with dark beer to wash them down, until Doc wasn't sure the TR3 would carry their weight. There did not seem to be any question of presenting a bill.

Doc parked the car in front of Ginny's building. As they went up the front steps, Ginny slipped in the fresh snow, and Doc caught her. He had a brief, wild thought of carrying her inside, but he didn't; just kept his arm around her shoulders all the way in. Ginny locked the door behind them. "You remember when I said there was too much suspense in my life?"

"Yeah?"

"Maybe I was wrong."

He found himself unbuttoning her blouse before she had quite pulled him into the bedroom. He had heard it wasn't difficult, after the first time. It was easier. He still seemed to weigh too much—the dinner was only part of that.

It wasn't that there was any difficulty. She seemed pleased, and that alone was enough to make him feel good. But something wasn't quite there: the Wild Hunt didn't ride, and he knew that she knew it. Still she sighed happily, and laughed, and held him all night.

Still, he knew what was locked up in his thoughts, and hoped desperately that she did not.

Monday night the usual poker crowd met at the Rush Street Grill. They sat over Flats Montoya's wonderful burgers with an uneasy quiet; Doc kept thinking of the Hopper painting, the diner at midnight. It was a relief to go back to the poker room, where quiet and blank looks were part of the game.

The Fox's game was way off form, and it threw everyone else's play off as well. After an hour, Kitsune tossed in her cards—an ace flipped upright—and said, "That's all. Good night, everybody."

Carmen said, "I'll get the box."

"Just say I'm tapped." She hurried out.

Stagger Lee counted Kitsune's chips. "Everyone agree we'll hold her share out?"

They did. "Who'll see her first? Lucius?"

"I'll take it to the Mirada. Shaker can hold the stake."

After another hour the raid alarm went off, and everyone went through the ritual of tossing in and covering up.

It wasn't the usual Copperbutton squad. It was Rico and Linn, with two very worried-looking Coppers trailing behind.

"Hello, Officers," Flats said. "Can I offer you something hot on a cold night?"

"Don't you love it?" Rico said. "Everybody here's the Welcome Wagon. Linn."

The elf went to the table where Doc and company were sitting. He looked at the people, then took a lens-shaped blue crystal from his belt. He gave it a snap of the wrist and it hung, spinning, in the air above the table, casting an electric-blue light. The tabletop turned transparent, showing the bucket of cards and chips beneath, the sitters' legs, a glimpse of their leg bones. Linn snatched the stone from the air with an easy movement and a tight little smile. He tucked it away.

Rico said, "The stuff that passes for cop work around here."

Carmen said, "We've got a seat open, Lieutenant. Maybe you'd like to sit in? There's room for two."

"Maybe some other time, honey."

"You mean that?"

"Yeah. I mean that."

"Look forward to it."

The police went out. The patrons dug into their pie and brandy.

A burst of gunfire came from the front of the restaurant, and a long crash of glass. Someone screamed. Stagger Lee, with a completely artificial calm, said, "Somebody's way off script."

Doc was on his feet by instinct, grabbing his bag. "Keep *down*, dammit," Lucius yelled, and Doc dropped into a booth-high crouch.

Just as he got to the front room, there was a brilliant white flare from outside, and the front of the restaurant blew in. The shock

knocked Doc down; he huddled for a few breaths against debris
and any second detonation, but the booth wall had protected him
well enough. He got up.

The room was smoky, and smelled of hot metal and burning.
People were groaning, but not screaming now. There was some
blood, but no immediately apparent critical cases. The front windows were pretty well demolished, and the oak front door was a
jagged strip of bare wood.

Lieutenant Linn came in, breathing mist. His white wand was
out, floating between his open hands; a black nimbus of negative
light surrounded it. He looked at Doc, who went outside.

Rico was on the sidewalk outside, sitting up against the front
of the building. Her left leg looked chewed, and her mirrorshades
hung broken from one ear.

Doc snipped away her trouser leg, sponged blood off. The
wounds were fairly minor; no heavy bleeders, bones intact. He got
some dressings on. "You should be okay. Got any drug allergies?"

"Yeah. To needles. Go ahead, kid."

"People usually call me Doc."

"Yeah. Shit, that's cold."

"That's thorncast salve. It'll pull any fragments out. Did you
hit your head?"

"Other end. Linn saw the bikes coming, got a ward up. Any
sign of our so-called backups, Linn?"

Doc was conscious of Lt. Linn standing behind him, but missed
any reply. He looked at Lt. Rico's pupils: they were even, but di-
lated. He pulled off her glasses—carefully, around a bad bruise on
her cheek—shone a light on one eye.

"Watch it! Those used to be Night Owls."

"Sorry."

" 'S'okay. Doc."

"Lieutenant Linn, would you help me get her inside?"

Linn picked Rico up, carried her in to a bench. Doc saw to the
other injured. Through some combination of luck and Linn's spell,
nobody had caught a bullet or major fragment.

There was no question of going on with the games. The place
cleared out quickly. Carmen left with Stagger Lee, and then it was

just Doc, Lucius, Rico and Linn, and Flats, who brought out real coffee with Kahlua and cream.

"You said they were on bikes?" Doc said.

"Did I say that? I must have been delirious."

Doc glanced at Lucius, who raised an eyebrow and half of his mouth.

Flats said, "How about you, Linn? You ever talk?"

Linn shook his head.

"You gotta have something," Rico said. "When you're trying to do a job nobody wants done, by flaky rules, in a hostile country, among people who don't want you there in the first place, you've got to have some way of knowing who you are. That or go dinky-dau."

"What?"

"Crazy. Something my dad used to say."

Doc said, "You'll be sore for a while."

"I've been torn up before, Doc. I'll make it."

Doc nodded. "Take you home, Lucius?"

"Don't mind, Doctor."

"Hey, Doc," Rico said. "Thanks. And hey, Jake Lingle."

Lucius said, "Yes, Lieutenant, ma'am?"

"I read your column all the time. Nice to meet you."

"Thank you very kindly, Lieutenant."

"Don't get killed."

Lucius snapped a salute. They went outside, their shoes crunching on broken glass.

"So which way's home?" Doc said.

"Drop me at the Mirada. I've got to give Shaker the Fox's stake, remember?"

"Yeah." Doc thought about Kitsune's behavior, about speaking of it. But he didn't. Instead he said, "Who's Jake Lingle?"

"Famed local reporter, from the real gangland days. The Capone boys shot him dead one day."

"Oh."

"There was a rule back then, never shoot three sorts of people: cops, judges, and reporters. Too much heat, you see. And what do you know but that Jake's paper raised a row that eventually did help bring Al down." He turned his head. "You know Capone's Four Deuces club—that was the street address, two-two-two-two—was just over there a couple of blocks."

"You *will* be careful, won't you, Lucius?"

"I haven't gotten to the punch line yet, Doc. Jake Lingle, mob martyr, was taking fifty thousand Depression dollars a year from Capone. It's an ill wind, eh, Doctor?"

He let Lucius off at the club, knowing that things were no better than they had been a week ago. Maybe worse.

DECEMBER

That was where matters stood for the next few weeks. There were no overt incidents, no horrors uncovered in the dark. There were movements in the corners of the eye, faraway gunshots, distant rumblings.

Every Friday night Doc took Ginny out, to a museum or a movie, and then up to her apartment. It was sweet, it was very sweet. And still there was something not happening.

She asked him a couple of times what was wrong. Nothing was wrong, he told her, because whatever was wrong was only in himself, down where he was afraid to go.

There was a shootout the second week of December, the night of the full moon. Doc wasn't there, didn't find out about it until eight dead Truebloods in carry-out bags arrived at the infirmary, to be probed and dissected for what had killed them. McCain had a splinter in his scalp, which of course bled like crazy until treated with hemlock root, and required a little hasty barbering as well.

Back at the corpses, Doc worked fast, drinking Irish coffee; on the fifth body, the knife slipped and he cut through his glove, almost into the finger. He stopped, breathing hard. Never mind the effects of *gwaed gwir*; an open cut during an autopsy could go viciously septic. He switched to black coffee, put on a Bach recording, and finished up without further incident.

The following morning all looked well, and bright again, in cold sharp December sun; McCain was as close to merry as he ever was, and the house barber had restyled his hair to conceal the wound and Doc's chopping.

That afternoon Doc went to Patrise's office, intending finally to ask what the lead mining was for. Once there, however, in the glare of light on wood and metal, with Mr. Patrise—who had never wronged him, never, so far as he knew, lied—seated calmly at a side table, reading an old leatherbound book, Doc choked on the question. He managed to get out, "There's something—I have to know. About, well, magic, I guess. . . ."

Mr. Patrise shut his book. "Are you afraid of the sources of power?" He stood up, sat against the edge of his enormous desk. "Do you think that someday you will open a door, like Bluebeard's wife, and find the sort of place you saw under the streets?"

"I just want to understand."

"I know that," Mr. Patrise said gently, "and there is nothing more becoming to want. But would you ever be satisfied with an answer? I could give you all the keys I have, and you could still suspect I had left out the one *key* key. Now Bluebeard, on the other hand, gave out the master key first thing.

"Here is something you should recognize, Hallow: the True Blood is psychically bound to dominant modes of thought—in plainer words, slaves to fashion. This once was part of their power, when their culture was all the culture on Earth, and we huddled under trees because the sun and the rain made us afraid. The Truebloods said to the hominids, *Do things in the way we tell you*, and we did, because they were more frightening still."

"Trees," Doc said. "Elves are supposed to be tree people, in the old stories."

"Congratulations, Hallow," Mr. Patrise said, with what sounded like real pleasure.

"Eventually the Truebloods went away, and after—oh, who knows how long—we started to forget that they had been real. But we kept the inspiration: we continued to do things by rules, whether or not the rules made sense, to act as the group did, even when the group was insane, to enjoy making a pattern and watching the crowd squeeze into it. In time we technologized the process, industrialized it, networked it. It was, if you like, our magic."

Doc said, "And when the Truebloods came back?"

"They were bewildered at first by what they saw. There are hints that they did not recognize us as human—they thought we were some otherworldly species that had colonized the Earth.

"As anyone may in such a circumstance, many of them panicked. That led to the fires. To open warfare, in many places. Eventually you will learn about that . . . about Asia, and Africa, and the Silent Zones."

Why will I? Doc thought without saying.

"I often wonder," Mr. Patrise said, "what they saw in television that made them decide it must be erased utterly. Not that any of this saved them. They could not simply impose their rules on a race that changed its hemlines and heroes with the turn of the seasons. They were no longer the arbiters; they were just one more designer label. And as I said at the start, they were vulnerable themselves to the mass demand, as are all societies that rule by code and force. They began to ride motorcycles, pose with guns, wear stiletto heels and wide-shouldered suits and four-in-hand neckties. They can no more fight this than humanity can, so they must try to do it better than we do."

Mr. Patrise tilted his head, just slightly, and fixed his eyes on Doc's. "Suppose I told you that you could have any of them you wanted: a Highborn, Rhiannon or Stane Belle, the Kings of Elfland's daughters, on their knees in front of you, dressed in spider gauze and cold iron chains, begging you to—"

"Stagger said the cold iron thing doesn't work," Doc said, trying to keep the image from getting any clearer.

Mr. Patrise looked surprised. It was not a typical expression for him. "Stagger Lee is a fine technician, but he will never be a great enchanter. Do you know why, Hallow?"

Doc almost said no, then waited. He had the feeling Mr. Patrise really wanted an answer. "Iron . . . doesn't have power over the Truebloods. But some of them believe it does."

"As I was saying, Hallow . . . they can be bound. Even by us. And why should that matter so?"

"I don't know."

"Because they are not mortal," Mr. Patrise said, his voice dead calm. "We are. Whatever we choose to be in life, that life ends. Whatever our condition, however hateful the service we are yoked to—one day it will end, *and we know it*. Not so for them."

"All right," Doc said, his throat tight, "but, it's still not something I want."

"What you might desire and what you might do are two different things, Hallow. But I think you mean what you say. Making it very important that you know such power exists." Patrise went to a service table behind the desk, poured two small glasses of brandy. He handed one to Doc. "The first night we met, I told you to wait a while and ask me if I knew you. You haven't asked."

Doc sipped the drink and said nothing.

Mr. Patrise rolled his brandy glass, took a swallow. "There will be a party for the winter solstice—dress-up, naturally. Will you be sure to tell Ginevra that she is invited, and to visit Boris for a fitting?"

For days before the solstice party the staff were hanging ribbons, holly, ivy—"No advance warning where the mistletoe goes," one of the maids said happily—and setting out candlesticks.

Boris Liczyk provided Doc with a long-tailed cutaway coat of green broadcloth with velvet lapels, narrow trousers, and calf-high brown boots. The shirt was gauzy and ruffled, the tie a broad ribbon. At first he thought it was a repeat of his Halloween mad killer's outfit; but with the coat in place, he recognized the look from pictures in books. It was going to be a Charles Dickens Christmas.

He adjusted his tie and braces and went downstairs. Below, all the lights were out, and candles lit; hundreds of candles, in sconces and holders of iron and brass and glass, so many that their individual flickerings merged into an even, buttery light.

"Good evening, sir, good evening," Boris Liczyk said from a dim spot at the foot of the stairs. He was wearing a white curled wig and a butler's uniform that looked black in the light but must be blue: Boris was very insistent about who could and could not wear black. "You are dressing well tonight, sir. There's someone waiting for you." He gestured with his rod of office.

Ginny was wearing an off-the-shoulder dress of heavy satin in a deep, iridescent red. It outlined her body closely to the waist, then fell in a fluid cascade to the floor. Around her throat was a red velvet choker with a black cameo, and her black, black hair was curled and swept high.

Doc felt himself want her, that instant. He bowed, crooked his arm. She curtsied and took it.

All the regulars were there, naturally; Carmen Mirage in a black lace gown powdered with gold, Kitsune Asa in a pink kimono extravagantly embroidered with cranes in flight, Matt Black and Gloss White in rather less formal costumes that Ginny explained were two dancers from the Paris Moulin Rouge, as drawn by Toulouse-Lautrec.

Alvah Fountain's dreadlocks fell neatly over his high wing collar to the lapels of a steel-blue tailcoat; his handling of the coattails got him an ovation just sitting down at the piano. Phasia wore a white-on-white Empire gown, and a triple rope of black pearls.

The party wasn't, in fact, just Dickensian. It was about—elegance, Doc supposed was the right word; some high Victorian and some Regency and a touch of Edwardian. Doc greeted everyone, enjoying the play formality of bows and "Enchanted"s and nods and winks. At Ginny's insistence he danced with Carmen, and Phasia, and struggled through a group dance without too much embarrassment. But mostly he stayed with Ginevra, and that felt very good.

About ten, Cloudhunter (who was dressed as elven nobility from an illustrated edition of Dunsany—it was so unlike anything real Truebloods wore that no insult could be implied) asked Doc aside. They went into an alcove, where Patrise was sitting, in ruffled shirt and violet coat, holding his silver-handled stick.

"We have a message," Patrise said. "A possibility of tracking down Whisper Who Dares. Do you think we should follow it?"

"You mean, right now?"

"That is what I'm asking."

Doc thought. "Is this going to be another—another like last time?"

"No."

"There's nobody else involved. Nobody innocent."

"Not that I know."

"Then the hell with him for now," Doc said.

Patrise's fingers played with his cane top. "I agree, Hallow. It's too fine a party, too rare a night. Have you slept well?"

"I suppose."

"Then what we will do is this: when the party breaks up, be ready to change and move out. About one o'clock, I should think. Drink lightly."

"All right."

"And now, I think, we need another dance. Find your partner." Patrise bowed. Doc returned it and went back to Ginny.

Before long, he began to notice something different between them tonight. It seemed odd to call it warmth—hadn't they been warm? Her hands were tight in his, and her eyes seemed uncommonly deep.

A clock struck eleven. Doc thought of Cinderella, waiting for midnight, and thought perhaps he knew what the change was: she was feeling his tension, the energy winding up inside him, and reflecting it back, expecting—

Not expecting him to run away from her at one, to join the monster hunt.

Finally he took her into another room and told her what they were going to do.

"It's all right," Ginny said.

"No, it's not all right. Why should I want to run out and help— kill somebody—"

"That isn't what you're going to do, and you know it. Mr. Patrise and your friends are going out to do something important, to stop something terrible, and you're going because they may need your help. Where *is* Mr. Patrise?"

"Over in the—"

"Come on."

Patrise was speaking softly and rapidly to Boris Liczyk. He stopped, turned. "Yes, Hallow? Ginevra? Do you wish to leave us for a while?"

"No, sir," Ginny said, politely but firmly. "I wanted to say that, if you should need to leave early, I'd be pleased to help keep the party going." She smiled. "I have some experience there, as you know, sir."

"My very dear." Patrise bowed. "I am pleased more than you know to hear that, but you are a guest tonight. Boris and the staff will have no difficulties. But will you do one thing for me?"

"Of course, sir."

"Give me a dance."

Doc watched them, with just a spark of something he knew was jealousy, though knowing it made him feel sick and absurd. Then Gloss White tapped his arm, and he swallowed hard and danced with her; but of course Gloss could make a sack of turnips look like Fred Astaire, and it did go well, the four of them waltzing to Alvah's music. Then they changed partners, and all evil sparks cooled and died.

At a quarter to one, Doc hugged Ginny, and she pulled him behind an armoire and made it an extremely definite kiss. He left her and the candlelight belowstairs, went to his room to change into something more appropriate for the evening's late entertainment.

Doc drove with Cloudhunter in the Triumph's passenger seat. The cars didn't convoy, so Doc took meaningless turns at Cloud's instructions, until they parked in an empty loading dock, in a spot surrounded by broken pallets and snow-covered cardboard. Cloud opened a metal door. Beyond it was a dingy corridor, another door, and then space.

The building had been a shopping center, three or four levels connected by escalators, ramps, glass elevators; aisles and balconies lined with bookshops, record stores, fashion and shoe and jewelry stores. All the retail spaces were dark and empty, deserted or smashed in, with a litter of broken-heeled shoes and split-spined books here and there in passing. Snow filtered through broken skylights, down the open spaces between floors, and the greenery in the balcony planters had been overtaken by coarse wild vines with leaves like lizard scales.

Patrise was leading McCain and Stagger Lee across a stretch of mildewed carpet. More of his people were following at a distance. Doc and Cloud closed with them.

Stagger was holding a box of some heavy gray metal, perhaps lead, that had copper-colored rods protruding from each face. It was making a soft, high-pitched squealing that shifted tone as he twiddled and slid the rods.

"There," Stagger said, and there was a burst of red light from overhead. Voices, elf and human, screeched, and half a dozen people came running from one of the second-level shopfronts. Two were Silverlords in padded gray leather, jacket and jeans, jacket and zippered skirt; the rest were humans of one sort or other.

McCain raised his Colts, fired from both hands. A human—a Loop Garou, Doc guessed—was hit in mid-leap and fell hard; the other shot brought the male elf down in a heap nearby. The Silverlord woman vaulted the railing, landed fifteen feet below in a snap roll, came up holding two long blades. McCain took aim.

There was a flicker of light behind the glass of one of the storefronts. Then the doors blew out.

Lieutenant Linn stepped through, light streaking out behind him. Lt. Rico came after, in a heavy dark-blue jacket with web straps and pouch pockets. It said POLICE in big reflective letters. She carried what looked like a midget Gatling gun in black metal.

The Silverlord spun to face them, leveling her blades.

Rico's gun coughed and spat a burst of vapor, and a six-inch metal arrow stuck in the floor between the Blood's shoes. The multiple barrels rotated with a click.

"Everybody," Rico said, *"cool it."*

Patrise said aloud, "It's a big stadium, plenty of room for everyone to play," and quietly to the people near him, "Diffuse. Stay in touch, but spread out. Hallow, stick to Cloudhunter."

Rico said, "I don't think you're receiving me, Little Caesar. Nobody is doing any more playing."

One of the Silverlords' people above popped up with an automatic rifle; he sprayed half a dozen rounds in the general direction of everybody else alive. People scattered; Lt. Rico went for cover behind a counter and leveled her weapon. Lt. Linn moved his hands in a complex pattern that hissed and sparked with red light. The shooter screamed and folded over the railing; his arms were wrapped in metal and wood, bits of brass and powder spilling to the floor below. Linn had apparently turned the gun inside out around its owner.

Everybody was moving then, Patrise's people, Rico and Linn, the Silverlords and Vamps.

"This way," Cloud said, and Doc followed him around a sharp corner into a broad, dim corridor with dead stores on both sides. It was lit by a string of glass tubes, the pale cold light of half-dead magic. They got ten yards along, twenty, and Cloud kept going. Doc said, "Shouldn't we—"

"There's a focus ahead," Cloud said in Ellytha. The word the books translated as *focus* literally meant "seam of destiny": it could mean a concentration of magic, a battlefield, a sacred place. Doc had also heard Cloudhunter use it to speak of Patrise.

Cloud stopped.

Light from the corridor slanted into a broad, wide-open shopfront. It had been a clothing store, though there wasn't a rag of fabric left. The mannequins—all female that Doc could see—had been torn apart, hacked, savaged: here and there a blade was still stuck in the plastic, and a yard of cycle chain wrapped a headless throat. Slogans had been painted on the dismantled dolls and the store walls: Elvish obscenities, symbols.

"Did the gangs do this?" Doc said.

"Before gangs," Cloud said. "From the first days of Return. That sign means 'Give Mortals Their Destiny.' That one, 'Leave None Whole.' "

Something white sailed out of the darkness. Cloud's sword reached out and intercepted it; it hit the floor with a crack.

It was a skull.

"Get back," Cloud said, low and hot, and Doc took a step backward. Smoke boiled out of the far corridor. Cloud gave the skull a vicious kick to the side; he threw out a hand, and a handful of throwing stars flashed through the haze.

A shape came out of the smoke: a bulky black cloak, no face, no form, with a long thin sword extending from beneath it.

Cloud said, in Elvish, "I am somewhat amused, Whisper Who Dares." He inclined his head to the black thing. Then his hand moved again, and another spot of light crossed the space separating them. This time the throwing star came bouncing back out of the smoke, and spattered elf blood on the floor.

Another black figure, identical to the first, emerged from the smoke; as it passed, the first shape crumbled into air.

The cloak was thrown back. Whisper Who Dares the Word of Words in Darkness wore heavy boots, a thigh-length black coat of wool and leather set with steel rings. Bones hung from the rings on thin leather thongs; small ones, carpals and phalanges. A human radius swung from his waist.

Whisper's milk-white face was flattened and scarred. Something dangled from his earlobe that coiled and twisted.

Whisper and Cloud spoke to each other in Elvish, too low and quick for Doc to follow. They crossed swords. The air sang.

Doc realized they were paying no attention to him. He had no more part of this than in the war between wind and mountains.

Cloudhunter cut, and cut, and cut, and some of Whisper's bones clattered to the floor. Whisper didn't seem to have touched Cloud. Doc took a step away, wanting to go for someone else, McCain, Patrise, Rico and Linn, any kind of backup, yet not wanting to leave Cloud. He took another step back, and collided with something rubbery and cold and wet. His guts turned over. He turned.

There was nothing there: just air like gelatin. It distorted the hallway; somewhere down there were Patrise and the others.

Steel scraped. "Doc!" Cloud shouted. Doc turned. Whisper and Cloud stood a little apart, swords leveled. Whisper had a hand to his throat, as if he had been wounded there. Then his arm snapped straight toward Doc. Doc tried to dodge, but the gluey air held him.

Cloud moved. His sword swept down. The creature that had been at Whisper's ear struck the floor in two scratching and writhing pieces.

Whisper lunged at Cloud's back. Cloud stepped aside easily, swung again, severing Whisper's sword in the middle of the blade.

The swordhilt vanished into Whisper's cloak. Whisper took a step to the side, toward Doc. Cloud blocked him. Step, block. Step, block. Whisper snarled something in Elvish; Doc caught the word "dishonor," but he knew that the word had infinite shadings; it could not be understood out of context.

Cloudhunter cut again. The long bone on Whisper's clothing leaped and clubbed it aside. Whisper spun a butterfly knife into his hand, sliced at Cloud's arm, connecting. Cloud spat a few words, swept an arm, and knocked the knife away. He forced Whisper back with his sword. Whisper said something with "death" in it.

Cloud replied; "dishonor" was in it twice.

Whisper folded his cloak about himself, seemed to lose a foot of height. He backed away rapidly. Cloudhunter stood his ground. When Whisper was a dozen yards away, Cloud turned. "Doc," he said, "tell the others—"

Whisper had drawn a shotgun from beneath his cloak. Before Doc could speak, he fired. The blast ripped into Cloud's flank. He turned around. Whisper fired again, into Cloud's chest, and again.

Cloudhunter stayed on his feet. He raised his sword, pointed it at Whisper Who Dares, spoke a phrase in something that wasn't Ellytha; whatever the words meant, the voice pulled and tore like a dull razor over the skin.

Whisper fled.

The air was suddenly thin again, and Doc stumbled. Cloudhunter turned, and fell. Doc gathered balance and ran to him. He shouted *"Patrise!"* as loud as he possibly could, and knelt by Cloud, opening his bag, spreading Cloud's jacket. The wounds were awful: a load of tight-choked shot and two solid slugs, son of a goddamn bitch. Sponges, he thought. Pressure bandages. He had one unit of IV D-five in his bag, a couple more in the car.

Cloud's silver eyes were wide, staring straight up. His hands went blindly to his throat, unwound the blue Nancy-silk scarf. "Calm down, Cloud," Doc said, "don't move."

Cloud hung the scarf around Doc's neck. His arms dropped away.

Doc was aware that other people had come in. Without looking up, he said, "Can anybody here start an IV?"

Patrise's voice said, "Where is Whisper?"

Doc gestured with his head. "That way." More pressure. Clamp the bleeder. Tape.

Patrise said, "Lincoln. Katherine. See if you can follow the trail. No friendly casualties, understand?" He leaned on his stick, lowered himself to his knees. "What can we do, Hallow?"

"You got a trauma team in your pocket?" Doc said. "How about an intensive care unit?"

"We can get them."

Tie off. Bleeders every damn where. "Do it quick," Doc said, and then realized what he was saying. More pain, more cruelty, wasn't going to help anything. What they needed was—then it clicked. *"Katie!"*

The woman stopped on her way down the hall, gun and knife out. McCain turned as well.

Doc said, "You told me your father was a bloodstopper. That he showed you."

"Yeah, but I never..."

"You gotta try."

Mr. Patrise said, "Come here, Katherine. Lincoln, do *not* go on alone. Get Rudy. Or the two detectives, if they're not *busy.*" McCain nodded. Patrise said to Doc, quietly, "What is a bloodstopper?"

"Folklore," Doc said, breathing hard. He tried to explain, as he kept up the pressure on Cloudhunter's wounds.

Katie set her gun down, bent over Cloud. "I just don't know."

Mr. Patrise said, "I believe you can, Katherine."

She closed her eyes, tensed. *"Seisote veri,"* she said, *"Seisote veri!"*

Cloudhunter heaved, gave a sigh that pulled tears into Doc's eyes. The hemorrhaging stopped as if a valve had been turned. Doc sponged again, groped in his bag for the IV set, knowing it was still hopeless.

No. Not hopeless. *Not* hopeless. *If they can crawl to Elfland*—"I can't do anything more here. If I can get him up to Division, maybe—"

Stagger said, "They'll never let you through."

Patrise said, "Try."

Stagger and Katie helped load Cloud into the Triumph. He made no sound. Doc unstoppered a vial of fairy dust, scattered it on the wounds, touched it to Cloud's lips. Cloud breathed it in. His face grew luminous, relaxed a bit. Doc pulled out of the alley and turned north. Away toward the lake, there was a hint of false dawn.

Pedal to the floor, Doc drove toward Division. He ran out of gears and kept pushing: he could always mend the engine, or Jesse could, or there would be other engines, other cars. He drove until the buildings to either side squeezed up and bent over before him, until the light turned purple ahead and red behind and the clocks ticked slow, and still Division stayed ahead. He thought he was seeing the same windows and doors and traffic lights pass again and again, like a chase in a cartoon; and then suddenly the road was broad and black and glossy, like the marble floor of his bathroom back halfway to the World. Ahead there was a vast Gothic gateway flanked by stone griffins. Elves stood all around it. Through the gateway was—nothing. Not darkness, not any kind of door or wall, just a dully luminous grayness, the color of a fainting spell.

Doc pointed the car at it. She hummed, skidded just a little; Doc doubled her down, gripped the wheel and Cloudhunter's wrist—

And stopped, without sound, effort, or inertia; the car was simply standing still, engine idling cool, five yards in front of the gateway.

Cloudhunter breathed in audibly. That was all. His eyes were open but seemed to see nothing. Or maybe silver eyes could see through the blind spot.

Doc blasted the horn of the Triumph at the gates of Elfland.

Most of the elves seemed to be ignoring them. A few were looking on *and the fuckers were smirking.*

Doc opened his door, yelled at the nearest elf. "Let me through, dammit! I've got one of your people here, and he's *dying*!"

"The mortal knows he may not pass," one of the elves said, "or else the mortal is a fool." The timbre was metallic; it scraped Doc's nerves. *This is how they talk*, he thought, *when they're not talking to us.*

"Then take him through! He's not stable here—dying, do you understand that?" *Do you fucking know what that is?* he thought.

"*Gwaed gwir* takes this risk beyond homelands," the inhuman voice said. "It is a risk honorably borne, honorably lost."

Another elf voice, a little milder than the first, said, "If the Trueblood wishes to pass through, then aye he may."

More of the Ellyllon turned to look. None of them moved a step closer.

Doc got out, opened Cloud's door. He couldn't get a pulse, but there was a faint trembling of the colorless lips. Doc pulled at his arm; Cloud fell on him, knocking him on his butt. Doc braced his feet against the car and pulled. He felt bone grate, and his heart flipped, but what was a little more damage now, a piss in the ocean: five yards away was the deep water of healing, if only they could crawl the distance.

He tried to lift Cloudhunter. Fresh blood welled up in the elf's chest, and he groaned aloud. The sound cut like a torch into Doc's brain, and his knees gave way; for a moment he was insensible, blind with tears.

Through water he saw one of the elves, watching them, hands pressed to his (or her or its) ears. Was it shock? Was it anything?

"Help me," Doc said, from his knees. "Please."

Nothing.

"Piss on you all," he said.

He tugged the Nancy scarf from his neck, got it under Cloud's arms and began to drag him. A dozen feet to go. Ten. Eight. He didn't know what would happen when he hit the barrier: would he just slam into it, bounce off, burn up, die? He would have to get behind, push—

A clear, sweet elven voice said, "How earnestly he doth shift the thankless burden. A thing almost noble 'tis, to bear a stone unfreighted of itself."

"You're lying," Doc said out loud, "You're lying, you want me to give up," but he looked into Cloudhunter's face and knew it was so; meat, that was all, elf meat.

He heaved one awful sob, and then stopped, because enough rage makes anything possible. He stumbled back to the car. Behind him, the elves began to move toward the body.

Doc brought up Cloud's sawed-off shotgun. *"Get AWAY from him!"* The elves stopped. He didn't know if the gun would fire, here, just on Division; he was ready and willing to find out. The Truebloods all drew back.

He got out the kit, carried it and the gun to Cloud's side. This was going to take a while. He hoped the elves hung around to watch. He hoped some of them got sick all over themselves.

An hour later, Doc threw what was his into the TR3's backseat, got in and slammed the door. The last thing he said to them, as he threw the car in gear, was "Okay, I'm a fool. And you *know* what you are."

Doc took the elevator up to Patrise's office. His hands were stuffed into the pockets of his coat, which had long thin streaks of Cloudhunter's blood across it. He was stained with dirt and snow. His fingers tightened and relaxed, bunching the cloth.

He knocked and entered. Patrise was standing in front of his desk, looking at a poster on the wall. It was a network of colored lines, the rapid-transit system of the city long before there was World and Shade.

"Hallow," Patrise said.

"I lost Cloud."

Patrise nodded once, slowly. He turned to face Doc, held out a hand, palm up.

Doc took a folded, bloody gauze pad from his pocket. Inside were the pellets and slugs he had dug from Cloudhunter's body, as he had taken so much lead from so many dead Ellyllon before this.

He had thought he would throw it on Patrise's desk, as . . . what? A statement? A demand? For what? Instead he just put it gently in the outstretched hand. Mr. Patrise's fingers closed on it, tightly.

"Was Cloudhunter taken through the gateway?" Patrise said.

"Yeah. After it didn't matter."

"It matters a great deal, Hallow."

"To who? Them?"

"Yes. This is a matter of what they believe, not what we want. I told you about that, about iron and faith. There is more to come of this, you may trust. Now, I believe Ginevra is waiting in your rooms." He turned, took a step toward the inner apartments.

Doc said, "About the bullets—"

"Another time, Hallow. I am selfish with my grief, and will not share it."

Doc lowered his head, turned toward the door. He stopped. "Did you get Whisper?"

Mr. Patrise paused. "No. As I say, there is more to come of this."

Doc went down to his apartment. Ginny was in the living room, asleep in a chair. She still wore her red satin dress; her shoes and stockings were placed neatly on the floor, her feet tucked up beneath her as she always sat. A book was open in her lap.

She had uncurled her hair, and it spilled down one cheek. He reached to touch it, then realized what he looked like, bloody and ragged, a nightmare for her to wake to. Moving as softly as he could, he hid the coat in the closet, went into the bathroom to strip and shower.

When he came out, wrapped in a bathrobe, Ginny was sitting on his bed, leaning against one of the bedposts. "Hi," she said.

"Hi."

"Boris let me in. You don't mind?"

"No, I don't mind."

"I like your place." She giggled. "It's big."

"I should have brought you here before."

She rubbed one foot against the other. "My legs went to sleep out there." She tilted her head. "Think I need treatment?"

He stepped behind her, found the zipper on her dress. She raised her hands to let him take it off. He touched the velvet band, close around her neck, and she purred.

"My God, it's dawn," she said, looking at the windows. "You were gone a long time."

"Yeah," he said, and then his throat closed up. He reached into his piled clothes, took out the blue Nancy scarf, wound it between his hands.

"That's Cloudhunter's," Ginny said. "He gave it to—" She pulled in a breath. "Oh, God, Doc, not Cloudhunter."

"We all fought it. Katie and—that's what I'm supposed to do." He was crying. It didn't matter. The toughest guys on the fire squad cried for this. You got handed somebody's life, and you held on to it with everything you had, and sometimes it still got away from you. If you didn't feel something then—"I'm not very good company right now. If you want to go . . ." he said, and let it trail off, not at all sure what answer he wanted.

"Where would I go?" she said plainly. "I love you. I've known it for . . . well, I know, okay? I've been scared to say it, because I didn't know what you'd do." She shuffled a foot. "Do you still want me to go?"

"I didn't. I just—"

"Then come here," she said, and held out her hands. He looked at her wrists, and the silk taut between his white-knuckled hands, and thought that it was good he was already crying. He unwound the scarf, folded it, put it carefully aside.

He needed to hold her so badly it hurt. And he needed to be in control. But if he said what was coiling up in his mind, and she pulled away—there weren't words for how bad that would be. There weren't even thoughts for it. And you fought the bad thing, right? Until you had nothing left to fight with. Like with any other life you were given.

So he just sat down heavily on the bed, and let her hold him, until the room blurred and faded into sleep.

When he woke, there was a note on the bedroom mirror: "I didn't want to wake you. If you want, I won't wake you New Year's Day either."

JANUARY

Doc turned over in bed New Year's morning, and felt his cheek warmed by Ginny's shoulder. She made a small noise and shifted, but didn't wake up.

At once he understood the not-waking thing, and how good it felt. He shifted around—carefully—to watch her. Was that soft-focus, movie-star glow real, or was there just film on his eyeballs?

The phone rang. Ginny's eyes snapped open.

"Let it go," Doc said.

"No, I shouldn't." She kissed him and rolled out of bed, tugging a robe on, stumbling into the other room.

Doc called after her, "It had better be—"

"Yes, Mr. Patrise," Ginny said. "Of course, sir. Just a moment." She brought him the telephone, moved a teacup still partly full of flat champagne to make room for it.

"Yes, sir?"

"My genuine regrets, Hallow, but your presence has been requested by one of the High Elves," Mr. Patrise said. "So that you understand: this means you go. That we go; as your patron, I am expected to accompany you. We will be around to collect you in an hour."

An hour later, Doc was breathing fog on the steps of Ginny's apartment building. Mr. Patrise's car pulled to the curb. Jesse was driving; Doc supposed there must be some reason McCain was absent, but he didn't ask what it was.

On the way, Mr. Patrise said, "There are protocols involved in meeting a Highborn. The one that concerns you most is this: don't speak unless I tell you that you may. Do not answer even if you are addressed directly. I'm sure that sounds arrogant, and I assure you it is."

"Is there anything else I shouldn't do?"

"Countless things," Mr. Patrise said dryly. "I would advise you not to look into the Urthas's eyes. You may find that difficult, and there isn't likely to be any real danger, but . . . If in doubt, look at the floor somewhere in front of our host."

They parked at a colonnaded building right on the lakefront, near the natural history museum.

"Are you fond of the Field, Hallow?" Mr. Patrise said.

Doc realized he had been staring at the museum. "I only went there once. With Cloud."

"Yes. I should have remembered that. This way, Hallow. Please."

Carved letters above the building entrance read JOHN G. SHEDD AQUARIUM. A pair of Ellyllon in green armor flanked the door.

"Do they own this place now?" Doc said quietly.

"The Aquarium is closed for New Year's Day. The Highborn has been courteously extended its use." Mr. Patrise pointed to the right of the aquarium building: a narrow finger of land extended out into the lake. A street down its centerline ended in yellow-striped barricades. "The breakwater was twice as long before the Shadow fell, and the Planetarium was on the end of it. Apparently our stargazing offended someone." He paused, looked into the distance. "The dome was bronze, on a marble base. It sank like a little Atlantis. The fire paused then—nobody remembers just how long; it might have been as long as five minutes. Then, suddenly, there were Ellyllon at the Art Institute, helping to save its contents. Draw what conclusions you choose.

"Now, we have an appointment. Remember your instructions."

One of the armored elves opened the doors for them. They entered a large, high-ceilinged space lined with aquarium tanks; in the center was an enormous cylindrical tank, clear all around. Inside were corals, and darting, brilliantly colored fish. There were half a dozen Ellyllon in green standing at attention around the room. They did not move. A weirdly ugly, flat-faced elf—a Mani, Doc supposed—appeared from around the coral tank; he wore a metallic green robe that trailed on the floor twice his height behind him. He approached Mr. Patrise, bowed, then bowed again to Doc.

They followed the Mani down stairs and around a curving corridor to a wide, domed space, an open auditorium flanked by green plants, stepping down to an expanse of open water. The Mani bowed again and left them there.

Mr. Patrise stood quite still before the blue pond, looking straight out. Doc did the same.

The water rippled. Small waves broke on the pavement before them, making thin puddles around their shoes. A figure in green and white, blue and silver, rose into view.

The Highborn woman wore a long, floating cloak of deep green stuff, which spread out on the surface of the water for two yards in all directions; it was fantastically puffed at her shoulders and fanned high behind her head. Beneath it was a tight-fitting garment that seemed to be made of fish scales. Her white legs were uncovered, and her very small feet were in silver boots. Her hair, which was elven silver with streaks of green, was circled by silver hoops that trailed blue-green ribbons.

Her face was angular and beautiful—though among Truebloods it seemed only the Mani might not be—and her silver-coin eyes were tilted, shadowed with deep green.

"You are good to answer my request," she said. There was a rushing whisper under the music of her voice. Doc had never been to an ocean, but he had held a seashell to his ear: that was the sound. He started to make some polite reply, then remembered not to.

Mr. Patrise said, "My lady Glassisle, I present to you Doc Hallownight, my household's healer."

"Was it then the Healer's oath?" Glassisle said. "It was our understanding that death breaks such vows." She looked directly at Doc, and—carefully—he looked back. When he caught her eyes, the echoing whisper beneath her voice grew louder, and he looked down. "Or was it the patron's charge, which we know well is not broken?"

"My healer and my swordbearer were in company of battle, my lady. Which well we know, also, is unbroken."

As the water calmed around Glassisle, her reflection steadied. Doc saw that it did not match the figure standing on the surface: there was still a woman there, the same size and shape, but the image below the water wore a cloak of green seaweed and a breastplate of scallop shells, and her bare arms and legs were white veined with blue and silver, like marble.

Doc turned his head slightly toward Mr. Patrise. His reflection also showed full-length in the water puddled on the stone floor, though that shouldn't have been possible given the light and the angle. Patrise's image wore a deep blue cloak lined with red, and bronze armor over red cloth, like pictures of Roman soldiers Doc had seen in books.

Doc turned back to Glassisle, and fixed his gaze on her reflection, suddenly very afraid to look down and see his own.

The water moved and the reflection shattered. A long-nosed dolphin broke water by Glassisle's feet. It gave a screech, then a sound like high-pitched chuckling.

"This is a paladin of mine, Healer," Glassisle said. "He has a question for you. A reply would be gracious."

Doc looked at Mr. Patrise, who nodded gravely.

The dolphin swam to the edge of the pond. It spoke: the words were squeaky, but recognizably English. "Greetings, Dockallownite."

Doc leaned forward. "Hello." *Okay, I've been a dinosaur, and now I'm talking to a fish.*

"How long," the dolphin said, "do you carry your young?"

"Nine months," Doc said, then, "Three seasons; three-quarters of a year."

The dolphin nodded, chirping. "How do you teach them to breathe?"

Doc thought hard. "Before we . . . emerge, our lungs are filled with fluid. That must be drained out. Then we . . . touch the child, enough to wake it. If it makes a good, loud sound, we know that it is breathing well."

"And if no . . . loud sound?" The dolphin sounded intensely interested.

"We can push air in. Sometimes we have to do that for a long time, with a . . ."

"Ma'sshine?" the dolphin said.

"Yes."

"Yes. We arrgga—" The dolphin ducked its head below water, came up making a gargling noise. "*Argue* over ma'sshines. But some are good. For life."

"Some of them are, yes," Doc said.

"Good thing to learn. Our thanks, Dockallownite."

The dolphin jumped, stood on its tail for a moment, then dove, splashing Doc with water. He stood quite still. Glassisle laughed loudly.

"We are pleased at you, Healer," she said, "and grant you the gift of an Ellyll's life. Use it well. As well we welcome you to visit us . . . if you learn to breathe water."

She sank out of sight below the surface; in a moment even the ripples were still.

The Mani led them out of the building, and the doors were shut with a bang. Doc felt a shiver, and told himself it was just that he was soaking wet in the cold moist air and the lake wind. At the car, Jesse had a towel over his arm; he tossed it to Doc, then draped a blanket over Doc's shoulders. They got into the car.

Mr. Patrise opened one of the drawers beneath the seat, handed two paper parcels to Doc. "Dry clothing, courtesy of Boris. He said—I quote exactly—'I suppose you're going to see that damp woman again.' "

As Doc changed, Mr. Patrise poured a cup of hot chocolate from a vacuum pitcher. Doc took it gratefully.

"That was important, right?" Doc said. "The damp woman."

"It was."

"Did she give me, or you, the right to kill Whisper Who Dares? Or did I get that wrong?"

"You were given the life of an Ellyll. If you can think of more than one way to interpret that—well, the Trueblood certainly can."

Doc thought about it. He felt a hollowness under his breastbone. "Cloud's life . . . ?"

"Is not anyone's to return. But thank you for the thought." Patrise leaned back and folded his hands. "Do you want to kill Whisper?"

"And then what? Cut the bullets back out of him?"

"You want to know about that, don't you, Hallow."

"Yes, I do."

Mr. Patrise said, "Do you know what alchemy is?"

"Turning lead into gold."

"Not really. Alchemy is a way of treating materials as if they had souls. Transforming matter by transforming its spirit. Gold does not tarnish or corrode, which makes it a metaphor for perfection, immortality, spiritual purity. All the alchemical processes are analogies of life processes, stages in the spiritual journey: birth, coupling, nourishment, fasting, shriving. Death and rebirth."

Doc started to speak. Mr. Patrise looked at him, plainly, placidly, and Doc was silent.

Patrise said, "Do you know who John Fitzgerald Kennedy was?"

"Sure."

"Yes. You are well educated for your age and time. The bullet that killed John Kennedy is preserved in a government archive. At least, it is supposed to be the bullet; it was found on a hospital gurney, not in a wound. And it looks barely damaged, perhaps unfired. Yet it is supposed to have blown through the President's skull and *then* caused bone-shattering wounds in another man's body."

"You mean it isn't the real bullet?"

"Much effort has been expended proving that it could be. You know who Kennedy was: do you know that he was confused with Arthur of Britain? That people believed he really was the Fisher King?"

Doc said, "That was a long time ago."

"Not as long ago as Arthur, but before Elfland returned, yes. More than thirty years before magic became visible. How long does a spiritual journey take, Hallow?"

"And what . . . happens to the bullets . . . once they're changed?"

"I use them," Mr. Patrise said in a very deliberate tone, "as Whisper Who Dares used those people you saw, in the red chamber."

Doc took a quiet swallow of hot chocolate. He didn't speak.

Mr. Patrise said, "I also offer the people around me what Whisper offers those who follow him: security, the comforts power brings, in exchange for loyalty and the best work they can do."

Doc said, "If you think I can see no difference between the two of you, you are very wrong. Sir."

"I am very glad to hear you say that, Hallow. While I very much hope that you see the right differences." Mr. Patrise picked up the car telephone, dialed. "Good afternoon, Ginevra. Yes, all is well. I wonder if you would be free for New Year's dinner with a few of us at the house this evening? Formal, yes, but leave that to Boris. No, Hallow has something to attend to at the moment, but he will be there. Shall I have Jesse collect you in . . . ninety minutes? Excellent. I shall look forward to seeing you."

He put the phone down, smiled at Doc. "Sometimes the Gordian knot just wants cutting," he said. "But it shouldn't become a habit."

On the sixth of January, Patrise asked Doc to arrive at the Mirada a little after eight. When he did, he found an EARLY CLOSING sign on the locked door. He knocked; Pavel opened up. "Do come in, sir. Mr. Patrise is expecting you."

Patrise was seated at his usual table, and with him Stagger Lee, Carmen, Kitsune Asa, McCain, and—unusually—Lucius. Ginny was behind the bar. There was no one else in the room. Since that first, late night, coming in from the cold, Doc had never seen the club so empty. It was disturbing.

"Thank you for coming, Hallow," Patrise said. "Take your seat. Ginevra, bring Hallow a drink. Anyone else? This party, and the death of a dear friend, would come near to make a man look sad. Ah. How could I have missed it. Stagger Lee, would you tell Ginevra to set out flutes for everyone. Then go down to the cellar and bring up two bottles of Taittinger."

"Sir?"

"I trust you to find a good year."

When Stagger Lee had gone, Patrise said, "Now that the immediate presence of magic is removed, does anyone feel less tense?"

Carmen said, "If you could have spelled out what you want, you'd have done it."

"Would I? Perhaps I love a mystery as much as the next person."

Kitsune said, "You loved Cloudhunter rather more than that."

McCain turned to look at her.

"Be calm, Lincoln," Patrise said. "Calmness is a great human virtue. Lucius: the night Flats's place was bombed, you did see something a touch suspicious, didn't you?"

Carmen said easily, "Do you mean something the rest of us didn't?"

Kitsune watched Lucius. Her black eyes had a terrible intensity.

Doc heard himself saying, "Let Lucius alone. Carmen's right; if anything happened then, we all saw it."

Kitsune pushed her chair back.

Lucius said, "Fox, sit down."

"Birdsong," Kitsune said, "you may love what will not be loved, but you cannot protect what will not be protected." She walked to the head of the table, bowed deeply to Patrise. "You've given me every benefit of the doubt, *oyabun*," she said. Her voice was very small, sounding near to breaking. "Someday I hope you'll know how much that's meant to me."

She put her hand on Patrise's forearm. There was a metallic whir, like a clock spring. Patrise gasped, and blood sprayed from the touch.

Kitsune stepped back. There was a four-inch blade, not much thicker than a needle, at her cuff.

McCain was on his feet, a pistol out before his chair could crash to the floor. He fired.

As he did, Lucius threw his dinner plate into McCain's face, and the bullet tore up the tablecloth and exploded a wineglass. McCain wiped his face and aimed again. Kitsune had stepped well clear of Patrise, making herself an easy target. Patrise clutched his arm; his face was compressed, congested, turning blood-dark. Doc was trying to get up; his chair wouldn't move.

Lucius threw himself at McCain, who batted him away, not so much savage as indifferent. The gun bore true. The Fox waited for it.

Fay sang out.

Only one note, not much more than a scream, but it was The
Voice screaming. Once at the Biograph, Doc had seen the film catch
in the projector gate; the image stopped still, then melted into light.
This was like that, with the whole world.

The note stopped. McCain was standing with his arms limp at
his sides, his face slack. Lucius was kneeling against the table, sobbing. Kitsune stood crookedly, staring into space.

A hand was on Doc's shoulder. He got up. Carmen shoved his
bag into his hands.

Patrise's head rolled back. His face was gray, blotched with purple. Not coronary, though, Doc thought. Poison: something not of
the World. Doc dove into the bag with both hands, searching for a
tarantelle cap. He got hold of one, pressed it to Patrise's nostrils,
hesitated. "Help me get him clear," he said to whoever was there.
Fay and Carmen helped him pull the chair back. Carmen pulled
Patrise to his feet, arms around his chest. "Do it!"

"Don't breathe—"

"*Do it!*"

Doc cracked the cloth-covered glass between his fingers. Carmen squeezed Patrise's chest in her arms and released it, forcing a
breath. Patrise's body stiffened. His arms flailed. His legs twitched.
Carmen dragged him down to the empty dance floor. And they
danced.

Patrise jerked and thrust and shook and spun, staying impossibly on his feet. Carmen led him away from railings and stairs,
mirrors and furniture. Now and again his arm struck her, with all
the energy of convulsion. She kept dancing.

Kitsune moved, turning in place like a music-box doll. Doc
went to her, grabbed her arm and held it out. He looked around.
"Ginny! Help me here."

She dashed from the bar. "See if you can get that thing off,"
Doc said. "Be careful. Please—be very careful." He ripped the
sleeve back, and Ginny unstrapped the spring blade. She dropped
it into a glass, covered it with a saucer, as if it were a live scorpion.
"Doc, look at this."

Kitsune's forearm was distinctly paler than her hand. Doc held
her head as gently as he could, looked into her face at close range.

He put a thumb gently to her eyelid, stroked firmly.

The epicanthic fold came away in a curl of tape and makeup.

Doc looked at the stuff on his fingers. He remembered Carmen's eyes, Halloween night. He turned his head.

Patrise was on the floor, his arms and legs out ragdoll-limp, his head cradled in Carmen's lap.

Stagger Lee came out from behind the bar, holding a champagne bottle under each arm. "What the hell—"

"You tell me," Doc said, and showed him the woman he was holding, the eye makeup. "Who is this? This stuff couldn't have made us think she was Kitsune, not by itself."

"Glamour," Stagger said thickly. "This is—I mean, *she's*—a simulacrum."

Doc said, "A what?"

"A double, a copy."

"So where's Kitsune?"

"Linked to this one. You run one from the other, like selsyn motors. Puppets."

"And what happens if this one dies?"

Stagger gaped at him. He looked around, at McCain, at Lucius, who was sitting up unsteadily. "What do you think happens?"

"Hold on to her," Doc said, "take care of her," and he went to see to Mr. Patrise.

Patrise's temperature was normal, his pulse racing, his face back to its usual unhealthy color. He seemed to be recovering, just utterly exhausted. Carmen's face was wet with tears, and Doc could see the bruises developing on her cheeks and forearms where Patrise, in the grip of the tarantelle, had struck her.

Mr. Patrise said, "Not . . . our . . . Kitsune."

"No, sir."

"Someone should call Chloe," Carmen said, "and tell her Jolie-Marie isn't missing anymore."

"Whisper," Patrise said. "Can we . . . find him?"

Stagger Lee had his arms around the dazed Jolie-Marie, a champagne bottle still clenched in each fist. "With both doubles alive, it'll be easy," he said. "But he'll know that."

"Then . . . we must be quick."

"Pavel," McCain said, "get my gear."

"I'll be right there," Doc said, finishing the dressing on Mr. Patrise's gashed wrist.

Mr. Patrise turned his head, looking Doc directly in the face. They were both still for a second, locked like that, and the room quieted around them, but nothing was said.

Doc stood up. "Let's go."

Patrise said, "Stagger . . . we'll want the wine. Don't drop it."

"So where are we going?" Doc said to McCain, who was driving one of the big cars. "Back to Hell?"

McCain gave a short laugh. "Not quite so far down this time." He was wearing a leather jacket, bulky with equipment hung beneath it; on the seat between him and Doc was a black steel crossbow with a telescopic sight. There was going to be no question of powder missing fire.

"The next one on the right," Stagger said from the back of the car.

McCain pulled up in front of a ruined office building, tarnished metal and big smashed windows. There was a doorway onto the littered sidewalk, or at least a dark, square opening. From somewhere beyond, there was faint yellow light, pale as piss on the ice and broken glass. "What else are you getting?"

"Could be a few people close together, but there's no crowd."

Doc said, "Could he be alone with her?"

"Depends on what he wants to show his audience," McCain said, with no humor at all. "Like Stagger said: the Fox is alive, so he knows we're on to that, knows we can find him. So he must want to be found. That brings us to the hard part. Who goes in?"

"What do you mean?"

"The elf's crazy, but he's not so crazy not to know the spot he's in. He must want some kind of a deal."

Doc said, "What are the choices?"

"If I go in, I'm going to kill him before I do anything else. You understand that? Whisper goes down, and then we pick up whatever pieces are left." He turned to look at Doc. "You don't look like you like that."

"Okay, that's what happens if you go."

McCain said, "If he sees Stagger first, they'll probably witch it out. You know I'm not Touched, but I know you've gotta concentrate—and I know what I'd do if I had a hostage and I wanted to mess up somebody's concentration."

"Down to me, then." Doc opened the car door. McCain's hand clamped on his arm.

"Don't just walk out on me," he said. "Tell me to wait."

"Linc—"

"Just say it."

"I'm going in first," Doc said carefully. "If the Fox doesn't walk out alive, then Whisper doesn't either. Right?"

"Yes, sir." McCain reached down, held out one of his automatics, grip first. "Katie said you did some shooting."

Doc picked up his black bag. "I'll play these."

McCain put the gun away. "You're gonna need more than luck," he said, his voice tight, "but luck anyway."

Doc went through the doorway. The source of the light was a stairway, maybe a hundred feet straight ahead through a glass-and-metal corridor; the stairs curved to the left and down, out of sight.

There was no place else to go.

The stairs ended in a tunnel, less than twenty feet wide, with an arched ceiling. McCain had explained that it was an old freight railroad, built forty feet under the streets to make downtown deliveries. Doc could see grooves on the puddled floor, and streaks of rusty rail. The light came from naked, dim bulbs dangling at twenty-foot intervals along the top of the arch. Cracks in the walls had grown spectacular icicles that twinkled in Doc's flashlight beam as he passed.

The tunnel curved around to the right. Reddish light shone on the wet floor, from somewhere still out of view. Doc got as close to the wall as he could and went on.

The red light came from a side door, framed in old brick. A derelict office desk and a couple of broken crates were to one side. Just beyond the door, the tunnel was blocked by a wooden wall—made of odd pieces of lumber nailed together, but not just piled debris: deliberately made and solid-looking.

The red light shifted, moved from side to side. Doc went to the door.

He was looking down a hallway some twenty feet long. At the far end was the shifting red light.

Hell again after all, Doc thought.

Doc waited a moment. His chest hurt. The tension, the damp and the cold, and the unsteady light were starting to make him sick, and if he waited any longer they surely would. He went down the hall.

A red bulb swung from a cord, throwing shadows back and forth. It did not seem to be an electric bulb, or an oil lamp, just a glass ball full of bloody light.

Kitsune stood just behind the light, her feet on a wooden stool, her arms outstretched. Her hair was brushed down straight, her head at a slight angle. She was wrapped in strips of gauze, spotted with what looked like bloodstains. As the light moved, it flashed on brass wires that came down from darkness overhead. They were twisted into loops around her neck and wrists.

There was a loud heavy flapping, and Whisper Who Dares appeared from the darkness. Instead of the Trueblood-sorcerer bones and charms Doc had seen in the ruined mall, he wore a rather plain black double-breasted suit, dark against darkness so that his face and hands seemed to float. His shining eyes were narrowed, and his face was shadowed below the winglike cheekbones. There was a single heavy silver ring, with a dull black stone, on his right hand.

"Put down your tools and conjures," he said. "Mischiefs abound in the levers of man."

Doc set his bag on the floor.

"You," Whisper said softly, "you are the one who carried death to the gates. And beat upon them. And now you come here, alone. Are you so terrible, then, in your courage? Or so steadfast in your vengeance?"

"All I want is her," Doc said. "After that—"

"You want *her?*" Whisper laughed, a bubbling hysteria that might have been funny in any kind of decent world. "Was the other a disappointment?"

"After that I don't care about you."

Whisper paused. His face twisted into a marble gargoyle's.

"This is no way to bargain! This of the pair is a trader, and the other goes for a price: what will either of them say to you, if you buy at the first offering?" He reached over to Kitsune. His foot bumped the stool, which wobbled. "Ah, cares, cares. Mortals are blind to beauty, but you appreciate the throat. So delicate, so vulnerable, so tight with wind and blood and nerve. Now. Here." He stood behind her, put his hands on her waist, slid them up to her breasts. "Oh, that's good," he said, and Kitsune's mouth mimed the words. He shook her. She groaned. "*Yes*, Whisper, again, please."

"Stop it!"

Whisper peeked from around the Fox's body. "Why? She can't stop *you*."

Doc thought furiously. There was no useful threat here. Whisper certainly had no shame or guilt to play on. If McCain was right, there was a bargain still to be struck; but there was nothing to bargain with.

There was only nothing.

Doc said, "Because I'm not interested."

"In what? This body? No?" Whisper took a step aside, arm out, showing the woman off like a car salesman praising a $200 beater. "Not even in *two* such compact and elegant bodies? Joined to do whatever—"

"In you." Doc climbed up on the stool, stepping carefully around Kitsune's bare feet, and reached to the wire around her throat. "I'm taking her and going away. After that you can go play with yourself."

"What?"

Doc looked at Whisper. From the stool, he looked slightly down into the Ellyll's shiny eyes, which were quite wide now. He supposed they were reading everything he'd ever thought about a woman. And he found he *didn't* care. Cloudhunter was beyond all hurt. Kitsune was alive, with another life hanging on hers. Whisper Who Dares—

Whisper was *his*.

"I said you can go shit your little elfin pants."

Whisper snarled and kicked the stool away.

Doc got his hand inside the brass noose with nothing to spare; it scraped his knuckles and cinched into the back of his hand.

At home, a farmer's wife had hung herself in the barn with fence wire. The stuff hadn't bothered to strangle her; it didn't stop until it hung up on her vertebrae. This stuff was thicker, but it would still be ugly fast if Doc lost his grip.

He clenched his teeth and pulled. Kitsune moaned, opened her eyes, looking straight into Doc's. "Hang on," he said.

Kitsune's arms pulled at the wires holding them, making a little slack in the strangling loop.

"*Now* you act like yourself, mortal! Dancing on air." Whisper applauded and stamped time.

Doc felt his heart twist, then pulled his brain back into Trauma Mode. He got both hands inside the loop—he was actually dangling from it, and his weight helped pull it wide. Kitsune pulled her head down, and Doc eased the noose over her head.

He let the wire slip away. His feet hit the floor, and his fingers started burning. He reached up to work at the wire binding Kitsune's right wrist.

Whisper leaned against the wall. "Not a bad show of faith, for a mortal," he said. "But somehow I don't feel my flesh burning at the touch of the Nazarite Christ."

"Didn't see any point in bothering him," Doc said, and freed Kitsune's other hand. She sagged against him. "Can you walk?"

"I'll try."

"Touching," Whisper said, and moved to block the doorway. "Moving, is that not what the mortals say, who have nowhere to go? I shall give her two thin knives, and let her dance on *you:* her sister will echo it to all your companions." He gave a wet giggle. "You'll *like it.*"

It washed over Doc. He had a vision, now, of what he was: there was plenty of darkness in it, but there was none of this. He said in Ellytha, "There is something in our way. Remove it."

"What, all rage gone?" Whisper said. "Have you forgotten that I killed Cloudhunter Who Keeps His Sisters' Counsel?" He stepped aside. "Or perhaps the thought of the mortal whore in his arms has supplanted all memories of a dead Ellyll."

Doc felt the anger rise again. Kitsune squeezed his hand hard.

Doc said, "You did not kill him. He accepted his destiny beyond the gates. You were only able to strike a blow because he had ceased to notice a coward. I am taking what I came for, and in return you may continue to be afraid."

Whisper was entirely still physically, but he *wavered*, as with rising heat. Doc made the effort to look away from him, and led the Fox down the corridor, into the icy tunnel.

A few steps past the door, Kitsune's breathing went ragged, and she leaned against some of the ruined furniture. Doc held her upright. "I'll be all right in a moment," she said.

From the inner chamber, there was a hideous, trembling howl, and the slam of boots. Whisper emerged, walking heavily, a knife in his fist.

"Look at my reflection, coward," Doc said, pointing at the wet floor, hoping this was a live card. "See what Glassisle saw."

Whisper Who Dares froze, his arm raised. There was a green flicker in his silver eyes. The knife dropped from his fingers; he clutched at his ring as if it burned him, and he backed against the wooden wall that blocked the tunnel.

Doc's eye caught a shimmer of black on black from the opposite direction, and he dared to turn away from Whisper. McCain raised his crossbow and pulled the trigger; there was a bass plunk and a hiss. The bolt nailed Whisper's right wrist to the rough wooden wall. Whisper Who Dares yelped like a kicked puppy and groped toward the arrow with his free hand. McCain pumped the bowstock, recocking it, and had another bolt loaded in five seconds. He placed it right below the elf's left collarbone, stapling his shoulder back. Blood splashed Whisper's cheek, his left arm went limp, and he groaned, a sound like tearing cloth.

McCain slung the bow, walked up to the pinned Ellyll. Whisper's left hand came up, holding a tiny stiletto, its blade stained with something like tar. McCain's hand slashed, and Doc heard Whisper's forearm snap; McCain didn't seem to have thought about it. Whisper began sobbing, calling out in some Trueblood language, not Ellytha.

McCain's fist hit Whisper's jaw like a twenty-pound sledge. "Shut up, Tinker Bell," McCain said. "Nobody believes in you no god damn more." He took a step back, unbelted his coat. Metal gleamed underneath.

Doc turned away. "Let's go," he said to Kitsune, and led her down the tunnel, helping her over the worst of the ice. They paused at the bottom of the curving stairway.

"Here's the hard part," he said. "I'd love to carry you, but . . ."

"Frankly, my dear, I don't give a damn," Kitsune said, and they climbed.

They found two cars at the curb. Stagger Lee opened the door of the new arrival. Inside, Mr. Patrise sat up against a pile of cushions, holding a slim delicate glass of champagne. *"Konban wa, Kitsune-sama,"* he said, his voice soft and a bit ragged. *"Dozo, ohairi kudasai."*

"Domo arigato gozaimasu, oyabun Patrise-san."

"Doitashimashite. There is tea hot. And perhaps a little brandy. Then Hallow and Stagger Lee must attend to you. And your sister-image."

"Yes, thank you," she said to Patrise, and then to Doc, *"Gokuro-san,* Doc. Thank you very much."

McCain stepped onto the sidewalk. He gestured. Doc went to him.

"You took him down," McCain said. "He's yours." He pointed to Doc's black bag. "Got everything you need?"

Doc nodded. McCain said, "I'll be at the car. Take your time, we got all night." As he went by, he said, much more softly, "If you need to think, think about Cloud." The doorway stood empty, lit dimly from below, just as it had before. It seemed like a much longer trip down this time.

Whisper Who Dares the Word of Words in Darkness was standing upright, arms outstretched. His chalk-white face was tilted, blood glaring red on his cheek and lips, a Pierrot puppet on wires.

He was held there by the two crossbow bolts, their steel fins quivering as he breathed, and maybe a dozen twenty-penny nails hammered through his clothes and his hands and one ear; some were driven through his boots into a slat of wood on the floor. On the concrete, little pools of *gwaed Ellyll* were glazing over.

The brass wire noose that had been around the Fox's neck was now around his, its trailing end twisted around another nail high up on the wooden barricade.

Doc set his bag down on the broken desk.

Whisper's eyes went wide open, looking at Doc and then away

from him, semaphoring pain and fear. Doc took hold of one of the crossbow bolts, pulled it out. Whisper shuddered.

Doc wrapped the bolt in a gauze pad, tucked it away in his bag. He took out another small object. He held his hand in front of Whisper's face, turning a tarantelle cap over in his fingers. He pressed the cloth-covered ampule against Whisper Who Dares's upper lip, which trembled. The elf's pupils looked as big as silver dollars.

Doc thought of the flaying rooms, of all the abuses and the sufferings. He thought very hard of Cloudhunter.

He closed the cap in his palm, turned to replace it in the medical kit. As he did, his fingers brushed a thin edge, an object Doc had forgotten was still in the bag. He pulled it out, held it up in the bad light. Whisper saw the movement and whimpered in absolute terror of whatever might be worse than the tarantella dance; he tried to shuffle backward, in spite of the nails.

"Ace of Clubs," Doc said, hearing his own voice rumble and echo in the arched hall, "not worth the effort." He threw it down at Whisper's feet, closed his bag, and climbed back up to the street without looking behind him.

Mr. Patrise's car had already gone. He slid into the front seat of the remaining car, beside McCain.

"Give me the phone," Doc said.

He waited for the connection. "Get me Lieutenant Rico. No, Officer O'Gara, I won't wait. I said *get* her."

When he finished delivering his message and put the phone down, McCain said, "No, huh."

"No."

"Everybody tries to guess, and nobody knows. Not till you got the motive and the weapon and the target in your sights. You just can't know till then."

As he started the car, the flare of blue police lights was visible far behind them.

Kitsune and Jolie-Marie were lying side by side in the surgery. Stagger Lee had put them both deeply under with spells, copper bands around their foreheads, lead set with amber at wrists and ankles. He had also explained how the operation was to proceed:

"There are five amulets placed beneath the skin of each double. The incisions may be well healed, but there will probably be wheals, and a mark will be visible. When you find and remove an amulet, go to the other double—the scar will be in the same place—and remove its mate. Try to remove them all intact; especially try not to break one inside the wound."

"And do you want them kept?" Doc asked.

"No," Stagger said quietly.

Phasia was there as well, sponging the sleeping women's foreheads, and Doc's, holding a coffee cup for him to sip from, bringing clean gauze.

The first cut was in the upper left arm. Doc reopened it with a scalpel, used a small retractor to spread the insertion channel. He shone his headlamp in. There was a disk of gray metal, the size of a quarter. A hemostat brought it out easily. It was carved with symbols. He dropped it into a basin and went to remove its duplicate.

The second amulets were of lacquered wood. Adhesions had formed, and he got a small ophthalmic scalpel, called for Stagger to retract and irrigate.

The third, under the left breast, uncomfortably near the heart, were of bone; finger bones, apparently. *Oh, the fearful wind and rain*, his mind sang.

The house shook somewhere deep down, and the lights went out. Doc's battery-powered headlamp made huge shadows on the tile walls. Stagger got out another lamp, and Fay brought in spirit lamps.

The fourth, over the right shoulderblade, were metal disks again; a different metal, badly discolored, with necrosis and pus around them. Doc had to open an area the span of four fingers, flush and cleanse and dress the wounds. Stagger adjusted the trance bands and stood away. Fay carried away the soiled sponges without a flinch. Doc argued with himself about putting in a rubber drain. They might heal more neatly if he just cleaned and closed, but . . . it was so damned *dark*. . . . He decided to trust to goldenrod and careful observation.

The last cuts were inside the right thigh, and the probe led to thumb-sized lumps of waxy white stuff, smelling faintly of camphor.

Doc held one up to Stagger's lamp. There seemed to be something buried inside them. Doc didn't ask what, or cut one open. He didn't care. He threw them into the basin, cleaned up and dressed his incisions.

They moved the patients into the infirmary bedroom, turned the lamps down.

Stagger Lee stripped off his gloves, said, "I really need a drink."

"Why don't you go get one, then."

"I—"

"Good night, Stagger. Thank you."

"Yeah, Doc. Good night." He bowed slightly to Phasia, left the infirmary.

"Flesh leyell ins'ta?" Fay said. "Kissna Kissna verdet well." Her face, lit from below, looked unreal. Doc thought she seemed near collapse with the effort of making words. He felt exhaustion like a hand rearranging his guts.

He made a sleeping gesture. She nodded. He took both of her hands and held them, not knowing how else to say thank you. There must be ways, he thought. Had they done enough with sign language?

She went out. Doc went to look at the sleeping women again. He should stay here tonight. He couldn't possibly watch them even an hour longer, but at least he would be here if something happened.

He called the kitchen. As they were connecting, the door opened and Lucius came in. Doc said, "I was just calling for some coffee and a sandwich. Would you like something?"

"Never to refuse free coffee, that is the Law, are we not men?"

Doc smiled and made the order. They sat down. Doc found himself nodding off in the chair. "What . . . brings you here?"

"Just a couple of things to say. One is thank you. For getting Kitsune out alive."

Doc thought about what the simulacrum had been made to say. "You love the Fox, don't you."

"Birdsong on love in one paradox: Nothing is more perfect than the unattainable," Lucius said, trying to make it sound like a joke. "See, the audience all knows that the lady's supposed to fall in love with the hero, even though she's running a clue short. So the hero has to go into the fire, or the ice, or the generally bad place, and come back with the plot coupon that says *Good for One True Love.*" He shrugged. "We don't do that anymore. Not if we're really heroes."

"What's the other thing you wanted to say?"

"Wait till the butler's come and gone. It's only for you."

After the coffee came, Doc said, "Well?"

Lucius looked at the bedroom.

"They're asleep."

"I *should* have told you this before. Or maybe I shouldn't. I didn't know what was going to happen when you found her. I suppose I thought things didn't need any more complication. And that, if she died, it might as well stay unsaid."

"What you mean is," Doc said, "she *did* sell Mr. Patrise out."

"Ah. I see you love a mystery too. But that isn't what I've got to say. Kitsune *did* try to deal with Whisper Who Dares, but it wasn't anything to do with street fights and *gwaed gwir* bootlegging. She wanted something she thought Whisper might be able to give her."

"Which was?"

"Truebloods lie about magic, did you know, Doctor? They know that in the Shades the spells that can reshape the stuff of reality itself work like a two-stroke lawn-mower engine with grubby plugs and bat guano in the fuel line. But magic's part of elf style. So they lie about what they can do. Or can't do."

"Okay . . ."

"The Fox is a consummate deal maker. I'm sure she expected Whisper to deal tough. But she probably didn't count on pure-quill Ellyll crazy. So she got caught. I wish I knew just *when* she got caught, when it started being the copy. Information *did* pass Whisperward after that, but that was different. I'll never know, though, because I'll never ask. Will you?"

"I don't suppose it matters."

"No," Lucius said, suddenly very still, "I don't suppose it does." He stood up. "Good night, Doctor. Thank you for the coffee and the attentive ear. And thank you again for my friend's life." He stood up, got his hat, went to the inner door and looked in on Kitsune and Jolie-Marie in their beds. His hands clutched the hat tight to his chest. Doc turned his head until Lucius came away from the women, headed for the exit.

"Lucius."

Birdsong stopped.

"Will you tell me one more thing?"

"Knowing that it will surely make none of us happy, why, yes, Doctor, I should be delighted."

"What *did* you see at the Rush Street, that night?"

"Remember that there was gunfire, before the explosion?"

"Yes."

"Were any windows broken when you got out to the front room?"

Doc thought back. "No, there weren't."

"I saw the bullet marks. They were all high and outside. Nobody's that bad a shot, except on purpose. All the gunshots were supposed to do was bring somebody out of the back room, just in time for the blast to get him."

"To get who?"

Lucius looked infinitely sad. "Someone who'd dash right out to help the shooting victims, without thinking twice." He opened the door to the hallway, smoothed his lapels and tilted his hat to hide his eyes. "It shouldn't be possible to forget, given all the strings round our fingers: Hammett, Chandler, Crumley, Macdonald and McDonald. Not to mention Oedipus the King. But we do. Something in the genes, in the winds of DNA, that says The Answer is Good. I really *can't* be trusted, you know, Doctor. Good night."

And he was gone.

Doc sat down heavily, and just stared at the wall for minutes on minutes, thinking.

There must be some reason for a thing like that, he thought; people didn't just kill each other for the amusement value. Another part of his mind answered back, *Wanna bet?*

But if there was a reason, what was it? What did he know? What could he do? He wasn't any threat to Whisper Who Dares, certainly not before the meeting with the Highborn Glassisle. Even afterward, he'd only used her gift as a bluff.

Unless the reason was something that Doc didn't know, and wasn't supposed to live long enough to find out.

Kitsune had wanted something from Whisper, wanted it so much that she had ended up selling herself out. What could anybody want quite that badly? What, Doc thought, would *he* do such a thing for?

So the hero has to go into the fire—
Birdsong on love in one paradox.

Of course. Not a *what* at all.

Doc checked on his patients: still sleeping quietly. He went around the room snuffing the lamps, until there was only the circle of illumination from his headlamp. He reached into his bag, took out the crossbow bolt he had pulled from Whisper's body.

The metal didn't look transformed, but neither had all those bullets. Did it *have* to be death that brought the power? Surely not.

He had no solid idea how to proceed. Where he had come from, there wasn't any magic, but people believed in it anyway—any of your neighbors might be bribing the Devil to blast your crops, sicken your stock, dry up your women. Nobody ever said exactly what the formula was for calling up Mister Scratch, but the evidence after the fact usually included blood and sharp objects.

Doc looked in on the sleeping women again. This was no place to experiment. He put the arrow back in his bag, called one of the house staff to watch the patients, and carried the bag down to the firing range next to the basement garage.

He had to assume that Kitsune had followed the right clue. He had to guess that there was something to the rule of fairness in magic, that no pain or sacrifice was ever wholly empty. He had to *try*, dammit.

What could the Word of Words be, anyway? The Word that commanded all others? That told language to flow, or be silent—or be confused? In darkness . . .

He turned out the light.

There was nothing at first. Then he saw a light from the arrowhead: not the cold blues or elemental reds of the magic he had seen, but a warm, peach-colored glow.

Maybe this was it. He felt dizzy, put his hands on the table. What next? Think. His fingers arched, as if he were probing the throat for a tracheotomy. No, that couldn't be right. It wasn't a structural blockage.

He didn't have any psych training, beyond holding an accident victim's hand while his partner pulled glass and metal out of the wounds. He had to heal a mind, and a mind was never meat—

In Darkness, the Word of Words.

The glow from the arrowhead warmed his hands, and in a slow flare sweeping through his brain he knew the Word that ruled all others, that commanded all tongues to speak or be mute. But it wasn't enough to know it.

He stumbled upstairs, seeing but not sure what light he was seeing by. He entered the dining room, which was lit by one oil lamp on the sideboard. A butler was there at once, asking what she could do to serve Doc.

"I would like not to be disturbed here," he said, and the woman nodded once and disappeared through the kitchen door.

McCain had taken orders from Doc, too, just outside Whisper's lair, just as if Doc had some sort of authority over him.

Doc put the lamp and his bag on the dining table, pulled up a chair to sit near them, facing the hallway entrance. This was the place, and the hour, he had first met her. Things like that were never insignificant, in the Shade.

He took the crossbow bolt from the bag. His fingers were unsteady, and he held it tight, trying not to cut himself with the bloodstained point. It looked ordinary in the lamplight.

He was horribly tired, and afraid he'd fall asleep just a moment too soon. Then he felt her approach—didn't hear, but knew it. She stepped around the corner.

Once again, the force of the glamour's physical aspect struck him like lightning. Again she smiled, and her eyes widened curiously.

A thought spun in Doc's head, of how much Mr. Patrise must need her, tonight especially. *Bad timing.* But it was too late to reconsider; he barely understood how he'd gotten this far.

He reached for the lamp. The last thing he saw before the light went out was Fay's face, and the expression there froze his belly. *Bad timing—*

But the Word was already in his mouth.

Whisper Who Dares.

Once long ago in the land of Iowa, someone—probably Robin—had told Doc that the French phrase for hangover translated literally as "My eyes are not opposite the holes."

How literal, Doc thought. His vision seemed to be rolling in the dark, with occasional flashes of brilliance as the pupils lined up with the sockets. Where the heck was he? He'd been in the dining room . . . he must have come back to his apartment. Which meant he needed his key, if he was going to get into the room, fall onto the bed, and . . . that was enough advance planning for now.

Where was the key? Here, key, key, key . . .

There it was, in his palm. No wonder he couldn't find it. Couldn't have been there long, though—it was cold, colder than a something's whatsit. He shoved the key forward, and punched air. Then he felt pressure against his back, all the way down to his heels. He'd fallen down.

This was a swell hangover; he hoped the party had been worth it.

Still clutching the key, he put his left hand to his eyes and fingered the lids open. Blazing whiteness poured into his brain. Then something eclipsed the light.

"Doc? Are you there?"

"Ssssurrrrrre."

The shape got closer. Hair fell across Doc's forehead, familiarly. Lips pressed his cheek.

"Ginny . . ."

"Glad to have you back," she said. It was filtered through the sound of tears, and Doc was suddenly a lot more awake. He levered himself up and fell straight back down. His bedroom started to take shape around the two of them. "Oh, wow."

Memory began to click in. "Fox. Jolie . . . I gotta see . . ."

"They're doing all right," Ginny said. "The staff's taking care of them. And Stagger. And me."

"An' . . . Fay?"

"Fay's just fine."

"Really?" He waved at his mouth.

"Yes. It worked, Doc. Now relax."

"Who . . . called you?"

"Mr. Patrise. Two days ago."

"How'd'e know—*oh*."

"You know I'm a good babysitter," she said, but the weeping edged back into her voice.

"C'mere," Doc said, with a gluey tongue. "Hug."

She wrapped her arms around him. It brought a much pleasanter dizziness.

"Ouch," she said, and pried the key ring out of his fingers. "What are you doing with these?"

"Uh? Oh. I got the Touch now, I guess. I wanted 'em, and they came."

She put the keys on the nightstand, gingerly.

Doc said, "I ought to get up. See some people. What time is it?"

"About four."

"What four?"

She laughed. "In the afternoon. Don't get in a hurry. Stagger Lee says you could have died."

"Now he tells me. I want to see Fay."

Ginny was quiet for a breath. "Fay's not here. She's—staying at my place for a few days, and I'm staying down the hall here."

"Why? I mean . . . why isn't she . . ."

"Things are changing, Doc. Fay wanted to be by herself, just now. And Mr. Patrise said he thinks I should move in here. It doesn't have to be with you, if you don't want that. Do you want that?"

"I don't know . . . you might not want me. All the time, I mean."

"I think I want all the time you've got, Doc. But . . . I have to ask you something."

He tumbled the possibilities over in his head. "Go ahead."

"Something's not there between us. I love what you do with me—I love *you*, Doc—but it's like there's something you're dodging, or afraid of, or—I've been wanting to ask for so long, but I was scared you'd just run away." She leaned over him. "You can't run now," she said. "I've got you prisoner."

He started to laugh. Then his ribs ached, and it finished in a long cough.

"What's wrong, Doc?" she said, alarmed.

"Not wrong. I think. It's . . ."

And he told her.

For at least half a minute she was perfectly still, looking down at him with her mouth open and her eyes wide. "That's it? I mean, that's really it?"

"Yeah."

"But . . . why didn't you just ask me?"

"I didn't want to . . ."

"Do it? That doesn't sound right."

"I thought maybe I could just not . . . be that way."

She said gently, "Your friend Robin, who can't get away from home, and doesn't even have you to talk to anymore—do you think that means he's not gay now?"

"It doesn't matter what I am, if you run away. You are not . . . a prisoner."

"No," she said, and her smile melted into the Gioconda's. "Unless we both agree that, for a little while, I am."

"There are things I won't do. I've seen . . . a lot of stuff. I saw Whisper Who Dares. And whatever I am, I'm not that."

"Do you think I didn't—*Whisper?* Do you think I could have believed *that?*"

He felt suddenly very small.

"And I know there are things you won't do," she said. "You won't ever do anything that makes me feel bad about myself, or about you. I trust you on that. Because trust me on this: you won't get the chance to say 'That'll never happen again'."

He nodded slowly.

"We got some kind of a deal, lover?"

"Deal," he said, and pulled her against himself for, oh, who cared how long.

Finally she said, "So do you want to get up and start the day? Your scraggly red beard is, I gotta say, pretty scratchy."

He rubbed his chin. "Yuck." He let her help him stand up. "I'll get cleaned up. And all of a sudden I'm really hungry."

"I'm not surprised. What would you like?"

"Uh . . . some eggs over very, very easy. And coffee."

When Doc got out of the bathroom Ginny was standing beside the service tray. Her face was taut. Without a word, she held out a copy of the *Centurion*, folded to Lucius's column.

THE CONTRARIAN FLOW

by Lucius Birdsong

It has been a while now that I have been writing this here colyum (as some of you choose to call it) and there is a question that many of you have asked, one way and another, and one way and another I have not ever answered it.

The question is not what you would call a stumper. It is Why do you call that column of yours what you call it? And since this may well be the last time I write it and you read it, things being what they are and all, your correspondent would like to finally let the thing out of whatever the thing is in.

You see, there are all these other questions. The ones you didn't ask.

You never asked why I have not taken you sculling down the old blood stream in a little paper boat, and pointed out the heaps of skulls that shoal its banks, nor the vacant eyes of those who troll it, nor the pale viscid nature of the so-called life it supports.

And you never wanted to know why children come here as if drawn by that cheeky chequy chappie with the woodwind wail; you don't know that story, because in the commercial version the children are a warrior and a wizard and a bard and a thief and a fledgling dragon, and they not only defeat the entrepreneur but get a bag of gold to boot; you never asked why the only ones to leave this place can never, age regardless, again be called children.

And corollary to that, no letter has ever arrived from the World beyond inquiring of your correspondent why the only children left out there are the damaged, the crippled, the already too lost to find their way, who are now confronted with the unspeakable possibility that they may be the children of fortune after all.

Indeed you never demanded why I have told you of this and that but never the other thing, of the rainbow but not the pot of gold, the dance but not the steps, the singer but not the song.

In this great city, we are supposed to have made a river run against itself. Now, while the water does indeed counter the tendency of the Continental Divide, no such thing happened, nor has it ever happened. What we did, at great trouble and expense, was adjust the river's circumstances: to lay down a red carpet strewn with rose petals and good intentions, and hope the stream would choose to go our way. We didn't command the river, because one cannot tell water where to go, and if the attempt is made the torrent will take a revenge that is even more awful for being without passion.

Your faithful reporter has tried to coax a trickle in a thirsty land, but he knows better than to strike the rock.

I am leaving you now, for an uncertain while, and hope to get just a peek at the place I shall not be going.

Doc dressed, kissed Ginny, and drove to the club. Pavel took his coat. Stagger Lee was in the lobby as well.

"Sorry I'm so late."

"Almost *the* late," Stagger said. "Next time—" He shook his head. "Excuse me. I've got to get the show going."

Patrise was at his table with the regulars; everything seemed normal, except that Shaker was on the bar and Ginny was nowhere in sight. Neither was Lucius.

"Glad to see you, Doc," Shaker said, setting a dark beer down in front of him. "I'm sure they'll be glad to have you over at the table. Unless you'd rather sit here? Show's about to start."

What kind of question was that? Doc wondered. He went to Patrise's table. Patrise and Carmen stood. She hugged him, Patrise gestured toward an empty chair. McCain sat quite still. Then Carmen sat back down. The lights dimmed.

Doc said to Carmen, "Aren't you—"

"Not tonight. Sssh."

The spotlight hit the stage. Stagger's voice came over the speakers, spoke a name Doc didn't recognize.

It was Fay that came onstage. She was wearing a pearl-gray suit with long trousers and a low neckline. Doc swallowed, wiped his damp hands on a napkin.

She sang. With words: clear, intelligible, certain words.

> *The evening descends*
> *The radio's on*
> *A voice in the air*
> *And solitude's gone*
> *But who have you got on*
> *That favorite spot on*
> *The dial*
>
> *The next voice you hear*
> *Whatever its source*
> *Will be coming through clear*
> *No static of course*
> *Let's close the request lines*
> *Since all of our best times*
> *Are gone*

She had a good voice, a very good voice, sweet and warm. Doc felt a warmth on his hand. Carmen was holding it. She was watching the woman on stage, and smiling.

> *The next voice you hear*
> *Will take you right back*
> *To flutter and wow*
> *That our broadcasts lack*

It's strange how the cold hands
Warm up to the old bands
Once more

"Alvah wrote it for me," Carmen whispered. "But I never could sing it. Nor ever can, now."

A wonderful voice. But it was just a song, after all.

We now leave the air
Here's station ID
We bid you good night
With hopes that she'll be
Forever the right choice
Whoever's the next voice . . .
You hear

The patrons applauded. Someone called for an encore, but Fay had already vanished through the curtains; she did not reappear. The room was rather quiet after that, and table by table began to clear out.

Mr. Patrise said, "You'll have to excuse me, Hallow. It's been a long day." He stood up. "Coming, Lincoln?"

"Yeah," McCain said, but he just sat there staring at Doc.

Doc said, "Have you seen Lucius, Linc?"

"I guess he's around," he said.

Slowly, quietly, Doc said, "If you'd rather not talk to me—"

"Anybody can *talk*," McCain said, in a dull, metallic voice. Then Doc understood, and knew there really wasn't anything to be said, not now, anyway. McCain got up and walked heavily out.

"I'd better go too, Doc," Carmen said. "Linc—well, when he sees his lord survive this loss, he will forgive you."

"I suppose . . . I didn't think she'd leave."

Carmen looked at him, her face soft. "Do you think she could have known it herself?"

Doc said, "Wasn't it what everybody wanted?"

"Oh, no," she said. "You did what was right. Big difference." She stood up, looked after McCain. "But you did make her happy. Some of us have to work hard for a lot less. Good night, Doc."

He was alone at the table, looked up and saw he was alone in the room, except for Shaker industriously wiping a glass.

Doc went backstage. Stagger Lee was unplugging some cables. He looked up. "Evenin' Doc. What can I do for you?"

"Is . . . um . . . she still here?"

"She left just after she finished the set. Didn't even change." Stagger put down the stuff in his hands. "You don't remember her name, do you?"

Doc opened his mouth, tried to think.

"I'm sorry, Doc. That was mean, and you've been through plenty. The lady's Shadow name is Phasia; changing it would take— well, acts of substance. That's one of the reasons she's gone. And that is your lesson in magic for this day, young sorcerer." Stagger gave a crooked grin.

"Thanks. Can I have one more?"

"Ask away. Just remember that we wizards are subtle and hard to light."

"Under Wacker Drive. Cloud said it was for power, so did Mr. Patrise. But—power for what? To do what?"

"You read Orwell, Doc? *1984?*"

"No."

"You should. It's in the library. The phrase you're looking for is 'The object of power is power.' You don't gather power because you want to cash it in for something. You do it because of how it makes you feel. It's a feeling you want more of. And if you get power the way most people do, you get scared that someone else might have more than you.

"As far as I know, Whisper Who Dares didn't have some kind of supervillain doomsday plot that needed derailing just as it counted down to zero. No reflection on what you did, Doc." He pulled some switches, and the lighting room went dim and silent. "Any more questions?"

"Not now."

"Yeah. Not now. Poker Monday. See you there."

Doc went back to the empty main room.

"Another round?" Shaker said.

"Is Mr. Birdsong's typewriter still back there?"

"Sure is, Doc," the elf said. His voice was light, solicitous, ready to listen. The perfect bartender. He set the typewriter on the bar. "He said you'd ask for it."

There was a note in the machine:

UNION STATION
PLATFORM 8
12:15 P.M.
sharp

Doc groped for his watch. 11:35. "Where's the Union Station?" Shaker gave him directions. "Do you want me to close up, sir?"

"Didn't Mr. Patrise—"

"No, sir. Mr. Patrise was quite specific. Your decision."

"Wait fifteen minutes," Doc said, unsure where the words were coming from. "If nobody's come in by then, call it a night."

"You got it, sir."

"Shaker, it's been a little bit—I mean, this evening hasn't been the happiest."

"They're mortals, Doc. They don't always take well to a change in fashion."

Doc turned the car into the station lot at twelve minutes after midnight. He ran up the steps, nearly falling twice, followed the signs to track eight.

Under the dark expanse of the train shed, a pair of red lights were just disappearing in the distance, and a whistle blew long and sad.

Lucius stepped out of the shadows, holding his coat collar up against the cold. "The train left at midnight," he said. "On time, but I wanted to leave a little safety margin." He looked down the platform, along the empty pair of rails, pointing away west.

Lucius said, "She didn't really want to say good-bye. But people have changed their minds about that. She did leave a kiss for you. You won't mind if I only tell you that."

"Where's she going?"

"There are only two ways you can go, relative to Elfland: toward and away," Lucius said, very patiently. "She's going away. To be somebody different from Phasia. Someone more like the way she is now."

" 'Elfland?' You didn't call it Our Fair Levee."

Lucius didn't laugh. "I never have, except on paper."

"Yeah." He looked at his feet. "Would you like a ride . . . somewhere?"

"No." The word was heavy, very final.

Doc said, "You're not leaving too."

"Leave Chicago? Not likely, Doctor. I'm taking a sabbatical from the *Centurion*, but I doubt it'll last. Ink and sawdust know where they belong. Hold on to my typewriter, will you?"

"I'll tell Shaker."

"A good fellow. He's still got the Fox's money, now that I recall."

"Then what do I do with myself?"

"You get to find out. A voyage of discovery, isn't that a wonderful prospect?" He looked up at the platform roof, a glimmer of moon above it. "Your era may be better than Patrise's. Kinder. Built on care instead of just control."

"My . . . what?"

Lucius said, "Will you take a last piece of advice from the pulpwood Indian?"

Doc started to protest, then just said, "Of course I will."

"Hold on to Ginny. You can do it. And you've got to. The Great Spirit made you out of better stuff than us, true clay with hot breath in your nostrils. But you weren't fired as we were. That's your power, as clay can shift when brick breaks, but clay needs a form. Ginny's your potter's wheel, Doctor. Lose her and you'll shift away to dust."

"Lucius . . . who *are* you?"

Then Lucius laughed, loud and ringing through the empty station platform. "Man flesh and Man spirit in Shadow time," he said. "And therefore part what I am made, what my will makes me, and what I might become."

"Lucius, please—"

"See you around, medicine spirit man." He reached out and fingered Doc's lapel, then turned sharply around and walked away, down the platform into fog and hard darkness, colorless as the ending of a Biograph movie. Part of Doc wanted to run after him, but a greater part knew that there would be no more running after.

Doc looked at his coat where Lucius had touched it. Thrust through the buttonhole was an eagle feather.

He got into the TR3, leaned over the dashboard, and said, "Go where I am going. Go. Go. Go."

It didn't work. Whatever higher powers had been slumming on the Levee had packed up their dates and gone home. He had to drive.

As he walked past the switchboard, Lisa said, "Mr. Patrise left word that he would like to speak with you, sir. At your convenience."

Doc dashed straight to the stairs, not waiting for the elevator. Mr. Patrise was sitting behind his desk, in black silk pajamas and a long black dressing gown. For the first time Doc could recall, Patrise looked old.

"You wanted to see me, sir?"

"I asked to see you, Hallow. But we'll let the distinction pass. Do come in."

Doc approached the desk.

Mr. Patrise said, "Did you speak with Phasia, before she left?"

"No, sir."

"That's too bad. She must have had remarkable things to say, after all this time. But then, you did speak with her, didn't you? Every chance you could?"

"I . . . tried."

"The best of mottoes. Perhaps you will have it engraved on your signet, when this office and this house are yours."

"What do you mean, sir?"

"Oh, I'm not handing you the keys yet, Hallow. You have a great distance to go before, like Alice, you reach the eighth square. And the Shade is a dangerous place: we may lose you before your ascension. But you've survived—what is it, three direct attempts to kill you now. . . ."

"Three?" Doc thought of the roadway ambush, and the attack on the Rush Street Grill. And— In a small voice, he said, "Cloudhunter? When he fought Whisper . . ."

"Truebloods are hard to kill, unless they're throwing themselves in the way of destiny. Grieve, Hallow, as is proper, but do not make grief your master: I think Cloud was happy to give his life for you."

Doc wanted to vomit.

"A question, now, before the night passes," Patrise said. "What is the secret of the Shade?"

"Secret . . ." Suddenly it was obvious; it should have been obvious the first time he'd met Mr. Patrise, traveling with a Trueblood miles from the Shade. "Magic . . . doesn't end at the Shadowline. It works everywhere."

"Just so. *Terminus non est:* There is no line of division. The Shadow, like all buffer states, is a political fiction meant to keep both sides comfortably separated. We of the Shadow Cabinet have made mistakes; you will make your own. But there will be no more Miami Craters. And when the time comes to conclude the secret—for people to understand that things have genuinely changed—well. Perhaps it will come on your watch."

"But how can that be a secret?"

Mr. Patrise tilted his head to one side. "Absolutely correct, Hallow. It cannot. That is, it cannot be secret from anyone who cares to think and ask questions. It is the second of the three great secrets—the one you keep from yourself."

"What are the others?"

"The first is the one kept from others. You tell me what the third is."

"The truth."

"You see, Hallow? How could you ever say that we did not know one another?"

"But I don't want the house. I wouldn't want your job, even if I could do it. I don't want—"

"To be consumed by the desire for power in itself?" Patrise said, with barely a flicker of emotion. "To become Whisper Who Dares?"

Doc stared at the carpet.

"I think you have been asking hard questions of Stagger Lee. Read Machiavelli after you finish with Orwell; you'll see yourself there too, but remember that the mirror never shows the person whole.

"You risked your life for someone else's, without the hope of gain. You were given the power of life and death, and left your prize to the judgment of others. With Ginevra . . . while I would not embarrass you, Hallow, what happens in my house is known to me."

"And . . . when I tried to summon the Word?"

"That too."

"But if you knew I could do that—if you even knew I had the Touch—why didn't you tell me?"

"I didn't know. But I also didn't ask you to try. As I did not ask Cloudhunter, or Stagger Lee, who I knew very well did have the Touch." He looked Doc directly in the eyes. "In no small measure you succeeded because you did not know any better. Think about it, Hallow: if you knew that night what you know tonight, would it have been as simple?"

"No."

"And you still, even now, cannot face the reason that I never asked anyone to do the thing."

"I don't know what that is."

"Yes, you do." Mr. Patrise stood up, leaned across the desk. "You can lie to Ginevra for as long as you like, Hallow, but you cannot lie to me. Not in my own house. Not about the fear of losing what you love with one, wrong, loving word."

Doc took a step backward, then another.

Patrise stood, walked toward his inner rooms. "Good night, Hallow. May it be pleasant."

"Good night, sir."

He waited for the elevator. When it arrived, Doc was startled by its occupant: a figure in a long dark cloak, hood raised.

"Good night, Doc," said a voice from within the hood, and the cloaked figure moved into the hall.

"Good night, Carmen," Doc said softly, as the doors closed.

The lights were on in his apartment. He started to throw his coat on a chair, then carefully removed the feather and carried it with him.

Ginny was sitting up on the bed, her legs tucked beneath her. She must have had the habit for years, but he had never seen her do it in front of anyone else. It was as if it were a pose just for him.

She was wearing one of his shirts, a few buttons done, and a tight, very short skirt of silk black as her hair—no, it was a scarf, black and shining with stars, silk that nothing mortal could damage. He knew it well enough. It could only have passed as a gift. From one lonely woman to another.

She turned, just slightly. Leather cuffs cinched her wrists to her upper arms, high and tight against the sweet curve of her back. She leaned back, falling against the pillows; turned to look at him, her hair spilling out in a dark halo. Her eyes were luminous and endlessly deep.

She was strong, he knew that, but from that position there was no leverage; she was all but helpless. Unless he did something about it.

Doc felt himself stiffen, his own breathing grow thick.

Quietly but firmly, she said, "Call the turn, dealer."

Then he knew. If he ever demanded more power over her than she held from him in return, she would be gone. And as Lucius said, he would fade to dust.

The Wild Hunt was gathering, and he could not stop it. As if he wanted to.

So here was the chance to do something right. Not that he knew what it was. He only knew what he was going to do, to hold her as she would be held, tonight with leather and silk and heat and pressure: she was trusting him, as she had been all along, and he had to stop rejecting that trust. Whatever happened in the morning, he was the master of the house tonight. And the monster. And maybe even the hero.

He leaned over her, spoke into her ear. "I will never harm you," he said, "and you will not ever allow me to harm you. Understand?"

She nodded once, slowly.

"Then give me your safeword."

She shut her eyes tight and whispered it.

He stroked the feather across her lips. She pulled in a convulsive breath.

He bent to kiss her bound wrists. She sighed from deep down. Her cheek was hot to the touch.

Enough, perhaps, for the two of them to keep out the cold.